Truth & Consequence

Sordid South Book 2

Aria Daze

Daze Dream Publications

Contents

Dedication

Dedicated to Femme doms, tenacious women, and men who are strong enough to be soft. You keep the world spinning.

Foreword

ACHM,

Hi again. You may have remembered the last book's foreword, the one where I discussed how my goal in life is to help lend diversity to romance. Well here we are, and guess what? This book includes diversity too, this time by touching on BPD. Borderline Personality Disorder is a mental health disorder affecting emotions, attachment styles, and self-regulation. Mental health disorders are often genetic, but they also disproportionately affect Black communities. That is due to environmental factors such as trauma, diet, and other stressors. Black people are also less likely to seek help managing such disorders, due to financial barriers. As a person who once fell into both categories, I feel like it is my responsibility to highlight and represent those who may be struggling with BPD or other diseases like it. We are still valuable, we are still deserving, and we are still capable. It is my greatest hope that the representation in this book affirms all of the above statements. Thank you for reading.

Content Warnings

B EFORE YOU DIVE IN, please check out these handy content warnings. Reading should be enjoyable, and some of the topics covered in this book may not be for you. Your comfort matters. Triggering topics include by are not limited to:

- Suicide (Attempted)

- BPD (Borderline Personality Disorder)

- Anxiety

- Depression

- Kidnapping

- Stalking

- Coercion

- Violent crimes

- Organized crime

- Drug use

- Murder

- Sexual Activity

- Inappropriate language

- Forced marriage

- Female domination

Your mental health is important, and if this story negatively impacts it at any time, please discontinue reading.

The Playlist

- SchoolBoy Q- Numb Numb Juice

- SchoolBoy Q-Ride Out

- Victoria Monet- Moment

- Joe- I Want To Know

- Sade= Is It A Crime

- Sebastian Mikael-Domesticated

- Adagio In E Major- Mozart

- Vivaldi-Spring

Genesis

ALISE

I always knew I would fuck him. I knew it from the minute I started getting hot in the pants. He was wonderfully tall and broad, and his eyes were so brown they were damn near black. They were the color of freshly roasted whole espresso beans, the good shit that people went bankrupt for. Then his skin wrapped around him like black mulberry silk; Fine, lustrous, opulent. So opulent that he would sometimes look blue in the moonlight. Especially when he smiled. Stars would fill his eyes while the ivory of his smile contrasted with skin just one shade lighter than midnight. He embodied the majesty of a thousand galaxies. I'd seen plenty of beautiful men, but none quite as eye-catching as Truth Greene.

Most women would describe him simply as handsome and dark skinned, and technically they weren't wrong. But there was so much more to his attractiveness than that. There was the confident twinkle in his eye when he addressed crowds. There was the way his ears lifted when he laughed. Then there was his gait: Long, calm, and unhurried. It told anyone who was willing to listen that he was walking with purpose and probably something heavy. Something powerful. Something mind-altering. So yeah, I was gonna fuck Truth Greene. Just as soon as I figured out how to get him to break his number one rule.

Truth

"No."

My sister slowly retreated to her side of the table and then looked at her screen one more time to make sure she was hearing me right. The woman she showed me as a blind date contender was indeed beautiful. Clear nutmeg skin, long black curly hair that was kind of wavy, bright white smile, an ass from what I could see. And yet I still said...

"No?"

"Yes."

"Yes?"

"No, yes to you confirming my no. I'm good on ole girl."

Liberty's shoulders sagged in defeat. This was her third recommendation this month. She was getting worse than our mama.

"What's wrong with this one!?" she signed furiously, her nails clicking as she did.

I looked my sister dead in the eyes as I signed back,

"How old is she?"

I already knew the answer: Not old enough.

But still I was curious to see how Liberty would spin it. She, like most people, thought my rules on dating were too strict. I didn't give a damn though.

"Truth," she sighed. "It's just six years difference."

Just as I thought, not old enough. I was turning 35 in December. My thirties were halfway over with. I had learned a lot about who I was and what I could safely handle, and younger women were not it. I wasn't gonna be keeping up with young girls and teaching them how to ride dick, and they weren't gonna be driving me crazy. For that reason, I had a personal rule of five years older, five years younger. Really it was 50 months, but I knew I couldn't reasonably enforce that.

Six years though?

"Nope, I'm good," I reiterated before sucking the meat out of my teeth.

I loved steak but I got an overcooked one every once in a while. Especially when they had the young ones in the back. Which once again proved my point. Man or woman, hardly anyone under 30 knew how to treat a steak.

"Truthhhh," Liberty groaned. "I thought you were serious about getting in the Senate."

"I am."

"A stable partnership could help with ratings."

"Yes, a stable partnership with someone my age," I nodded.

"She is... Boy you know what-"

"What?" I smirked. "Is Lele mad because I'm standing on business?"

Liberty was the baby of the family, and the only girl out of five, six if you counted Boogie. We rode her nerves while growing up with all the nicknames, pranks, and teasing. So I half-expected her to reach across the table and pop me on the hand. Instead she collected her shit, disconnected her cochlear implant, and walked out.

"Aye! Forgetting something?" I called. "Where is your money at?"

I knew she couldn't hear me but she could feel the vibrations of my voice, and as a response, she simply threw her middle finger in the air and scoffed. That was fine. We both knew I was paying anyway and that's why she let me eat her leftover fries. Plus it was only fair since she was working so hard as my matchmaker. Even though I had fired her months ago.

Marriage was important in my family. It protected our interests, our money, and our reputation. With Boogie getting married in a week, that made me the next victim. Everyone's pestering, pandering, and plotting fell on me. Especially since it aligned with my upcoming candidacy for a Senate seat. Liberty was right, spouses did make quite the difference in ratings, but that wasn't a good enough reason for me to bite the bullet. A lot of us Burry boys didn't believe in divorce, me included. So if I was gonna do this shit, I was gonna do it right. Whoever I dealt with had to meet my standards. I needed someone intelligent, independent, determined, and in possession of some kind of sense of humor. I wanted an equal. I wanted her to be able to understand my past and appreciate my present. And I wanted someone my own damn age.

"Greene!" Simon whooped as I stepped off the elevator into my office. "How's my favorite future senator doing?"

I tried not to cringe at his greeting, but the truth was I'm a cynic at my core. Future senator sounded too certain for such a tumultuous task. I was running against a 3 term incumbent in a red state with a very progressive campaign. Simon had a habit of making things sound easier than they really were. A symptom of idealism I guess.

"Hey, Simon. I'm not too bad. What brings you by?" I replied.

He tipped his head towards Mariah then we slipped into my office quietly to avoid disturbing my secretary's diligent scheduling. At least that's why I hoped we had gone into my office. Last time we talked it was to get ahead of the potential smear campaigns. Luckily I didn't have many notable scandals.

"Nothing much, I wanted to see how you were feeling," Simon shrugged while settling into a chair.

He got comfortable in a way that reminded me of a fat cat lounging in the sun. For some reason that bothered me. However, I brushed it off for the time being. I found plenty of things bothersome.

"Fine. Confident but cautious," I answered honestly.

"That's a smart approach," he nodded. "Logical."

"Well I am a lawyer at my core."

"Ha. You don't have to remind me. Your work speaks for itself. It makes for good optics. Speaking of optics..."

Shit.

My record was clean but that didn't stop my heart from falling into my ass. I've always had terrible anxiety which seemed to worsen with age. Every year I had more and more to worry about. Was I getting enough fiber? Did I hit my step goal? Were my siblings ok? Was my mom getting sleep? All things I didn't give a second thought to in my early and mid twenties. Back then I was just surviving off of fast food, a weekly phone call home, and the occasional basketball game in the park. Now my schedules had schedules and I had to worry about shit like "optics". There was simplicity in youth that was unattainable in your 30s. Sometimes I found myself missing it.

"Relax, it's not a scandal or anything," Simon chuckled.

I was about to sweat out one of my favorite suits and here he was laughing. Typical optimists.

"You know, sometimes I think about firing you," I tutted.

"Oh, please. But back to the topic at hand, Alabama is a red state."

"As I am painfully aware."

"Glad to have you up to speed," Simon clicked. "To that point though, constituents like to see their representatives aligned with their values. Values like beliefs, interests, families. You know marriage-"

Apparitions of the altar haunted me relentlessly, both personally and professionally. Wedding bells rang in my ears like a horror soundtrack, and ghosts of veiled women flashed before my very eyes. Marriage was a suggestion I couldn't seem to escape.

"I'm gonna stop you right there, chief," I interjected. "I do not have a wife nor am I currently seeking one."

"May I ask why?" Simon sighed.

"Because women are a terrible amount of work if you plan on being a good husband, and I don't plan on being a bad one. You know my family doesn't believe in divorce."

"Ok, so just get a fake fiancée. That checks off the commitment box, but prevents a divorce. Problem solved."

"My mother would kill me. With her bare hands, and you know she could do it."

"Ah yes, Aster," Simon chuckled fondly. "How's she doing anyway?"

"Just fine. How's your wife?" I asked curtly.

Simon Richards was a man of many talents, including collecting mistresses. He attended high school with my parents and while he respected my father, he never quite got over his crush on my mother. When Dad died he would occasionally let his admiration be known. However, that was a hard line in the sand for me. Yes he was one of the best campaign managers in this half of the country, but when it came to my family, anyone was replaceable.

"Message received, Greene," he replied with a respectful nod. "We'll brainstorm on this fiancée thing some more later this week. Maybe we can do the whole, 'She lives in Canada' thing," he laughed.

"I'll think about it," I sighed while slumping back in my chair. "No promises, Simon."

Walk On By

TRUTH

We were nearing the end of the week and I had, by a miracle of Big Sandals himself, evaded all other questions regarding my lack of a relationship. I'd been forgotten about with Boogie's wedding rush. RSVPs had to be counted, seating charts finalized, and travel plans made. No one was tryna get me to meet up with the daughter of some woman that sold them Avon 30 years back. No one was questioning my rules. No one was trying to get me to break them. Life was great. I was in control and feeling good.

Right up until I pulled into the lot of Victor's.

"What are the girls doing here?" I asked, climbing out of my truck.

We were supposed to be at our final suit fitting, but instead of seeing fades and line-ups I was looking at the tops of lace fronts, pineapple fros, and directly into the eyes of one Hatchette daughter in particular. Alise held my gaze for way longer than I was normally comfortable with, and the mischief in her gaze made my stomach drop when she finally strutted away.

I didn't like that feeling.

And I was wholly unprepared to deal with Mama Hatchette's matchmaking attempts. For whatever reason, she almost always successfully conned me into a date. I don't know what it was about that woman, but she could get the devil to do her bidding. Maybe it was the smile. I noticed her daughters had inherited that too.

"They have their final fitting upstairs, and Mama Hatchette wanted to make sure everyone looked cohesive before the rehearsal Friday, so we just decided to sync times and check this off the list," Boogie grumbled. His tone held ire, as if it was his second or third time explaining it. But I knew it was just because my cousin was stressed.

Reason number two that I wasn't in a hurry to tie the knot. He and Dre weren't even technically in a relationship yet but I could see that she was eating up his mental bandwidth. We talked a few days prior, and he mentioned wanting to fire all of her staff. But he didn't have a good enough reason and he also didn't want her to know he was a certified basket case this early on. So he stewed instead, and the thoughts of Andrea and all her naïvety had settled into his eye bags and decided to stay a while. His skin was dull and tired, making him appear like a phantom of a tortured man. A man whose steady and predictable routine had been blown to pieces. I felt bad for Andrea whenever she finally decided to give that nigga some ass. Yeah, Boogie was footing the bill, but she would be paying for all those last minute changes.

"Just 4 more days," I reminded him with a shoulder pat while entering the shop.

"Just a fucking lifetime," he hissed back, following behind me.

Victor's always did an amazing job. They had been our family tailor for years, and for good reason. I took a sip of my champagne before twirling in my suit and then hitting a jig. I was happy to see neither my pants or shirt riding up. A little light trickled through the small egress window above me and made the green shine brighter. I couldn't explain why, but I felt lucky as hell in this suit. The emerald complimented the brown of my skin quite nicely, as I suspected it would for everyone else as soon as they got done getting dressed.

If they ever got dressed.

I don't know how my cousins and brothers managed to complicate suits, but it took them twenty minutes to figure that shit out every single time. Denim-loving simpletons. I started to open my mouth and tell them to hurry up, but Mama Hatchette interrupted me with that syrup-sweet smile.

"Oh, Truth. You look so handsome, sugar," she cooed.

She grinned at me with her eyes full of joy and pride, like I was one of hers. I heard that Andre was a menace back in his heyday like Dexter, but I never believed it on account of his wife. She was too sweet and dignified to be dealing with some shit like that. Now that I was older though, I could tell she domesticated his ass. Turned a rowdy wolf into a loyal lapdog.

"Thank you, ma'am," I smiled back.

"Mhm, Victor's has always done a fine job with you boys," she said while examining the fit of my threads. "Come on up, they can get a picture of you since you're already dressed."

What I wanted to say was, *"hard pass"* or *"I'll wait on the rest of the guys."*

But what ended up coming out of my mouth was,

"Sure thing, Misses Joy."

Then I promptly trailed behind her like a lost puppy. She made me fall in line just like that. I wasn't a praying man anymore, but when I laid down that night I'd be sure to pray for Boogie. Because I was sure Mama Hatchette's powers were genetic, and he'd be done for when Andrea turned that charm on him.

She abandoned me by the windows to check on the girls. So I was ready to stand off to the side and catch-up on some emails while waiting, but then I heard the one name I was trying my best to forget.

"Alise?" Mama Hatchette called. "Come here, sweetheart."

As if her name commanded the heavens themselves, the sparse clouds parted so the sun could shine a spotlight on the pair of endless, soft, mocha-colored legs rounding the corner. Legs that would probably be running through my mind all the rest of this week and the next.

Legs belonging to none other than Alise Asasi Hatchette.

We used to call her Baby Ax coming up, but she was a baby no longer. She was tall, lithe yet curvy, and breathtaking. With supple rich skin, round, curious eyes, an upturned nose, and bow shaped lips that looked like the definition of kissable. Alise was practically a living Barbie.

"Yes ma'am?" she sang, breaking my concentration on her mouth.

I snatched my gaze away and set it towards the hardwood floor, hoping my sneaky glance wasn't obvious. I had no business staring at Alise Hatchette, and certainly not with the intent to notice how beautiful she had become. Anything involving that woman was a hard no. We were 14 years apart, and outside the fact that Boogie very well might put aside his beef with her brother, Dexter, to beat my ass if I tried it. I had my rules but she was really too young. Her reputation hadn't even been sullied. She was still only known for her birth order, the youngest Hatchette. Dre Senior's sweet baby.

"Oh, you look so pretty, sweetheart," Mama Hatchette cooed, bringing her hands to her chest to soothe the swelling emotion.

Alise looked more than pretty in that champagne gown. She looked downright angelic. That was a given for her though. She caught the eye of everyone in the shop, and even some random men walking past the windows outside. Same thing with the Governor's Ball last month. She walked in after Andrea and the room stopped. Maybe even the world. Right then though, it was affecting my heart. My shit was pounding like a bass drum, skipping around, and flat out racing. I feared I was about to drop dead in the middle of that damn shop.

"Thank you, Mama," she smiled before looking at me.

That mischievous glint remained steady in her gaze when she addressed me.

"Truth, you look handsome too. You always did well in jewel tones."

My head began to spin from the sudden increase in my pulse. I don't know why, but something about her tone made my nervous system riot. I simultaneously wanted to run out of the shop and draw into her. Alise's attention felt like a drug. I wanted more even though I knew I shouldn't. That contradiction made me uneasy. Burry's were historically immune to drugs.

"Thank you," I responded hesitantly.

"He does, doesn't he?" Mama Hatchette agreed. "Anyway, baby. Come pose with Truth so we can take a few pictures for the florist."

Alise came to my side to oblige her mother and this time I opened my mouth to say no, but instead my refusal was replaced with a soft plea from Andrea.

"Mama, can you come here real quick?" she whispered out the cracked door of her dressing room.

"I'll be right back," Mama Hatchette called while abandoning us. "Don't move."

Fuck.

Her mama had left but Alise was still touching me. I was uncomfortable at best, but I knew better than to show it. Alise never said anything untoward to me, yet instinct told me to avoid her. Maybe it was because she had eyes like a predator, dark and observant. Or maybe it was because of my own fucked up thoughts in recent months. Either way, I needed to make space between us. Or at least distracting small talk.

"How-"

"Is something the matter, Truth?" she interjected.

I stared at her again. This time unabashedly. I let my eyes rove over her high cheekbones, over her wide nostrils, and down the gentle peaks of her lips to the slope of her chin. She was a woman, soft and innocent. I was certain of that. So once I was done, the same question appeared but with a new context. How? How did she know? I was a politician and lawyer for a damn good reason. I had a poker face like no other, and when it came to mind games, I was the game master. But somehow in that moment, 21-year-old, fresh-faced Alise Hatchette had me pinned.

"No, I'm fine," I lied. "Just a long week."

And a long dick, but she'd never know that.

"I agree," she nodded. "Although I keep saying that, and yet somehow I'm surprised it's almost July."

"Right? This year is moving. It was just January in my mind."

"Mhm. We were just at Easter dinner," Alise agreed. "But, Truth."

She said my name while turning to face me, and once again, I found myself weighing the option of fleeing. If anyone saw us, they'd think we were about to kiss. The optics were terrible and yet the idea of peeling away from her became more unsavory the longer I considered it. She was so damn pretty. Like an embodiment of a blooming springtime. She even made my heart flutter like falling petals. I'd seen and experienced beautiful women before but none of them made me nervous. It was such a novel feeling that I thought it may have been a fluke the first few times, but now I knew for sure that her eyes made my pulse race.

"Y-yes?" I choked back.

"You don't have to be scared of me," she chuckled softly. "I don't bite. We're friends, remember?"

"Right. Friends," I nodded back.

We'd been cordial before but right then there wasn't a friendly fucking thought in my mind. I was thinking about getting a better sniff of her perfume and then licking it off her neck. I blinked and my hands were on her body, squeezing her ass tighter than that dress ever could. My lips were folded into hers, her body was pressed against mine, and those long claws of hers were dragging over my stubble before digging into my shoulders. I became dizzy and restless from her touch.

Because Alise was everything I feared she'd be.

Addicting, torrid, and passionate. Against all the rules.

I blinked again and I was back in reality. In Victor's, where we were close, yet not close enough. Her gaze dared me to meet her somewhere in the immodest sliver of space between us and test the fullness of her lips, and I wanted to.

God knows I wanted to.

I couldn't do that though. So I tried to ground myself by focusing on the world around us, but the romantic classical music playing in the background of the shop only deepened my desire. The rich notes of the piano facilitated surreal visions of Alise's dark body lying against a bed of rose petals, with those curious eyes demanding all of my attention and strength just like now. I knew I could have her underneath me if I really wanted to. I could pull her closer. I could make my fantasy a reality and draw breath from her lips...

Before I could decide on how much of my common sense I wanted to cash in to sate my lust, Mama Hatchette burst back in the room in a fury of unsuspecting laughter. I didn't touch Alise, yet my heart pounded against the linen of my shirt when I saw her mother's skirt swish around the corner. I stepped aside as if I had almost gotten caught stealing from the church, however, Alise remained as she was. That made me wonder if I was overreacting.

Until the little temptress smirked at me.

"Ok, pictures!" Mama Joy clapped.

"Actually..."

I leaned away to try to save my sanity and cement my pending excuse of having to locate a restroom, but Alise rejoined my side and placed her hand in the center of my back. Her claws dug through the jacket into the sensitive nerves of my spine, forcing me upright.

"Smile," she said gently, but with a certain bite that made her demand irrefutable.

I made a living from refuting. From fighting, from arguing. But when it came to that voice, those hands, and those jaguar-like eyes, it was impossible to do anything but bend to her will. I nosedived into a spell of eager compliance, happily doing whatever Alise wanted. Smile, spin, laugh. Even with my boys looking at me like I was an entity in a Truth skin-suit, I couldn't stop. I did everything as directed. All until she was satisfied. All to earn one soft smile and a gentle pat on the shoulder.

And it was almost as satisfying as I imagined fucking her to be.

In the grand scheme of things, there was a lot I didn't know or understand. I didn't understand the science of identical twins, or the theory of relativity, or the purpose of the half-nail on my pinky toe. I didn't know what made people want to settle down with one person. I didn't know why the days got longer in the summer outside of daylight savings. Yet there was one thing I knew and understood with absolute certainty.

I knew I needed to stay the fuck away from Alise Hatchette.

First Comes

ALISE

My sissy was getting married. She had been draped in cream and crinoline, plucked, primed, and moisturized, and now she stood in front of me as a glowing bride in a veil the length of an extendo cab Silverado. The feeling hit me like a gust of chilled wind in the fall. Andrea was really getting married. Her room had been cleared out that morning while we were getting our makeup done. Boogie's team had relocated everything in a matter of minutes, and her new address had been updated that morning in the company database. She'd be a Burry in an hour.

It was a bittersweet moment for me. On one hand, I truly believed Boogie would be good for her. But on the other hand, I was terrified with the new reality of having to share her. I had access to Andrea my entire life. She taught me how to paint my nails, pick out good fruit, and find my skin's undertones. She was the one I cried to when some dumb boy broke my heart. She knew all my secrets and habits as if they were her own. We were sisters by more than just blood. But now she'd also be a wife. Probably even a mother once her anger softened. Possibly by next week if she used that box right.

Either way I had my name suggestions ready.

"It's time, ladies!" The coordinator called.

My heart leapt from my chest at the announcement. It was the end of an era. On the plus side, getting Andrea married meant more time for my personal endeavors. Namely hunting Truth. Normal people would say pursuing, but hunting seemed more apt for this situation. Truth didn't want to be pursued, he wanted to be in control at all times or left alone. He wanted to stick to his little rules, play the games he had already mastered, and keep it safe. Which is exactly why I wanted to tussle in his sheets. Any man wound that tight would be something magical when he unraveled. Something unforgettable.

Maybe even something dangerous.

We floated down the Mansion's expansive East hall where we met the groomsman outside of the grand ballroom. Boogie had bought a small country's worth of flowers to fulfill Andrea's vision, and they, like everything else, were perfect. From the linens, to the food, to the wedding party. There wasn't a hairline, bra strap, beard hair, necklace, or tie out of line thanks to Joy Hatchette. Our auric champagne gowns sparkled in the afternoon sunlight, while the boys dazzled in their emerald and white. Especially Truth. I wasn't lying when I said he looked good in jewel tones. Color complimented his complexion no matter the occasion, and there in the hall with the sun beating down on his back, the rich green and crisp eggshell made him look like the definition of Black masculinity. Strong, yet endearing and gentle.

I placed my hand in his and gave him an innocent smile. Truth and I were coupled together as the Best Man and Maid Of Honor, which I appreciated. It made it easier to soften his will. A subtle squeeze here, a touch there, a smile, a look. Anything to get his heart racing and his mind running.

"You're very handsome today, Mister Greene," I said as the doors swung open.

I heard his breath hitch in his throat and it sounded like a deferred groan. A thrilling indication of my affect on him. We took two slow steps forward in silence before he returned my compliment.

"Thank you," he whispered. "You look beautiful, Alise."

His gaze roved over me momentarily before we reached the aisle, and I could see the restraint clouding in his dark eyes. I wondered what he was thinking about. Did he want to touch me back? Did he want to taste my lipstick? Did he want to defile me amongst all the sunny daystars and romantic peonies?

Probably all three. I could have surely found out the order of which that night, but I decided against pressing my luck since it was my sister's day. So I relaxed the reins and let us glide down the remainder of the aisle with the music narrating our silence. Besides, the seed was already sowed. If I wanted to remain a lady, it would be up to him to water it.

And I didn't ever doubt that he would. Especially not with what happened next.

Our road began to diverge when we reached the altar so he could take Boogie's side and I, Andrea's, but his grip on my hand tightened when I pulled away. It took him far too long to realize what he'd done. However when he did, he took his time with my captured hand, rubbing his thumb lazily across my knuckles before abandoning it at my side.

Possessive and uptight?

Oh I was gonna have fun with him.

I recovered from Truth's firm grasp and settled into my spot on the right of the Pastor to wait on Andrea. The girls fell in line with me one-by-one until we were all gathered, and we waited until the next melodic cord of the organ struck out to announce Andrea's entrance. The oak doors were pulled open once again to allow her and Daddy inside. Sun cascaded through the gigantic windows like soft rain and highlighted her cherubesque face as she clutched her overflowing bouquet, eliciting awed gasps from the crowd. Boogie seemingly grew impatient as he watched her glide down the aisle, with his arms and hands straining against his sides as to not go and simply pluck her from the floor. That wasn't surprising to anyone who'd been paying attention. Nathaniel wanted her.

He had always wanted Andrea.

More unexpected was Andrea's reaction to it all. Instead of cowering, or finding something or someone else to watch, she stared right back until she reached the altar. Only breaking their shared gaze when the men exchanged conversation. Then once they were done and their promises were made, her eyes returned back to the man who was about to be her husband. I released a relieved exhale as soon as they settled.

This would be a very good thing for her. I wouldn't have to be as concerned.

Now the only thing I had to worry about were the dark, desire-filled eyes watching me.

Truth

"You're staring."

I spun around on my heels, irritated that I had gotten caught. There was no denying that statement. Everyone in the room was staring while Alise danced.

With the exception of Boogie's ass.

He was too focused on Andrea, the woman he spent years swearing up and down he didn't want.

I understood it was her sister's wedding day and that the after-hours reception was still a family affair, but the Hatchette's should've made Alise go home with them when they left. Because the way that woman rolled her hips and bounced her ass on that dance floor had me mesmerized. It reminded me of when I was young and I would get lost in the swing of my grandfather's pendulum clock. I lost at least an hour watching her.

I wanted a bite. I wanted her to sit that shit on my face. I wanted her to dig her nails into my back again.

"Shutup," I hissed. "She shouldn't even be doing all of that."

I knew I was wrong as soon as I said it.

This shit with Alise was getting out of hand. I had never been the type to police women and mind their business. Aster Nicole had raised me better than that. Which is why I could hear my Mama's voice scolding me before Boogie even said anything. But then his additional two cents certainly didn't help.

"Damn nigga, you got it bad. You know she grown right? You can't stop her from dancing just cause it makes you feel like a nasty-ass old man," he chuckled.

I understood why women were so quick to throw drinks during conflict because that's exactly how I wanted to react to my big-mouth-ass cousin. Flick my wrist and shut his ass up with a rum and Coke to the eyes.

His triumphant laugh was irritating, but the worst part of it all was his accuracy. I did feel like a nasty-ass old man while watching Alise. I wanted her in a way that made me sick. I could barely be honest about that reality most days, and I certainly didn't need other people peeping that. Boogie always did know how to get under folks' skin. It was simultaneously his best and worst quality.

"Go away," I scoffed.

"Why, so you can be a peeping Tom in peace?" he teased. "Nah, I ain't gotta do shit. This my wedding."

"Right, which is why your wife is dancing with another nigga."

He spun around so fast you would've thought that he was a tornado. His expression filled with spite and malice while his back and arms tightened with the strength of rushing adrenaline.

He was ready to go to war.

Until he spotted his wife in the corner with her cousin Mae, having an animated conversation about God knows what. His posture slowly relaxed along with his previously accelerated breath until he returned to normal. It was like watching the Hulk shift back into Bruce Banner in real time.

"Looks like I ain't the only one being terrorized by a Hatchette," I scoffed.

Boogie nodded, seemingly in defeat. Until I saw the glint of his wedding band align with my face.

"Andrea's a Burry as of 3:43 this afternoon," he chuckled back. "I found a solution to my problem. You better hurry up and figure out yours."

He left me with that and hobbled off to go bother his bride. I wanted to ignore what he said, but in his absence I had to admit he was right. My reaction to Alise was a problem. I was possessive and way too eager. I needed to figure out what to do with those feelings and figure it out fast. My campaign was starting in September, and I couldn't afford to be caught sniffing around her young ass. Simon would have a fucking fit.

I was busy running a thousand different possibilities and solutions in my mind when one of Boogie's drunk friends, Von, wandered over to my table. His once-pressed dress shirt was wrinkled and rolled up at the sleeves while sporting pasta and sweat stains. Haggard was the word that came to mind. He was fucked up and it was evident.

Which is why I should've ignored him when he said,

"Damn Baby Ax done got thick as fuck. She got my dick hard as fuck."

His swords came out in a mostly unintelligible slurry and he had to lean against the table to avoid eating the tile. It was clear he wasn't in his right mind, and again, I should've ignored him.

But I didn't.

Instead I snatched his ass up by his collar like he was a wayward child, lifting his entire body off the ground.

"Watch yo fucking mouth before I cut yo ass open," I hissed, sending spit flying.

My saliva landed on Von's brow and he jumped like I poured acid on him. His previously wide, unassuming smile quickly faded into a regretful grimace before his hands extended in surrender.

"My bad, T. I ain't know Baby Ax was you. She been by herself all night," Von stammered.

Technically, she wasn't mine.

The logical thing to do in the moment was to deny his claim and pass my anger off as simple familial protection.

But I once again ignored logic.

Instead I chose to correct the latter portion of his statement to make myself feel better about what I was gonna do next.

"Quit calling her that shit. Her name is Alise," I grumbled while returning his bitch ass to the ground. "And mind your fucking business."

Von's comment took me outside of my calm public character, but the only reason I didn't fuck him up for it was because it made me realize I needed to stake my claim. The wolves were always out when it came to beautiful women from good families, and Alise was no exception. Regardless of how bothered I was by the fact.

I stuck to the shadows to avoid Boogie. I knew we'd have to talk about it eventually, but not tonight. There was only one conversation I needed to have tonight. The woman haunting my dreams stood in the right corner of the room, dancing to a sped-up remix of Surround Sound.

A blue bill accompanied my request to the DJ for something languid and romantic which he happily obliged. Sade began to flow through the speakers by the time I reached my final destination, interrupting the unsuspecting woman's rhythm. She turned to face me, her expression indicating that she was capable of being surprised. Her curious eyes were big and analytical while her mouth twisted with an unverbalized question.

"Dance with me," I demanded, answering her.

Alise's shoulders softened as she smiled up at me. It was a haughty smile. One filled with arrogance and pride.

One I wanted to lick.

"Truth, that's not the way you ask," she chuckled. "I know you have better manners than that."

Actually, I didn't.

So I ignored her request for a respectable proposition and pressed her body to mine.

And it felt so damn right.

A low groan ripped from me as her curves molded to my body. She was soft and warm and she smelled just like she did in Victor's. Spicy and rich like ginger and cashmere. Then another smell I couldn't quite place. It drove me wild regardless. So I left just enough space between us so that Alise could see exactly what she was doing to me. Just enough space that I could still feel her warm breath on my neck.

Eventually Alise let me have my way, and we began rocking to the steady rhythm of Is It A Crime.

Honestly, a fitting song for the occasion.

Here I was dancing chest to chest with her young ass. Someone who broke all the rules. Those who knew me and my rules stared in disbelief, but I didn't give a fuck. I'd been craving her touch all week.

"What is this about, Mister Greene?" she asked while tucking her head on my chest.

Her soft smirk indicated this was a test. So I should've answered with tact. Kept the truth close to my heart.

Instead I once again defied logic when it came to her.

"I don't like the way you make me feel," I whispered while nuzzling her neck.

"Why? Because you're not in control?" she giggled. "You can't be in control all the time."

"Yes I can."

"Nah," she shrugged before digging her nails into my shoulder. "And I don't think you wanna be either. Do you, handsome?"

Now it was my turn to be surprised. By both my reaction and my response. My spine tingled while my belly fluttered with anticipation. Being told what to do sounded strangely appealing. Especially when it came to her. That revelation was terrifying, so I said nothing. But Alise was fine with that because my body spoke for me.

"Careful, Truth. You're not gonna be able to hide that if you keep thinking about it," she teased.

She widened her stance just slightly and let her pubis rest against my raging erection. Then she resumed rocking as if she wasn't driving me into madness. My heart pounded from rising anxiety. I'd never been so hard in my life and I feared I might've nutted in my pants in front of my family. From the machinations of a woman I shouldn't have even been talking to at that.

"I'll leave you alone," she laughed while wiping sweat from my forehead. I assumed she'd do what every normal person did and wipe it on her clothes or mine, but instead her thumb came between her lips so she could have a taste. I quickly realized how this dynamic between us would end.

And that was with me in a psych ward, playing with my top lip.

"After today I'm staying away from you. Because if I don't, you'll make a monster out of me," I confessed while pecking her forehead.

Alise sunk further into me as my lips departed her silky skin. This time her hand traveled to the curve of my neck so she could rub behind my ear. I melted on the spot even though I knew what she was doing.

She was making an example out of my goofy ass.

"You don't have to worry about that, Truth," she said after a while. "After all, we're just friends. And I always look after my friends."

Her soft lips placed a promising kiss on the top of my Adam's apple, making tensions soar. Then once she was satisfied with my silence and frustration, she slipped away, retreating back into the safety of her cousins and siblings. I stood there for a few breaths watching her. My nervous system was a wreck but she floated about like it was just a regular Monday. Instinct had served my ancestors well, and every single one of my instincts was screaming danger when it came to Alise Hatchette. Yet as I watched her chest rise and fall from an innocent laugh, I couldn't help but once again pull out my umbrella when it was raining common sense.

Out Of Office

A^{LISE}

"No thank you."

Mama looked at the egregious bouquet of tri-colored roses in her hands with profound bewilderment. The vibrant peach and pink ones were particularly breathtaking. I understood her confusion. I should've been swooning.

"Alise, I'm by no means rushing you. But can I ask why not? He's quite handsome. Very smart too."

Her question was in reference to the sender, Terrance Holmes. He was very handsome and very smart. With smooth almond butter skin, an endearing dimpled smile, a muscular frame, and hair that was the textbook definition of the low-cut Caesars with the deep waves that Our Lord and Savior's, Destiny's Child, were singing about.

Yet I was completely uninterested.

Looking at him felt like the visual equivalent of eating Weetabix.

Boring.

"He's just not my type, Mama," I shrugged. "He doesn't do it for me."

Mama went deathly quiet while placing the bouquet back on the counter, almost like she'd seen a ghost. I watched her anxiously wring the hem of her dress for a moment before her lips parted with a question.

"Can I ask you something without you getting offended?"

"Of course, Mama."

"Are you... Are you a scissor sister, Alise?"

The way she asked left me no choice but to spit out the tea I was sipping. "A WHO!?"

"Are y'all calling it something else nowadays? I know we ain't really supposed to say dyke and bulldagger no more. But you know what I mean. Do you like girls? If so, I'm not mad. I just need to know so I can change my approach."

"Mama, please," I wheezed while taking her hand to silence her. "I am not gay."

"It's ok if you are. Andrea's gay. She's had a couple of girlfriends."

"Mama, I'm not gay. I like boys. I just don't like that man."

There was a skeptical glint in her eyes, and I almost wanted to shake her to get my point across, but luckily she relented with a dismissing nod. "Alright... But if you ever wanna tell me something. I'm here for you, sugar plum."

Mama went back to arranging the bouquet into a vase while I returned to my lunch. I bit into a single chip and the sounds of my crunching filled the entire kitchen. Sip, crunch. Sip, crunch. That's all you could hear. The house had never been so quiet.

Being the baby, you got used to people being around. Animated older siblings, their loud friends, cousins, and childless aunties who spoiled you rotten with sugar and gifts. That was all I had known for the last 21 years. Now Dex was pushing on forty and grew more and more resentful of unnecessary noise on a daily basis, while Andrea was busy sorting out her marriage. While I still preferred quiet most days, I was slowly realizing that quiet without any noise was maddening.

It had only been a week but I was getting lonely.

"I think I'm gonna call An-"

"Andrea! Calm down, baby. It's not that serious," Daddy sighed while shuffling in the kitchen.

Speak of the devil and they shall holler in your ear. I could hear my sister's argument clear as day. According to her screaming and pleading, it was that serious. So serious that Daddy skipped right over the healthy seltzers Mama had gotten for him to sip and thumped the cap off a bourbon older than him. He only briefly debated a glass before shrugging and tipping the bottle straight into his mouth. I watched in awe, both horrified and amazed at the sheer volume he swallowed before he needed air. Unlike my sister, whose mouth was still running a mile a minute.

"Daddy, he is MURDERING people! I saw him cut off a man's hand. He was making it dance like the fucking Thing off Addams Family!"

There it was, the inevitable.

See, Andrea lived in a world of rules. Murder was wrong so she didn't kill. Stealing was wrong too so she didn't do that either outside of the time she stole a tube of red lipstick from the MAC counter at 15. She felt horrible about it and the guilt ate her alive, especially since it was a tester that made her face break out something terrible. So no, my sister didn't steal, or conspire, and she certainly didn't believe in the personal sport of murdering.

Yet she was married to a man who committed every crime and sin there was to commit. Truthfully, the murdering wasn't really the problem because I always believed in the concept of opposites attract. I knew Boogie would protect Andrea and that she would eventually soften his wrath.

But they at least should've told the girl. She had been terrified of her husband since her wedding night.

"Andrea," Daddy sighed. "It's no-"

"DON'T YOU DARE SAY IT'S NO BIG DEAL! IT'S A BODY PART!" she screeched.

I heard Mama retch into the sink in response to the vivid description of events. She always did have a sensitive stomach, and while I had no firm moral opposition to casual murder under the right circumstances, even I could admit that the situation was harrowing. A gun wound was one thing, backyard dismemberment was a whole nother piece of pie. Yet my father remained silent. From either the shock or stress of it all. Honestly though, what do you say to that?

Sorry I married you off to a serial killer, he paid me a lot of money?

If I was Dre and Daddy told me that, I'd poison his bourbon. Silence was the best option, even if it pissed my sister off as a side effect.

"You know what, fuck it. I'm calling Dex," she huffed.

The disconnecting beep rang through the kitchen, making my parents jump. Everyone knew Dex wouldn't be able to save her from Boogie and Andrea was hell when she was pissed off. We had about 35 business minutes before she started cussing everybody out. So I fetched a wet rag to clean Mama's face while Daddy attempted to clean up the mess he made by calling Boogie.

Which was a mistake.

Daddy tried to open with a joke because, truthfully, Boogie scared him. The problem there though was that Boogie didn't do jokes.

"What do you need?" I heard him hiss.

My Daddy gulped. Nathaniel Burry had him sweating just like that. All of the Burrys were capable of demon time, Boogie was just the worst. His temper was shorter than freshly waxed coochie hair and he was particularly unforgiving. Even though everything had worked out in his favor regarding the acquisition of Andrea, I knew that the process immensely eroded his respect for my father. Andre Hatchette's authority was waning.

"I'll be back," I sighed, scooping my keys out the bowl.

My lunch sat pitifully on the counter, abandoned and half-eaten. This was the second time this week. Family management was getting increasingly difficult, but somebody had to do it. I could only imagine what would happen if I left these folks to their own devices. Dex would've made me an aunt ages ago, and I'm sure Mama would've been balding from stress by now. Don't even get me started on Andrea.

Luckily, I knew just what to do.

Truth

I hated driving to and from Boogie's house. I was supposed to be back in my office 40 minutes earlier to get through some of my preliminary paperwork, but then I had to escort Andrea home. Which means I basically took a day trip since that crazy ass nigga moved all the way out to the sticks to build what is essentially a survival compound. Don't get me wrong, I had no doubts that he could make it through Armageddon on that muhfucka, and I knew where I'd be living if it came to that. But the damn near two hour commute there and back, plus the random piles of cow shit would keep me in my place as an occasional guest. Besides, I preferred living within 4 miles of a Cook Out in case I needed a 1 am insomnia shake.

Speaking of insomnia, my restlessness was starting to catch up to me. Sleep had been elusive ever since Alise almost made me bust in my slacks. Phantoms of her touch raced across my skin while that sweet, innocent laughter rang in my ears. I even craved her scent. It was all I could think about recently. She was both everywhere and nowhere. It was like trying to catch wind in my palm. Impossible to grasp even though I could feel it all around me.

I still didn't know what to do about Alise. Our interactions were limited and brief yet she still managed to tilt my world off its axis. I wasn't sleeping, I wasn't fucking, and I had even accepted Liberty's most recent blind date attempt for next week just to get her off my mind. Honestly, I didn't even really know if it was reciprocal. Women were flirts, maybe Alise was a natural one. Or maybe she was just fucking with me. Or maybe I was living my worst nightmare and I was now a creep. I knew my feelings for her were wrong. Lusting after a woman nearly half my age was disgraceful, but I didn't know how I ended up here. Most days it felt like I was losing my fucking mind. I could even hear her sing my name from where I sat at my desk.

"Mister Greene, you have a visitor."
Mariah's voice rippled through the speaker clearly. Right along with my supposed visitor's. I knew that melodious laughter anywhere. It was haunting my memories just a few minutes ago, matter of fact. I sat silently, rolling my tongue over my teeth while wondering if she was conjured by a simple thought.
Maybe I needed to get some sage smudges from Liberty.
"Mister Greene, did you hear me?" Mariah repeated.
"Yes, I heard you."
"Would you like me to send her in? Her name is-"
"Yeah," I sighed, scrubbing my hand down my face. "Send Alise in."

Seconds later, I heard the soft snick of the turning knob before Alise strutted in. This time she was wearing frilly, ruffled shorts, a corset top, and a coordinating bow in her hair. She radiated youth, something that rightfully unnerved me. But she also radiated power, which I found equally disturbing. Especially since I found myself rushing to pull out the chair across from me so she could sit.

"Hi, Truth," she smiled. "How's your day been?"

The sun was starting to set behind us, casting an heavenly glow on her divine brown skin. So instead of replying like a normal person, I stared at her. The swell of her breast was slick with oil and silver body glitter. Her lips were painted a sheer rosy red, and her eyes were still predatory, roving over her surroundings like she was on a hunt. Yet she remained a lady. One leg crossed over the other, quietly and patiently waiting for my response.

Hopefully it came before I did.

"You have to excuse my dress," Alise hummed after catching my lingering gaze. "I just came from home."

"You're fine," I sighed longingly before realizing my tone.

I tried to recover.

"I mean you look good, you look nice."

But alas, I failed.

"Thank you. So do you. How was your day in court?" Alise repeated with a soft smirk.

"Routine. I've requested a lighter caseload so I can prepare for campaigning."

"Senator Greene," she cooed slowly. "That has a nice ring to it."

Alise spoke my surname with reverence and possession, as if we shared it. I'm not sure why she thought I was the one to play with. I had tried my best to put space between us since our dance, yet here she was willingly in my office, taunting me. Her unrequested presence in my space was akin to someone waving a leg of lamb in front of a starving man chained to a chair. Everyone acts like I'm weird for my rules, but rules keep people safe.

Soft, sweet, unsullied women included.

"Alise, Is there a reason why you're here? Did you need something?" The longer I stared at her profile in the dim, golden light of my desk lamp, the more inclined I became to poke holes in our family's agreement and find a way to keep her for myself. That was both greedy and morally bankrupt since Boogie already took Andrea, but I was starting not to care. After all, it wouldn't be the first time my family bent contracts to suit their will.

It also wouldn't be the last.

"As a matter of fact, I did come to ask a small favor," she nodded, full lips pulling into a slight pout.

"What do you need?" I rasped.

I recognized the urgency in my tone, and while I desperately wanted to swallow it and appear collected, I needed her to get the fuck out. Everything about Alise was created to drive men wild, and a God, I was not. I was just a man with limited self-control and rapidly decreasing blood flow to his brain.

"So, I'm sure you're aware of what happened to Andrea's PA," she started.

"I am."

"Are you also aware that she asked for a divorce?"

"Shit. I was not."

Well that complicated things. Besides divorce being a no-no with Burrys, Andrea and Boogie's marriage was acting as insurance for a very fresh and volatile business relationship. If we were flying straight, the Hatchette's and Burry's would be competitors outright, so having personal ties to each other was the best bet to get everyone to play nice. Both sides had plenty to lose if shit between them went left.

"Don't worry, she doesn't mean it," Alise said assuringly. "She's just in shock. Andrea's a planner and she didn't plan to end up with someone like Boogie. The real Boogie. No offense of course."

I took no offense to that, because the real Boogie was definitely an acquired taste. He was rash, violent, and impatient. But so damn observant and calculating. There was also an immense amount of pressure on him to ensure the success of our families, and I didn't envy that not one bit.

"So what do you need from me?" I asked, pushing away my paperwork. Family matters always got my undivided attention, and this one was urgent. If we needed to be their chaperones while they figured out their relationship, then so be it. I'd tranquilize that nigga if I had to.

"You don't have to restrain him," Alise chuckled, as if she didn't just display her telepathic ability front and center. "We just need to encourage communication with them. Communication and healthy resolutions. No kidnapping, no killing, no fleeing the country."

"Have you met Boogie? Like in real life? No murking is easier said than done."

"Truth, just talk to him. You can be a voice of reason when you want to be. I've reviewed plenty of your decisions proving so."

I snatched my head back in shock. Out of all the reasons I was expecting to be provided, that wasn't one of them.

"You review my case decisions?"

"Of course, you're our family judge. A formidable judge at that. Plus I hope to be a lawyer in your court someday soon."

While the latter suggestion was a massive conflict of interest, the former acknowledgment validated so many of my recent feelings. My decision to pursue law was always going to be beneficial for my family, but that's not why I did it. Only 7.5% of sitting circuit judges were Black, which was truly a wild juxtaposition when you took into account the demographics of those often being legally persecuted. Black people were also being handed harsher sentences more often than their white counterparts, even for the exact same crime. The only two things I had to do for absolute certainty was be Black and die. So if I had to dedicate time and money to something, it was going to be for the greater good of my kinfolk. Alise saying what she said made me feel seen.

"Ok, I'll talk to him," I nodded. "All you have to worry about is Dre. Anything else?"

Alise had given me yielding, innocent smiles the whole time up until I asked her that. My anxiety rose tenfold when a minacious grin stretched across her plump lips. Our conversation was so easy that I'd almost forgotten that I was playing with fire.

"What are you doing for dinner tonight?" she chuckled.

Every part of me knew that question was a trap, but when she asked I pictured her in front of me instead of the patty melt and fries I'd been craving all day.

"Time for you to go," I exclaimed while pushing out of my chair.

"What? Too forward?"

"Absolutely."

I rounded the desk and pulled out Alise's seat, eager to get her wherever she was going before I became Bham Now's scandal of the week. I could see the title now, "*Be The Jury Of This Judge.*" Nine years of hard work would be circling the drain just like that all because of some lip gloss and a pair of ruffle shorts. Absolutely not.

"Such a goody two shoes," she teased, accepting my extended hand. "But in all seriousness, I would like to have your number in case something else happens. I hate driving to the city."

I pressed my business card in Alise's open hand as she stood, lingering only briefly to enjoy the tenderness of her palms. Hands could tell you a lot about a person, and hers were unblemished and callous free. That reminded why she was off limits again. I was too rough for someone like her. Besides, we were practically family now.

"Text me and I'll save your number."

I watched her fold the card into her wallet with a polite but seemingly distant smile. She probably felt rejected, and while I wanted to assuage those fears, it was probably for the best. We needed to kill whatever this was between us before it grew roots. I didn't need to contribute to my growing possessiveness with dinner.

"Okie dokie," Alise sighed. "I'll get out of your hair."

Her disappointed little pout twisted my heart around like a wrung-out rag, and I got the horrifying urge to do everything in my power to fix it. That's exactly why I needed distance. I could only safely handle Alise in small doses. Small doses and public places. Unlike the private office we were currently in.

"Here, let me walk you to the elevator," I offered, trying to fix what my emotional guards had rightfully broken.

I was still acutely aware that my attraction to her was wrong, but my willpower was waning. So I placed my hand on her upper back, ready to guide her, but she stopped me with a hand to the chest.

"Truth, that's not necessary," Alise protested.

This time, there was no smile accompanying her response. Her expression was unyielding and her stare battled my own to determine situational dominance. This was my office and she was my visitor. Both of those things were hard facts. Yet I found myself questioning reality due to the way she looked at me. She watched me as if she already owned me.

"Alise," I groaned as she pulled me closer.

We met for a bruising kiss. A liplock that made me realize that I'd never *really* been kissed before.

No, not really. Not like this.

Not with soft hands lacing through my locs, or long fingers walking across my back, or hunger, or passion that made me forget everything about myself and the world around me. A single kiss wasn't enough, but ten may have been too many. A long-withheld moan slipped free on the 11th and Alise pulled away. That was really for the best, but I was already addicted and going through withdrawals. So I pressed forward again, hoping to satisfy the animalistic urge to fuck Alise on every available surface, only for her pretty claws to catch my throat.

"Aht, aht," she chided before placing one single kiss to the corner of my mouth. "Stay."

The Truth Greene Show immediately paused with Alise's demand. My mind, which was usually a mess of to-do lists, local regulations, laws, and pop-culture trivia, became an uncomplicated pool of white noise. I can't tell you how long I stood in the middle of my office disheveled, erect, and disengaged, but I can tell you that I was not happy to find Alise gone once I came back online. I first searched behind the furniture because it made perfect sense to my dizzy mind that a 5' 10" woman would be hiding behind a love seat. Then when I inevitably failed to locate her, I rushed into the tenth floor lobby to find the woman responsible for my recklessness. The air around me still smelled like ginger, cashmere, and what I now knew was lust, yet her absence taunted me.

"Mister Greene, are you alright?" Mariah gasped.

I was so determined to catch Alise that I'd forgotten that appearances and professionalism were important. I caught a glimpse of my reflection in the freshly polished gold doors of the elevator. My loose tie hung from my disrupted collar, my hair was pulled free from its usual knot, and I was drooling like a rabid dog. I scrubbed my hand down my face, more frustrated than embarrassed.

I had finally figured out why Alise's eyes reminded me of a predator. She had that in common with Jaguars, and to me, they were the same kind of monsters. Because they would mesmerize you with their beauty while they killed you, and you would enjoy the pain of death simply because you knew the risks of getting too close.

Bad Habits

A **LISE**

"Who are you talking to?"

I rushed to lock my phone even though I knew it was too late. Mae had probably been watching my text messages in the cafe window for the last minute. Luckily though, they were mostly innocent. Truth was invoking distance since our little kiss. Well, as much distance as he possibly could. He wouldn't see me in his office anymore, but he'd always respond when I reached out. Most of the time he even reached out first.

"Nobody," I smiled.

"TG. Who has the initials TG that we know?" Mae asked, tapping her pointer finger to her chin.

I quietly watched my cousin flip through her mental rolodex. Her eyes asked me for a hint but I wasn't going to help her blow up my spot. I preferred to do my dirt in private. The less people who knew, the better. I didn't need anyone to try and talk me out of it. My mind was already made up.

"Alise no," Mae finally gasped.

"No, what?" I asked innocently.

"Nah, don't try to play that ditzy bitch card on me. I know you too well. Truth Greene? Seriously? He's almost old enough to be your damn daddy!"

"First off, fourteen years does not make someone old enough to be my daddy. He's closer to unc age. Besides, we both know I've never been too interested in nephew and them."

"Girl, age thing aside, he's a Burry!"

"He's technically a Greene, and we squashed the family beef when Dre and Boogie got married."

"Ain't no technically, nothing! His mama may have given him his daddy's last name, but make no mistake about it, that man is a Burry. He grew up right alongside Boogie. They have the same training, the same grit. Alise, I don't know. Did you talk to Dre about this?"

"Why would I need to talk to Dre?"

"Nevermind, I already know you haven't," Mae chuckled. "Because if you had, she would've told you that Truth is a crash out in recovery. You like to play games, and that's gone get you in trouble with a man like that."

I did like to play games, and while I was a bit more adventurous than my opponent, I still only waged the most in the ones I knew I could win.

"He's a sitting Judge. He's not gonna jeopardize his position over little ole me. We're gonna keep things private and see what happens."

"So you're already fucking him?" Mae pressed.

"Not yet," I admitted. "I'm currently aiming to start in about a month."

"Yeah ok. Let me know what the wedding colors will be," Mae chuckled. "This is gone be your first and your last time plotting on a nigga."

"Don't be dramatic," I chided. "Marriage between us is highly unlikely. I ran the numbers."

My cousin cast me a skeptical side-eye, a silent indicator of her disbelief. She had her reasons for her cynicism but I had this handled. Relationship management was my specialty.

The house was empty when I got home. Dex was probably still working, while Mama and Daddy sent me a text saying they were off to dinner.

According to the text I got from Boogie, Andrea was somewhere on a Grecian beach drinking expensive wine and eating fancy cheese. That left me alone with my thoughts. I had a full to-do list outside of driving Truth crazy. I was coming to the end of my gap year and I needed to start applying for law programs. I also needed to schedule my mentee's next catch-up session, audit my earnings account, deep condition my hair, and study for the LSAT. The five year plan was still thriving, but my curls were not.

Forty minutes later, I was sitting under the dryer with a peach Bellini and a processing cap full of hair mayonnaise. I had gotten Symphony, my Black Girl Magic mentee, all scheduled for next Monday, and my data for my account was downloading. So I was ready to relax. But then Truth sent me a text. A poll on which coffee he should get.

I caught myself returning to an old anxious habit of nail biting while waiting on his reply. Which made me consider Mae's warning. Maybe I did need to talk to Andrea.

Originally my pursuit of Truth was purely sexual. He was fine and I wanted to fuck him. Plain and simple. My Mama had her thing with Allen Iverson and I too wanted the experience of someone like him to keep me company when I grew old and gray. I was capable of that degree of introspection.

But the more I learned about him, the more complicated that goal became. Truth was kind, and funny, and refreshing. He liked eating at hole-in-the-wall diners, watching MAFS, and sipping shitty, sugary, coffee drinks. But he was also possessive, like his cousin. So possessive that some of the men in our social circle had begun to flat-out ignore me, citing Truth as the reason why.

Burrys married, and they seldom participated in the ritual of divorce. That was a fact I knew well.

Meanwhile I was pursuing one while simultaneously harboring plans to remain unattached. I had at least a decade to get through before I entertained the idea of committing to anyone. Yet this man had put a claim on me and I didn't necessarily hate it...

I was still determined to fuck him at least once, but now I understood that I had to take steps to protect my heart. Because if I didn't, I'd belong to Truth Greene in a year.

Truth

"Yeah, I was nervous when Liberty brought it up since I'm not really a blind date person, but now I'm glad I came."

"Same," I laughed.

My date sat across from me in a deep red jumpsuit, coordinating heels, and a fresh curled blowout. She had a complexion that reminded me of toasted rye, high cheekbones, and a big animated smile. Her name was Makayla, she worked as a private Nanny, and she was beautiful.

"Ooh, let's try their chocolate cake!" she exclaimed.

"It's actually one of my favorites," I admitted with a laugh.

"Mhm, I knew I liked you."

The good news? We had chemistry.

"It feels like we've been friends our whole lives," she chuckled.

The bad news? It wasn't the romantic kind.

"Right?" I agreed.

AT. ALL.

I didn't know how I was gonna explain this to Liberty. Makayla was great, but I didn't wanna jump the broom with her. However, I could see us opening a food truck together. Her Mister Right was out there, but it definitely wasn't me. I think she knew it too subconsciously, which is why she kept bringing up friendship. Normally that might offend me, but I couldn't care less about that classification, simply because she wasn't Alise.

Fucking Alise.

I was learning that I could be friends with anyone else except her. She consumed my day even when I was busy, and especially when I wasn't. I had her put on the no visitation list at my office but that hadn't created as much distance as I hoped because I made the mistake of giving her my number. It was supposed to be for emergency use only but that didn't last long. We hadn't talked about that kiss, but it didn't matter. I had quickly discovered I could talk to her about anything. Conversation was always easy with Alise. We spent hours talking about everything from top five anime, to out favorite foods, to music, and hobbies. She has so many cool hobbies. I never expected her to be so complex and sure of herself at 21, but seeing it made me oddly proud, and I told her that every chance I got. Even if I had to seek her out first.

We were two weeks in and I was sharing more of myself than I originally planned to. More than what I had ever willingly given anyone else.

Maybe that's why this thing with Makayla wasn't working. I had nothing left to give since it was all tied up with Alise.

Fuck this was terrible.

After I inevitably set my career on fire, Uncle Nick was gone kill my dumb ass, and Dexter was gone help.

"So hey," Makayla started, interrupting my panicked thoughts. "I had a lot of fun, but I have to be honest."

Ah shit, I knew what came next.

"*It's not you, it's me.*"

Suddenly my shoulders were in my ears. I didn't like Makayla like that, but it was almost reflexive to tense in preparation for bad news, or in my case, indifferent news.

"Relax," Makayla chuckled. "I just want to be upfront about my dating situation. I'm seeing multiple people right now and I wanted you to be aware before we start anything. I understand if this changes how you feel about me."

I felt... Absolutely nothing.

"Oh, that's fine. So am I."

I don't know why I lied. I wasn't dating anyone. I was being terrorized by Alise, but that was it. However, it did make it easier to end this after another date or two. I could pretend that I chose someone else. Liberty wouldn't ask too many questions once I told her Makayla was seeing multiple people. She knew I had a possessive streak, and she'd stay off my back until I licked my theoretical wounds.

Then I could figure out this thing with Alise.

"Aw, Truth. These are lovely," Mama cooed while fluffing the petals of the arrangement.

I watched her enjoy the surprise for no longer than twelve seconds before she got back to business.

"How was the date?"

I threw my head back silently. I was annoyed yet I knew better than to sigh. Yeah I was in my thirties, but I still wasn't grown enough to be doing allat in my Mama's house.

"It was good, Ma'am. She was pretty. The conversation was nice."

I thought that was a sufficient amount of information to share with my mother about my first date. A respectful amount. And still...

"Mhm. If it was all that then why y'all ain't back at your place?"

"Mama, please! I'm not a whore," I groaned.

"I beg to differ," Justice wheezed.

That nigga was about to fall out of his seat from laughing. As if he wasn't in the same damn boat. He'd be next just as soon as I got married off.

"Shut Up," I hissed. "Cause you don't want me to get started, Mister itchy nuts."

"Nuhuh! Take that outside," Mama demanded, pointing towards the patio. "It's too late for y'all's bullshit. I got church in the morning."

The glass door closed behind us with a loud thud, then I heard the curtains slide in place. It's a miracle Mama didn't lock us out and make us climb over the fence, but she knew Justice had a bad back.

"So what really happened on the date?" he asked, taking a fresh joint between his lips. "She ain't have no booty?"

I hated the ringing sound Justice's electric lighter made when it was ignited, but I was happy to overlook it when the rich smell of cannabis filled the backyard.

"Nah, she was cool," I admitted, accepting his peace offering.

I took a long drawl while I considered what to say next. Me and Makayla wouldn't have made it far either way, but I immediately envisioned Alise and the way her lips felt on mine. I hadn't smoked in a hot minute and I didn't miss it, but after just one hit, one kiss, I was craving Alise.

"She just wasn't for me," I shrugged.

I took another hit before passing it back and this time I coughed.

"Damn, is this Boogie's shit?"

"You know it is," Justice laughed. "His crazy ass will return a nigga to ashes and dust just so he can use them in his tomato garden."

"Nahhhhhh," I chuckled. "People are flower food. Them tomatoes are the product of pure, grade-A cow shit."

"Damn, not we out here smoking boo-boo blunts," Justice howled.

It took our stupid asses four whole minutes to recover. Even hearing Mama fuss couldn't stop the free-flowing laughter. We got it together eventually though.

"So, who is she?" Justice asked, once the night's quiet returned.

"Who is who?" I queried.

"Who's the woman you really want? Cause you're feeling somebody. I know you."

Again I pictured Alise. Tall, dark, and gorgeous. Flawless skin. Flawless smile. Thick, dense, curly hair. Everything that drove me wild. I pictured all of it in front of me. All of her.

"It's not like that," I protested while watching the wind disturb the lawn. Watching thick blades of grass bend to accommodate the evening breeze brought me back to our moment in my office. It was a perfect metaphor for the way her touch glided across my hot skin.

"I think I just need to fuck," I tutted.

My brother smirked, but his laughter didn't join mine.

"Aye, be careful Truth," he warned. "You gotta let scars breathe. Otherwise they'll take over."

I swallowed my next joke and let my brother's advice marinate. He had made peace with his past, and I'd like to think that I had to.

But only time would tell.

"I'm good, I promise. I got this all under control," I said confidently.
I knew I would be a lawyer at the age of seven. Not because I was good
at arguing, or debate, or exploiting loopholes. Even though I was great at
all of those things, that wasn't the reason.
It was because I could lie so good that I could even convince myself.
That was the real skill.

That's Normal

A LISE

Mondays were always routine for me. I'd wake up early, have my tea, then head to headquarters to collaborate with our brand awareness team. After I finished work, I'd either have lunch with Mama or harass one of my siblings, then head home and study before we started on Monday dinner. The men would play cards, we'd all eat, then I'd get in bed and catch up on TV.

That was normal. That was routine.

So seeing Andrea in HQ bright and early that morning told me this Monday would be anything but.

"What are you doing here? I thought you were staying at the North division." I said, slipping in the seat next to her.

"Nat moved me," she grumbled.

"Oh because of Thomas?"

Thomas Cisos, or so he claimed to be, was Andrea's now pulverized personal assistant. The Burry's have their own intelligence team that investigates all new personnel, no matter which side of business employed them. My nail tech had even ended up on their radar because of my growing proximity to Truth. So of course Boogie had my sister's PA triple checked.

"You know about Thomas?" Andrea gasped.

"Sure," I shrugged. "I know lots of things. Truth keeps me informed."

Andrea cast me a quick but noticeable side eye. My big sister might have been a bit naive when it came to believing our father, but she was no fool. She likely had her own concerns. Especially since this was a life-long pursuit on my end.

"What's going on with you and him?"

For the first time in a week, I allowed myself to think of that kiss. It was a test for his boundaries originally, but all it did was piss me off in the end. It was rough and satisfying, and his touch reminded me that I was a woman. But I knew I couldn't fuck him in his office with his nosey ass assistant listening. I made a choice to spare his professional image, and he'd been avoiding me ever since.

"Oh, nothing. You know I'm too young for Truth," I damn near hissed.

The irritation in my tone surprised me. I wasn't one for emotional outbursts and here I was raising my voice during a simple discussion. I probably needed to flick the bean. Sexual frustration was a mother fucker at times.

"Is that what he told you?" Andrea asked.

"No, but you know he's firm on his five year under five year older age gap rule. For now," I smiled.

I resented that rule for a long time, but now I was kind of grateful for it. Truth was steadfast and dedicated. A man of principle. A man of morals. Honestly I respected it, even though I had plans to break every single one of his little rules. It made the chase that much sweeter.

Andrea wasn't thrilled to learn that Boogie was bringing her by the house after work, but I was excited. I wanted to hear about her honeymoon, and also get the scoop on why Boogie's assistant ran to her car crying. Plus cooking with my mom and sister brought me some much needed normalcy. Everything was changing so fast. Families, careers, homes. I didn't mind the change so much, but the pace was frightening. It put time into a different perspective for me. Five years was so little time to get my entire life together. My to-do list was growing out of control.

I was so spacey on the drive home that I didn't realize I was hungry until I heard my stomach rumbling like a spring thunderstorm. Which made me grateful that Boogie was bringing me a bun even though our group chat stressed Andrea out. I think she was still holding on to the idea that she could somehow weasel her way out of her marriage. So to her, Boogie's integration with the rest of us was further complicating things. But that man wasn't letting her go, and if push came to shove, she wasn't letting go either.

Once I parked I checked all my notifications, and Boogie was right on time with the menu. Also, some vintage pictures of Andrea wearing an obscene amount of galactic blue eye shadow. I was too young to remember anything about that era, and I'm grateful. I'm not afraid of much, but clowns terrify me.

Her and Bobo The Clown could've been twins.

"Going somewhere?" A familiar voice rumbled.

I looked up from my phone and into the eyes of Truth. He extended his hand to help me out of the car and I couldn't stop the smile that stretched across my face when my palm touched his. Mister Greene looked very handsome. He was still in his suit but he had his hair flowing freely down his back, and in the absence of his tie I spotted a heavy gold chain tucked against his exposed chest. Dark, thick curls swirled across his skin, reminding me of the majesty of Van Gogh's Starry Night. He was a masterpiece.

"Actually, I live here," I smiled.

I expected Truth to grow uncomfortable with the reminder of my family being near however he smiled instead. Then he pulled me close by placing one large hand on my hip. He was so close that I could see the chaos in his grin. A shiver ran down my tightening spine as we locked eyes. The chill was a physical warning. Mae was right. I did like to play my games, but I started to realize I might've met my match.

"You didn't text me back today, Alise," he whispered, bringing his lips to my ear. "That hurt my lil feelings."

Cinnamon spiced breath tickled my neck while the smell of rosemary, bergamot, and cotton filled my nose. I could feel the exact moment my pupils dilated, making my eyes sting from the intensity of the bright July afternoon. My body reacted to his touch like it was pure opium.

Reciprocity had begun to make me anxious instead of excited. Touching him was like getting a fix.

"Andrea's back," I croaked in response to his earlier statement.

"Mhm. She's at HQ now," Truth nodded, while nuzzling his nose in the crook of my neck. "Boogie wants her close. I think possessiveness runs in the family."

If nothing else about the moment was a warning, that statement certainly was. This was gonna be a short term thing, and I'd do well to remind him of that. Just as soon as figured out how to leave his orbit. If that was even possible.

"Oh my lord," I whispered as he placed a hot kiss on my bare shoulder.

His lips traveled up the length of my collar, until he reached my ear. Then he gently tugged at my earring with his canines before kissing it better. Goodness he could kiss like no one's business. His lips felt so good on my body that I started moaning.

Until I saw the sun reflecting off my family crest when I came to. I remembered that we were barely in the car park. Someone could easily spot us, and heaven forbid it be either of my parents.

"Stop before my Daddy sees us!" I hissed, pushing Truth back by his throat.

"Why? You don't want Senior to know that your hot in the tail ass been driving me crazy?"

"So that's what this is about? You're upset at me?" I chuckled.

"You damn right I'm upset at you," Truth grumbled. "I had to ban you from my office cause you had me out in broad daylight drooling like a wild animal."

"It was just a kiss," I cooed innocently.

"No it wasn't, Alise," he growled, stepping closer. "No it fucking wasn't. Every time the sun sets in my office, I imagine you. In front of me, on top of me, underneath me. Meanwhile you're safe at home, pretending like you're not driving me insane. So I started thinking: Why should my imagination get to have all the fun? What would happen if I just gave in?

Ain't that what you want anyway, sweet pea?" Truth asked while pulling me back into him.

His erection came to rest between my thighs, hard, hot, and heavy. My heart thumped like a rabbit's foot. My poor mind couldn't keep up. And my body? She was itching to show him exactly what she wanted.

"You wanna fuck me, don't you?" Truth chuckled, swiping his thumb across my cheek.

"I'd like to continue this conversation at a later date," I replied quietly.

"Nah, You wanna fuck me. You just don't want your Daddy to know, and best believe if I touched you in this house, he'd know."

Father God in heaven.

I was so wet I thought my period started early.

A prayer hadn't graced my lips in 40 days and 40 nights, but I uttered one right then. I needed a heavenly miracle before I got opened up against the hood of Truth's Highlander.

Suddenly my phone rang.

Hallelujah! It was a prayer answered.

I scrambled to answer the call, not knowing or caring who was on the other end, but luckily it was Boogie.

"Hello?" I gasped.

"Hey Lis, text me what you want. We're ordering the food now," he said.

"Sorry. I just got home. I'll do it now."

Boogie paused as if he could smell my bullshit through the phone. I knew he was the wrong one to lie to, but I couldn't tell him I got distracted because his cousin was trying to tie me in a knot. No matter how smug Truth looked watching me sweat.

"Alright," Boogie resumed. "See y'all in forty minutes."

A frown was creasing my lips before he could finish.

Somehow he knew something was up.

Boogie hung up the phone and I wasted no time taking the opportunity to flee to the safety of the porch. Don't get me wrong, I was definitely going to fuck Truth, but I hated being caught off guard more than anything. I had a plan but his impatient ass was going to ruin it, and during Monday dinner no less. The rest of the family would be arriving shortly, and they didn't need to witness the final results of my relentless pursuit. Besides, Mister Nick would get ideas. He wanted a full integration and another marriage was sure to do just that. I loved Andrea and I understood that she made a sacrifice for the rest of us, but I wasn't going out like that. No matter how tempting his nephew was.

Truth

I wanted Alise.

A month ago, I would've rather died before admitting that out loud. However, after spending the whole weekend dreaming about the way her body fit against mine, I decided that acceptance was the first step towards recovery. She was a grown adult. A grown adult capable of deciding that she wanted to sleep with me. That was a terrible decision, really, but so was my decision to try and stop her. I had learned that she was determined. Which meant she was gonna keep torturing me until she got what she wanted. So I just eliminated those extra steps. We could get each other out of our systems with these next few weeks before my campaign, and then I could focus.

Alise ran off after her call with Boogie, so I waited around until someone else arrived. Luckily it didn't take long for my uncle's limo to pull into the Hatchette's drive. I loved punctual ass old men. Uncle Nick believed if you weren't early then you were late. That meant I had plenty of time to get my payback on Alise.

"Hey, Nephew!" he cheerfully exclaimed as we walked up the steps.

My uncle's voice reminded me of Louis Armstrong. It was something he had gotten from his father. A deep and gravelly hum that was still rhythmic. Boogie inherited the depth and I inherited the rhythm. My brothers all fell somewhere between us. Sometimes that made me wonder about my future children. If I ever got around to having any.

"You ready to lose some money tonight?" he asked.

"I can only afford to lose $20," I laughed. "Anything more and I'mma have to start swinging."

"Ha!" he wheezed. "Ain't gone be no fighting. Yo cousin's supposed to be here."

"Never mind. I definitely can't afford a Boogie ass whooping. I gotta take my campaign photos in a couple days."

"Shit, can't nobody afford a Boogie ass whooping. You see how fast they married off Lil Dre don't you? They scared of his crazy ass. Quiet as kept, they're scared of a lot of you boys. As they should be," he chuckled. "If y'all wasn't mine I'd constantly be screaming, *"Police!"* like that one hoe who reported that bird watcher."

I don't know why that bit of information felt good to have, but it did. Maybe I'd process the reason eventually, but right now I needed to smile in Senior's face so I could rearrange his daughter's guts later. Everything else could wait.

"Hey, how y'all doing?" I greeted as we settled into the living room.

"Hey!" we heard in return.

The Hatchette's had a full house. Three out of five of Mama Joy's sisters were there. Two had brought along their men, while their sons and daughters were hanging off nearby couches and chairs.

"Damn, everybody here huh?" Uncle Nick chuckled while shaking Senior's hand.

"Yeah, Boogie and Dre's wedding turned into a family reunion," he laughed back. "Speaking of which, they should be here in a minute."

Alise was already in the kitchen with her Mama and cousins, so I found a spot near the bar and waited for Boogie. It was bridge night and I ain't need nobody else calling dibs on his good cheating ass.

"So what you been up to, Nephew?" Uncle Nick asked, grabbing the seat next to me. "Ya mama told me you started seeing somebody."

My heart started to descend into my ass until I remembered she probably told him about my date. He was talking about Makayla. Not that I was seeing Alise anyway. I was just obliging her request. She wanted this dick and I was gone give it to her. Nice, deep, and slow.

"Nah it ain't like that," I shrugged, still thinking about Alise.

I wondered what she was in there cooking. Could she even cook or was she just making a salad or something? I'd have to ask next time we talked.

"Shit, that smile got you looking like you might be next at the altar," Unc laughed. "Meet me at the altar in your white dress..."

I made the mistake of envisioning Alise in a white dress, and a big veil, and pearls smooth and lustrous. I saw her hand resting in my own as a I slid a perfectly set silver wedding band on her bony ring finger. Then I saw her lips utter my name as we exchanged vows. I could damn near hear it. Chills rushed down my spine at the thought of Alise being mine. Even though I knew that absolutely could not happen.

"Maybe," I mumbled, trying to shake my goosebumps.

It seemed like Boogie and Andrea initially had other plans, but there he was sitting next to me at the game table while his wife occupied the kitchen. Mama Joy could sell shit to flies.

"I wanna go home," he huffed as he folded yet another hand.

It was too many of us for a good game of bridge, so we ended up switching to three-card rummy. Maybe that was a good thing because Boogie was irritated and it was drop day. I would've lost $200 by now if I was dealing with him.

"You know all Dre's gonna do is fuss at you as soon as y'all get there right?" I chuckled.

"For what?" Boogie tutted.

I looked over at Dexter's triple wrapped palm, and then slowly brought my eyes back to my cousin. He gave me a questioning shrug as if my warning was somehow cryptic. But that was fine, because I didn't mind spelling it out.

"Probably for stabbing her brother," I nodded. "Definitely, for stabbing her brother."

"I wasn't gone shoot my sister," Dexter grumbled.

"I don't care. You had a gun pointed at her person," Boogie hissed while throwing in his hand.

Regret squeezed me tight, because it took no time at all for the table to devolve into complete chaos. Boogie was a lot of things, but one thing he could never be was a bitch made nigga, especially not about his wife. So it didn't surprise me when I saw murderous intent flash in his eyes at certain comments. Hell, I thought he was going to drag faux-unc off by the neck. But apparently he just went to find Andrea. I hoped she could talk him off his ledge before we had to get a late-night crew involved.

"Truth, what happened?" Uncle Nick asked once Boogie completely cleared the room.

"Hm?" I hummed back, knowing damn well what he was talking about.

So my cousin's wife had asked for a divorce. If it had been any other threat, the family *might* have minded their business, but divorce was untenable. It was the one thing we didn't participate in. But I really didn't think she meant it. Andrea was just upset to be blindsided.

Understandably so.

"Dre asked Boogie for a divorce," Uncle gritted.

"She was just mad because she didn't know what Boogie was capable of. Y'all should have told her," I shrugged.

He then turned to face Senior with the same look of shock, his graying brows shot high and wide.

"She really didn't know? Andre, I thought that was a joke! How is that even possible when Alise knows?"

"Joy wanted them to be normal," Dre sighed. "It was already too late for Dex so we chose to shelter Andrea. Alise is something else entirely. She figured it out on her own. Too smart for her own good."

"Jesus," Uncle hissed, sinking into his seat.

He ran a weathered hand through his tight curls slowly so his rings wouldn't catch. He wanted to step down in a few months' time, but that wouldn't be possible if Boogie didn't have his wife. That nigga needed a balancing force and Andrea was it.

Always had been.

"You need to fix this shit. Money and contracts aside, this is a problem. That boy will burn your house down before he gives up your daughter," Nick warned with a pointed finger.

"Don't worry," I interjected, growing uncomfortable with the tension. "I'm talking to him, and I got somebody on Andrea."

"Tuhuh," Uncle chuckled. "Don't worry my ass. We got an entire merger on the line. Matter of fact Dre, what's going on with your niece, Mae?"

"For who?" I choked.

"You that's who," Uncle said, snapping his fingers. "You tryna get into Senate with a hope and a prayer. You also need a wife."

A wife?

Again I pictured Alise. Soft dark skin, gentle hands, endlessly long legs that ran through my mind all day and night. Then soft, sweet lips that called my name like she owned it. Hell, she just might own my shit. I could be her husband...

"Absolutely fucking not," I snapped.

I was speaking more to myself than anything, but the sentiment still stood. And if it couldn't be her, then it wouldn't be anyone.

"Look, Unc. I appreciate it, but I'm seeing someone."

"I thought it wasn't that serious!" he harrumphed.

"I lied. I like her a lot. I don't wanna have this conversation again. So please keep me out of the schemes."

Silence filled the room like cigar smoke. Then I heard my uncle laugh, "Damn, nephew. Do that girl know she got you that bad? Probably not. Condolences to her father."

"Condolences indeed," I whispered while looking at Senior.

It was the third Monday in July. Today I heard six cases and decided on two. Tonight was card night. The Hatchette's were hosting.

Everything about today was normal. Routine even.

Yet I felt it in my spirit that this would be the last normal day I would endure for a while. Maybe even the rest of my life.

"I'm going to go check on the girls," I said, dismissing myself from the table. "See y'all at dinner."

Alise

I was starting to remember why I liked silence.

"Boogie, can you take this to the table?" Andrea giggled.

She drunkenly floated around my aunties who were busy talking about their next matches, and my cousins, who were arguing over music choices. Mama was busy rinsing mashed potatoes from the big pot before they dried and became a crusty mess, which meant there was the sound of metal banging on metal adding to the chaotic symphony every few minutes.

Talking, and singing, and scraping, and banging. All of the noise was making me tense, and I was about to slink off to find some quiet until I heard some calm cut through the storm.

"I saw Boogie setting up the table. Y'all need any more help?" he asked with a melodious chuckle.

The room stopped moving to watch Truth shrug his suit jacket and roll up his sleeves. Normally I'd be territorial at this point, but I understood his allure. Fine was an understatement. Truth was the definition of country-thick. Muscular but yielding where it mattered. His smile was never flashy, but it was charming and wide. Plus all of the Burry men were tattooed, and Truth was no exception despite his profession. The only difference was where his ink stopped, right below his elbow, and the vivid red he chose for some of the designs. Namely his family crest and the scarlet flax adorning it. Scarlet like ice-cold steeped hibiscus. Scarlet like the blood running through me and creating a mess of my mind.

"I think Alise could use some help frosting her cakes. Other than that we're all done," Mae replied.

I could hear the smile in her tone. For as much as she disagreed with my little pursuit, she had my back. She was always gonna be my wing woman.

"Gotcha, let me grab an apron," Truth replied while staring at me.

The kitchen was always a little warm, but the heat between our silent stares had it feeling like the second tier of hell. An impulsive thought crawled forward and begged me to take my clothes off, but fortunately I still had enough sense to push it away.

"Come on y'all, let's get everything in the dining room," Andrea instructed. "Alise probably needs a lil break from us anyway. Y'all know she don't do noise."

I knew I'd owe Andrea based on the little side eye she cast me when everyone was looking away, but I couldn't help but smile despite it. Everything had changed but Dre was still my mischievous big sister. The one that always had my back. I was blessed to have her and Mae.

"Y'all wanna leave her with Truth?" My cousin Felicity scoffed. "Can he even ice a cake?"

Dear, sweet Felicity. She'd been on my nerves all fucking night. I don't know why she was so concerned with what I was doing, but it was getting difficult to hold onto my smile. My motto was charm, don't alarm. Which was something that had historically worked well for me. Folks would see my Mama's smile and leave all their reservations at the door, no questions asked.

Except for now.

Change was in the air, but not the same change that was present on Dre's wedding day. It was volatile and uncomfortable instead.

"Oh please," Mama said, waving Felicity off. "Truth is harmless. We can barely get him to acknowledge anyone under the age of thirty. Let's go."

Everyone filed out behind my Mama, leaving just Truth and I in the peace and quiet of a once bustling kitchen.

"Ok, I'm ready," Truth said, tying the borrowed apron in place with a surprisingly extravagant bow. "What do you need me to do?"

I loved that he was always ready to serve. It made things much more enjoyable. Even when it was just everyday things like this. I flicked the frills on the hem of his smock before pointing to the walk-in cooler,

"Grab my cakes please. It's 6 in total. I'm gonna finish the vanilla buttercream then fold in some strawberries."

"What does that mean?" Truth chuckled. "What does fold in the cheese mean?

"Wow, I wasn't expecting a Schitt's Creek reference from you," I giggled as he whisked through the kitchen.

"I'm versatile," he shrugged while setting down the first three cakes. "Like American buttercream."

There was something endearing about a man not being completely useless in the kitchen. Even just possessing basic culinary knowledge. I tried not to hand them points for the bare minimum, but I had to give it to him. I doubted that most southern grandmas knew the differences between buttercream recipes.

"You bake?" I smiled while leveling off my powdered sugar.

"Absolutely not. I watch others bake though. Mostly on Is It Cake," Truth explained.

He then began unwrapping my cakes without further instructions, discarding the plastic and cardboard as he went.

"But I didn't know you cooked," he said after a while.

"That's because I don't. Touching raw meat makes me sick, so I stick to pastries. I deal with scallops on occasion if I'm feeling brave."

"Hm, that's good to know."

"Why?" I laughed.

Silence filled the air between us, humid and heavy while we locked eyes. I took pride in being the predator, in driving his uptight ass wild. Although I got the distinct feeling I was the prey in this particular situation when I felt my nipples tighten. Truth seemed to grow closer at first, taking interest in my state, but then he returned to his task of unwrapping the cakes.

"What now?" he asked.

"Let me portion you some frosting," I mumbled, avoiding his gaze.

Because otherwise it might set me ablaze.

I scooped two cups of fluffy white icing into a bowl before gathering his tools. The kitchen was too open for us to start anything, so I wanted to keep our interaction brief, but I made the mistake of sucking a speck of buttercream off my pointer finger.

I couldn't even get my hand out my mouth before he was behind me, staring like he'd never seen a woman before.

"Alise," he growled.

"What's the problem, Truth?" I laughed.

He bracketed me between two strong arms then pressed my hips into the counter with the force of his own. His erection surprised me and I dropped the bowl on the counter, splattering icing on my face.

"How long are we gonna play your little game?" Truth asked before licking the buttercream off my cheek.

One of his hands gripped my hip while the length of his other arm was tucked under my bust. He was showing me rather than telling me about how I affected him. And while I appreciated the sentiment, I was the one in control here. I attempted to remind him of that face to face, but I was locked into position with all of his weight. So instead I reached behind the apron and cupped his sack. It was heavy in my hand and full of promises. Just like Truth's whimper.

"We're gonna play this game until I say so," I laughed while stroking his print. "And since you're such a good boy, you're going to wait."
His zipper dangled in the center of his fly and I, being ever the opportunist, tugged it downward to slip my fingers inside.
Lord, be with me. His tip had the same circumference of a tangerine. Then he was so damn responsive that I had to hold his hips in place to keep him from knocking me over the edge of the counter.
"Alise," he simpered while rutting against my palm. "Please, sweet pea."
His request was so damn perfect that I almost agreed. I was a sucker for pleading just like any other dom, and Mister Greene was so good at begging.

"Frost my cakes, Truth," I whispered while pumping his length. "Let's see how well you follow instructions first. If you're a good listener you might get a reward."
"Ok, ok," he groaned, slipping out of my hands. "Let me get a spatula."
I smiled while watching him scurry around to do my bidding.
I loved to be in charge of good boys who listened well.

A Trick For Yo Ass

TRUTH

Hatchette women were demons.

Or maybe Goddesses.

I couldn't tell you which one for sure, but I knew they were otherworldly. I could be a model for a Viagra commercial, while Boogie looked like he was high on life.

"Did you get your dick sucked in the bathroom or something?" I mumbled. "I swear it's like night and day."

My nigga was on cloud nine. If the chairs were any taller, he would've been kicking his feet.

"Nah," Nat laughed, shoveling a bite of food into his gullet. "I think I was just hungry."

"More like hangry," I scoffed. "I thought you was gone break ole dude's nose."

He shrugged. Which meant he likely would've done just that and then some.

But again, Andrea was that man's calming force.

Even when she was a vulgar, tipsy mess.

Me and Alise exchanged a look as Andrea loudly proclaimed Boogie's nasty ass to be a munch. Everyone else was disturbed, but we had to withhold our laughter. That was another thing I enjoyed about Alise. Her sense of humor mirrored my own. We could bounce jokes off each other all day. We probably would've done just that if not for what happened next.

The table creaked and groaned with the weight of two men until one slumped against it.

"NATHANIEL, STOP! HE'S DEAD!" Andrea hollered.

What I initially brushed off as a heated but necessary conversation between Dre and Senior, turned into a full out murder when Boogie got involved. I had a feeling ole dude wouldn't be walking out of here in one piece, but I didn't think Nat would take him out at the dinner table either.

He dropped the man's head back on the table then checked his pulse before confirming that he had gone to meet his maker with a sigh. Everyone at the table looked rightfully horrified, including Senior, Mama Joy, and Uncle. I was too irritated to look at Alise. Instead I said a prayer for all the kitchen foreplay that would now be laid to rest with this talkative dickhead. Gone were my hopes of finally sliding in between her long legs. Instead I'd be facilitating a late night clean-up.

After confirming that ole boy didn't have any close family, Nat provided instructions. Everyone would sign an NDA and Joy's sister would get a hush payment to soothe the pain of her expired boy toy. The Hatchette girls cleared the table soon after with the help of Dexter, and everyone else including Boogie and Dre had evacuated. Now all we had to do was get S&D in here. I meant it when I told Boogie I was staying straight, so I didn't have to be involved beyond legal paperwork. Yet, I found myself setting up a prep station anyway. Old habits die hard.

"Need any help with the replacements?" Alise cooed.

I almost knocked myself over when I spun around. Alise had been watching me from a chair in the dark corner for God knows how long, thinking about God knows what.

"I thought I was in here alone," I whispered back.

"I was curious," she shrugged. "So, the replacements?"

The Sanitation And Dismemberment Department did exactly that. They'd clean every inch of a crime site, rendering it practically sterile and doing it all without the use of most detectable cleaning solutions. However, there were times when total replacement was a more cost and time effective option, especially when it came to porous surfaces like wood and fabric. I.E the high back dining room chair where a man's dead body currently sat.

"No, I already got replacements ready. I figured it was inevitable since Boogie was marrying Dre," I answered. "But how do you even know about that?"

Alise tilted her head to the side, like a little fox confused about something. But I soon realized she was just calculating how much she wanted to tell me.

"I know lots of things. I'm relatively quiet and easy to talk to. Plus I can blend in when it's beneficial," she explained.

My brows married amid my mounting confusion. Alise had done an excellent job at convincing everyone that she was aloof and benign, neither of which were true. I don't think I'd ever met a smarter woman. That revelation both excited and terrified me.

"Alise, S&D is a shadow department. They leave no trace. So how do you know about them and their inner workings?" I asked again.

She offered me a smile in response, and while I'd normally accept it, these weren't normal circumstances.

"Alise," I warned again, shuffling across the carpet to reach her.

"I just found out one day," she whispered. "There were men in white hazmat suits moving furniture out of your Uncle Nick's office. A week later it had been announced that one of the event vendors was missing. I put two and two together. He got killed in your Uncle's office and then a special team reset the space."

I remembered that. He tried to short sales by claiming damaged goods and my uncle found out and sent him packing. I was probably 22 or 23 when that happened. So Alise couldn't have been more than eight?

"You really are too smart for your own good," I said, shaking my head. Again she offered me a smile in reply.

That warning instinct was back again. Yes I wanted her, but I wanted to maintain my peace more, and it was becoming clear to me that Alise thrived in Chaos. I had decided long ago that me and chaos didn't mix.

"Go upstairs, Alise," I whispered while taking a step back from her. "The crew is gonna get started in a little bit."

Whether she was disappointed or delighted with my response, I couldn't tell. Nor did I particularly care to find out. I let myself slip into a fantasy before, but now I knew that me and her absolutely could not happen. Alise Hatchette would most certainly make a monster out of me, or maybe even worse.

Alise

"Thank you," I smiled, as the bartender slid my drink over.

It sat pretty and pink in a martini glass that reminded me of Sex And The City, beckoning me to put my lips to it. I took a sip after taking a picture and smiled. Raspberry lemon drops cured all. Even the trauma of witnessing a bare-hand murder up close and personal. Despite the straight up shock of tonight's events, I couldn't be mad at Boogie. There was a certain level of respect that came from killing a man for insulting your wife.

Even if it scared the shit out of 90% of her immediate family members.

"Are you waiting for someone?" A man asked as I crossed and un-crossed my legs.

I glanced at my phone that laid face down on the counter. I sent him a text two hours ago asking him to meet me here and he never responded, but the read receipt was reassuring.

"As a matter of fact I am," I nodded.

I hated overly horny men and the stranger didn't bother concealing his intentions. His eyes dragged up and down the length of my legs, cataloging every feature and muscle before he convinced himself to sit down in the stool next to me. Irritation rose in my throat but I still managed to give him a disarming grin.

"A lady such as yourself should never be kept waiting," he said, voice distorted from faux charisma.

For a second I thought he was going to really commit to the act and kiss my hand, but he quickly decided against it when my eyebrow shot in the air. I wouldn't entertain someone like him even if I wasn't actively pursuing Truth. He was too malleable, too eager, and too stupid. Really though, that was my fault. I seemed to attract those in droves. They usually couldn't read the warning signs until it was too late. Tonight's petitioner was no exception. But I was bored so I'd fuck with him a bit before I tossed him back.

"What's your name?" I asked, tilting my head onto my shoulder.

"Daeshaun," he answered, trying to withhold a goofy smile.

He inched closer, mistakenly believing he had sold me into a night of quick, unmastered pumping, followed by a Muver ride home then a consolation Black Bean Crunch wrap. The thought was amusing more than anything else. It was amazing to me how much confidence men had. They truly thought they could wipe their balls on everything in the world including women. Sometimes I'd let them naively believe that, but I had to stop Daeshaun when he reached out to place his hand on my thigh.

"Daeshaun, I once cut a man's big toes off and pickled them because he touched me without permission," I laughed. "So would you like me to send them back to you via FedEx or UPS? I include tracking."

The club's strobe lights passed over his paling expression just in time for me to see his throat bob with a nervous swallow. Even if he didn't want to admit it, I knew he was scared. I loved seeing men cower with fear. They lived life too confidently for my taste. They didn't believe women had the capacity to do harm and that's why they were so entitled. If I wasn't committed to doing good, then I'd probably spend my days fixing that narrative.

"Alise," Truth barked.

I turned to face him in all of his glory. Tailored pants, crisp dress shirt, a whore's chain, and a coordinating watch. He was still handsome and dapper, but his aura was menacing. Irritation and yearning darkened his gaze. It appeared that his patience with me had finally run out.

"Hi, Truth," I smiled.

I got a smirk in return before he took the unoccupied stool to my left.

"Who's your friend?" Truth asked, pulling my seat closer.

There he was, staking his claim.

Then there I was, allowing it.

"This is Daeshaun. He was just-"

"Leaving," Truth supplied, with a tilt of his chin.

Daeshaun scurried off without another word. Which tickled me because he was scrappy, but I guess he figured whatever was under that suit wasn't worth the risk of dealing with a woman who threatened to slice his toes.

"Is that your type?" Truth scoffed, as Daeshaun rejoined the crowd.

"This is a bar, Mister Greene. He approached me. As most men tend to do with pretty women."

Truth seemed to nod in agreement until he noticed my outfit. Then he became still. The only visible movement coming from his flaring nostrils while he surveyed my change of clothing. It was a simple lavender colored layered handkerchief dress with a halter bust and a matching bow in my fresh braids. Andrea dressed like a succubus, but I was more like a faerie, preferring flowy silhouettes and soft pastels. Comfort still took priority for me, even when I was trying to be seductive.

"What's wrong?" I asked, noticing Truth's pinched brows.

"You look like a flower," he tutted. "I feel like the big bad wolf."

How sweet. He was worried about me.

"Looks can be deceiving, Mister Greene," I giggled while knocking back my drink. "Flowers can be beautiful yet thorny if you're not careful. People can be the same."

Despite the analogy, Truth crept closer. His big body filled the space between us like a rain cloud. Then once he was satisfied with our proximity, his hand tipped my chin upward just slightly so that my eyes could meet his.

"Are you gonna prick me with your thorns, Alise?"

"Not unless you ask me to," I replied while batting my lashes.

I watched Truth's pupils dilate and fill with desire before that pesky self-preservation kicked in. Why did he have to have a conscience? A lesser man would've gleefully took me for everything I was worth.

"This is a bad idea," he groaned while nuzzling my neck. "You're no good."

"I disagree," I laughed. "I'm chaotic neutral. And as long as you keep kissing me like that, this is a very, very, good thing."

His bitching turned into silent adoration as his lips trailed the length of my neck. His lips on my skin were electrifying and so tortuously perfect. Before I knew it my nails were curling into the width of his shoulders, and he was tilting me backwards so he could gain better access to all my sensitivities.

"This is giving Pepé Le Pew," I giggled when he reached my earlobe.

He once again tugged at the hoop dangling there.

"Whatchu know about that?"

"Listen, I know I'm young. But I'm not Ipad kid young," I scoffed. "I watched Looney Tunes, wore slips, and listened to Luther Vandross on Sundays while mopping just like you."

"Who told you I wore slips? It was only one time cause I lost a bet," Truth chuckled.

I folded onto his chest with an obnoxious snort then sucked in a few breaths to quell my laughter. His ability to spin a joke in every situation was impressive yet distracting. I had almost forgotten that I wasn't trying to be his friend tonight.

"Shut up and dance with me," I snickered.

We glided onto the dance floor with the ease of a seasoned couple. Dancing hip to hip, shoulder to shoulder, and back to back to whatever was playing. Trixxie's was a mixed bag when it came to eras and genres, so it didn't surprise me when we eventually landed on a square dance.

"You're way better at this than I thought you'd be," I admitted as Truth heel-toed me into a twirl.

"Don't let the smooth taste fool you, baby. I got a city job but I'm still a country boy at heart."

"Ok, big country," I chuckled. "Look at you being full of surprises."

"Speaking of surprises," he said, dipping me low. "How do you know about Trixxie's?"

"Andrea. She took me here last month for my 21st. Also my 18th. I like the crowd."

"For people watching?" he queried as he rocked me close.

I was appalled even if I wasn't showing it. Truth had called me out on my shit, something rare and currently unenjoyable for me. There weren't many people who could do that successfully, and those who could spend years developing the skill.

That did not bode well for my grand plans of eventual distance.

"I do not people watch," I protested. "I am simply observant. I'm-"

"The word you're looking for is nosey."

"Shush, you crass man. You think you know everything," I snorted.

"No, not everything. I still can't quite figure you out," he admitted in a soft whisper.

"I know," I nodded. "And that's why we work."

The music slowed while the energy between us shifted. Soon we were pressed chest to chest. Our breathing and heart rates synced while we danced to I Want To Know, with all the tension between us kindling into passion, smoldering yet inextinguishable.

"Since when is there a We?" Truth sighed in response to my earlier statement.

Oddly he didn't sound irritated. His response was more akin to uninformed surprise. Which was fair. I wasn't known for being upfront. So part of me was shocked when I told him,

"Since you let me kiss you in your office."

My heart slipped into his shirt pocket when he grinned. It was unassuming yet proud, like he had mastered something inexplicable. Something like the art of arranging a perfect sunset.

"I let you kiss me?" he hummed.

"Of course," I nodded, recalling the event.

"I don't know if I let you. You kinda just went for it. Took me by force."

"No," I giggled. "You let me, Truth. I only have the power you give me. The fact that you let me get away with so much means you like giving up that power. Don't you?"

Mister Greene's Adam's apple bobbed with a nervous gulp, and I once again pressed a kiss to it. Despite our progress, Truth responded like he always did: By denying himself the pleasure of inevitable.

"Alise-" he groaned in protest.

He wanted it to sound like a protest but it wasn't really. In reality it was the sweet sound of deteriorating self control and the emergence of insatiable desire. Which I would happily encourage.

My hands greedily laced through the back of his thick locs and a raw, reckless growl ripped from the belly of Truth Greene. Then his hands moved from their respectful station on my lower back and came to the swell of my hips just beside my ass. Our pelvises were pressed flush from the force of his grip and for once I was grateful about the obstructed view Trixxie's dim lighting offered. We might've been reported for indecency otherwise.

"You never answered my question, Truth," I teased as we spun in a circle. We were still too close to be anything but scandalous. I knew just as well as he did where this night was leading.

"Please?" he whimpered against the curve of my neck.

His pleading was quieter than it had been earlier, but I found it just as impactful. Deep rippling voices tended to do that. Especially compliant ones.

"Please what, Mister Greene?" I giggled, testing my control.

"Let me have you," he replied, squeezing my arm possessively. "Just for tonight."

I was highly doubtful this would be a one time thing, but we'd iron out all the details later. We needed relief right then. Before we ended up on someone's police report for hunching in Trixxie's. The last thing I needed was documentation explaining that I had tortured a man into fucking me.

"Well as long as it's just for tonight," I smiled, tugging him along by his collar.

Truth

One night.

I could handle that.

Even if I was already addicted to the taste of her lips on mine. Even if the little voice in the back of my head told me otherwise. I could manage one night.

I had to.

When she first texted me with instructions to meet her at Trixxie's half past nine, I blocked her. Part of me was still spooked about the sheer amount of information such a little woman contained, but the other part was desperate for her attention. Desperate for her criticism and praise alike. Her kisses and her scratches. All the darkness hiding in that light, melodious voice of hers. I had long learned that I needed to stay away from Alise, and what happened after dinner only confirmed it. She was too smart for me. Too forward. Too perfect. Alise Hatchette was everything I ever wanted in a double dose. The only problem was that she was wrapped in poison.

Opium, cocaine, ecstasy, or simple table sugar. Something mind-numbingly enjoyable and deadly.

I knew this to be a fact, yet I still found myself sliding into my truck at 9, driving to Trixxie's, and seeking out my demise. Now I couldn't remember how the fuck I got home even though I was half-certain I had driven.

And I couldn't even blame it on liquid bravery. This was all Alise.

We stumbled into my loft in a flurry of tangled limbs and equally tangled hair. I don't know when she found the time to let down her braids but she did, and seeing them fall around her angelic face only worsened my desire to rid her of that too-pretty dress.

"Have some patience, Truth," she chided, as I worked to unlace the back of her garment.

Patience. What an endearing quality.

The problem with utilizing that in the moment was that all my patience had dried up between Alise jacking me in her Mama's kitchen, and then seeing men float around her like fruit flies at Trixxie's. I could respect some of those who hoovered out of sight, but the one that was bold enough to sit in her face really pissed me off.

Which is exactly why I had a van come collect him from the parking lot. That would be a week's worth of paperwork itself because niggas had families and shit.

So I was clean out of patience. Luckily I was in abundance of hard dick and I had two working opposable thumbs. Ones that I intended on using before I fully submitted to my caveman instincts and mauled her.

"I said slow down," she hissed while pulling me back by my hair.

The whimper that came out of me was unrecognizable. I should've been embarrassed to be handled by my scruff like I was some out-of-control tomcat, but instead I was hypnotized. She was so beautiful, but so strong, and so damn determined.

"Alise," I pouted as her lips grazed mine.

"Truth," she whispered. "We do this my way or not at all."

Part of me suspected that she expected push back, but after everything that happened this week her way sounded wonderful.

"Okay," I nodded.

Long, nimble fingers traced the hem of my suit jacket before carefully popping the buttons holding it to my waist. Those same fingers trailed up to my chest and coiled the curls present there around the tip of her nails. Rich cashmere flooded my senses while Alise pulled me into another hungry kiss. My jacket hit the floor with a gentle thud, then my shirt followed soon after.

"You know you really are quite beautiful," Alise said softly.

Whatever misguided fears I had that this was one-sided vanished the moment I noticed how she looked at me. Alise looked at me with both awe and appreciation, then fondness, and maybe even a little pride as she traced my scars. It felt strangely humanizing to have someone see my flaws and still find beauty in them. I couldn't recall a single time someone's gaze made me feel anything except for maybe grateful that I still went to the gym.

"Thank you," I replied, kissing the palm of her hand.

"My pleasure," she chuckled.

I was too hypnotized to realize that Alise had also unbuckled my belt. The edges of my mind simply started to darken as she tugged at my length through my briefs, encouraging all logic to abandon my brain. The push and pull of her devious, nimble hands became too much for me when she placed another hot kiss on my throat and the thrilling but awkward sensation of completion started to surround me. Awkward, because who the fuck came from a hand job at this big age?

"Alise," I groaned. "I really don't wanna cum in these pants. They're expensive to get cleaned."

"Then let's take them off," she said easily.

I was happy to oblige her. It took no time at all for my pants and drawers to join the rest of the clothes on the floor. Right along with Alise's jaw. Seriously, she unhinged that thang like a python. I didn't think humans could do that.

"Lis, you ok?" I chuckled.

Her eyes met mine, and I saw a flash of submission for the first, and probably, last time. I thought I was hallucinating but she shook when I reached for her. Like I pulled a gun out of my pants.

"Alise, are you nervous?" I queried.

She looked down at my dick then back at me, her lips twisting into a disbelieving pout. So I was a little bigger than average, but that wasn't my fault. I was tall. Surely she understood the correlation?

"Unfortunately so," she mumbled against my chest.

"I ain't gone hurt you, sweet pea," I assured her while massaging the knots from her back. "I know how to use this muhfucka. I'm licensed to carry."

"Shut up, sniper number 4," she chuckled dryly. "And get my shoulders."

As always, Alise only had to tell me once. I went straight to work rubbing the knots from her surprisingly tight shoulders. Which she rewarded me for with the lightest of pleasured grunts. My dick was so hard that I feared I would bust if I sneezed. Strangely, I didn't mind though. Touching her like this felt a whole lot safer than when she was touching me. Plus it was a simple comfort. Niggas like to pretend their love language is physical touch to get in unsuspecting ladies' drawls, but I really did enjoy non-sexual physical contact. Especially when it came to Alise.

I could do this all day if she let me.

"Mkay, that's enough of that," she announced, interrupting my bliss. Unfortunately that wasn't the case though.

"Ugh. You just tryna fuck me," I said, rolling my eyes. "What if I just wanted to cuddle?"

"Boy, please," Alise shot back. "Ya dick all out on display. You're tryna get fucked with yo hoe ass. Go lay on the couch."

"The couch? But there's a perfectly good bed upstairs," I stammered.

"Yeah, but the bed is intimate. I'll be all over your sheets and this is supposed to be a one time thing, remember?"

A one time thing.

That is what I agreed to, and suddenly I hated myself for it. Just one night of Alise's touch and taste? Now that I had it, I knew once wasn't what I wanted. This wasn't what I wanted. Usually once I came to that conclusion, I'd back out. But I was so desperate for anything that she gave me that I couldn't stop myself. I followed her directions with minimal fuss.

"Come here," I cooed once I stretched out.

My world tilted on its axis as she did just that. The room seemed to pick up and spin as she crossed the floors on the tips of her delicate toes, abandoning pieces of clothing with each step. I held my breath when she raised her arms to pull off her dress and I almost passed out from a lack of air when she finally got to the lacy purple thong hiding beneath it.

Then finally she stood in front of me, bare and ethereal with the exception of the jade waist beads clinging to her curves. Yes, she was beautiful beyond this world with her endless legs, and her soft belly, and her big predator eyes. She was close enough for me to touch yet still too far away to end my suffering and suffocation.

"I used to think Springtime was the prettiest thing God took the time to make, but clearly I was mistaken," I said softly.

"You must not own any mirrors then, Mister Greene," Alise smiled.

"Not any good ones anyway," I replied as she moved to straddle me.

My mind began to quiet when Alise pressed against me, then I lost my smart aleck reply to the void. In fact, I lost most coherent thoughts to the void. Thinking felt like trying to breathe while drowning. So instead, I gave up and focused on worshipping the woman on top of me. Her mouth, her jaw, her shoulders. I pressed my lips to every part of her within my reach and drank in every soft pant and moan she sang out. The pitchy notes imprinted in my brain like a needle on a fresh vinyl record.

This was supposed to be just this once?

Imagine getting a day pass to heaven then having to go back to ghetto-ass

Earth.

Preposterous. I now knew too much.

"You can touch me, Truth," she whispered as she laced her hands through my hair. "I want you to touch me."

That was when I noticed where my hands were; firmly on her waist. I guess it was a last ditch effort at chasteness even though we were both ass-naked on my sofa.

"I was trying to be respectful."

"Yeah, you can stop that shit," Alise smirked. "I'm not tryna get fucked respectfully. I'm tryna to put this birth control to the test. I want my lash extensions to be eyebrow extensions by the end of the night."

Shittttt. That's all shawty had to say.

She had been dripping on me for the last 10 minutes. So I slipped my hand between her thighs to see just how wet she was and Alise rewarded my light touch with a belly-wrought moan. Her nails sank deeper into my arm with every wrist stroke, her face began to flush, and her hips bucked to chase my fleeting touch.

"Are you gonna cum for me, sweet pea? Pretty please, baby," I gasped.

My heart hammered against my ribs while Alise chased her orgasm, and I chased a different high. It was oddly exciting to see her unravel in my arms. She was unguarded, uninhibited, and uncontrolled instead of her usual calculated and collected, and I loved that because this was the one time I knew exactly what would happen between us.

Or so I thought...

"Fuck, Truth," Alise hissed as her pleasure overtook her.

She rocked against my hand slowly, whimpering with undeniable frustration. Somehow she looked more unsatisfied than she did 10 minutes ago despite the fact that she turned my lower abdomen into a Slip 'N' Slide.

"What's wrong?" I asked, pulling her braids behind her back.

"It wasn't enough," she sighed while stroking my erection.

"Yeah, I know. That's why it's called forepl-"

I stopped mid-sentence as she aligned my tip to her entrance with it all wet, tight, and pink. My hands dug into her lush hips with the goal of grounding, then all the air was knocked out of my lungs when Alise pushed the entirety of my dick inside herself in one fell swoop. Pleasure rushed me first from the comforting warmth of her, then panic when I realized I had been met with unexpected resistance. My gaze moved from her eyes that were brimming with tears down to the point of our connection, where I found the tell-tale sign of blood.

Shit.

"Ok, well that hurt," Alise winced while trying to regain her rhythm.

I immediately locked her hips into place. Seeing that she had no plans to address what just happened, the responsibility fell on me.

"Alise, are you a fucking virgin?" I sighed, raising her forward.

Her legs quivered from the pain, which confirmed my suspicions. That information would've been nice to know beforehand, mainly because I didn't do virgins. It was selfish, but I didn't have the patience to teach and direct, plus blood made me squeamish. Fuck being gifted 40 virgins upon entering heaven. I wanted 5 ran-through squirters and a cream factory.

"Truth," she sighed, attempting to sink back down. "Virginity is a social construct."

"A social- You're bleeding on my dick!"

Suddenly it all made sense. Her sensitivity. Her skittish nature. The way she reacted when I took off my pants. All my instincts were right. She really was unsullied and I was too grown for her. The one time I broke my rule, it backfired immediately. Guilt for handling her so rough was overshadowed by another feeling.

I was pissed.

"Truth," she sighed again as I raised onto my elbows.

"Alise, you should've told me," I fussed.

"It wouldn't have made a difference."

"Yeah, for you! Unfortunately I have morals and-"

"Truth, please hush."

"No, woman! You gone hear what I have to say because you-"

"Oh my goodness, Truth! SHUT UP!" Alise hissed, pinning me back to the couch by my throat.

I choked in a half breath under her grip, barely enough air to keep me alive. Especially since my dick was so hard.

My eyebrows damn near shot into my hair. Who was this woman and what had she done with the Baby Hatchette? Who did she think she was talking to me like that?

Why did I like it so much?

"You can't tell me what to do," I bit back with a quiver.

Historically, I made a great deal of effort not to talk myself out of pussy. But here with her, being difficult felt right for some reason. So I tried to shuffle off the couch and of course Alise's grip tightened around my neck. The sensation of getting choked further eroded my common sense. It reminded me that I wasn't in control nor did I have to be. Her hands on my body also reminded me that I had a naked wet woman on top of me and so I bucked upward into her only for her to withdraw from me with a wicked smile.

Oh, I was in trouble.

I was also so fucking hard that I would probably nut if she hummed near it. I almost begged her to slide back down and finish my pitiful ass. What was happening to me?

"Actually I think I can," Alise smiled while leaning down to kiss the corners of my mouth.

"Fuck," I hissed as her other hand curled into my bicep.

The pain was just sharp enough to excite me. I needed more and I tried to get it by capturing her lips again but Alise wouldn't give me the satisfaction. Instead she kept me pinned in place by that tight grip on the sides of my throat.

Alise then teased me further by moving out of reach, and I, ever the proud man, whined at her absence. I whined like a kicked dog until she came closer. Only for her to pull away again after one feather light kiss. I was dizzy and desperate, and I wanted to feel all of her on top of me. But she wouldn't give me not one more inch.

"Please?" I finally whimpered. "Alise, please?"

The evil little thing laughed as I writhed beneath her. She would hover on my tip, inch down slowly and then shoot back up before I could adjust.

She yoyo'd back and forth like that for a few minutes until my whining turned into consistent whimpering. I knew I wouldn't be able to take it much longer. I had never been God's strongest soldier. Then when I was on the brink of insanity and ready to black out from the lack of blood flow, something happened:

I begged.

"Alise please, baby. I'm sorry. I'm sorry," I cried. "I'm quiet. You won't hear no more fussing out of me. I promise, please."

"Are you sure, Truth?" she cooed while stroking my hair. "I need you to be sure because only good boys get rewards."

"Yes, sweet pea. I'm sure. Please just fuck me. I need you to fuck me."

"Hm, ok. But only because you asked so nicely," she replied sweetly. "Just one more thing."

"Anything."

"Open your mouth for me, handsome."

I did as I was told and after a hot, sloppy kiss, she pressed the pad of her thumb to my tongue, letting the edge of her nail hook into my bottom lip.

"I don't wanna hear you say anything unless I give you permission. Do you understand me?" she hissed.

I felt the chaotic programming that was my mental state turn off like an old-school TV after her demand. My mind slipped into the safety of a white room with padded walls. However, instead of fear, I felt over-whelming comfort and pleasure. I don't remember agreeing but I must have because Alise smiled at me then resumed her strokes. Tortuously slow, but wonderfully deep so that her round ass crushed my balls with every bounce. With her perfect cacao nipples hovering above my open mouth like a Kisses' Christmas commercial. Everything about Alise was surreal.

Just like I feared she would be.

I also feared I wouldn't last long because I wanted her so bad, but Alise eased up when I got too close. And I ain't even have to tell her. I wasn't new to sex, not by a long shot, but I was new to this. I was new to being powerless. I was new to begging. I was new to taking direction. I was new to her. Then even though I swore to myself this would be a one-time thing, I knew for certain it wouldn't be when after the hardest nut of my life, she called me her brave boy then wiped me free of her virginal blood. I was delirious, hungry, and exhausted, but I had every intention of doing it again. That was bad enough without the little voice in my head whispering, "*Keep her.*"

I was fucked.

Figuratively and literally.

Hot Seat

T^{RUTH}

"Damn, Truth you late as fuck. Ya hair all raggedy. What happened to being 15 minutes away?"

"My bad, nigga. I overslept," I sighed.

Overslept was an understatement. My back hit the hardwood at 11:00 am when a leg cramp knocked me off the couch. Alise was nice enough to tuck me in with a blanket and leave me a dose of Tylenol before she slid out of my apartment, however, she didn't bother to say goodbye. Therefore my attitude started before I opened my eyes. Never mind the fact that by that time I had already missed two dockets. Mariah covered for me with some story about Liberty being sick which saved me from work, but I still had to deal with Boogie.

Observant, nosey, murderous Boogie.

"Since when do you oversleep?" he asked, clocking me immediately.

"Aye, we ain't here to talk about me!" I fussed while sliding into the seat across from him. "We're here to talk about you and that lil show you put on at dinner last night."

"What show?" he grinned.

"You know damn well what fucking show," I hissed. "Don't piss me off. I'll spend the next three days fucking up your paperwork."

The humor drained from his expression at my threat of administrative chaos. For all the things Boogie definitely was, unorganized he was not.

"Listen, I know I got carried away. But she was crying. You know I don't like that shit."

Oh, I knew. Boogie had made Andrea cry a grand total of one time in our entire lives and he spent every day since regretting it. Her displeasure was like poison to his system. Which I'm sure would become problematic eventually.

"I've arranged for you to see a therapist again," I sighed. "And I don't wanna hear any excuses. I know you got Mondays at 3:30 free now."

"So now you're managing again?" he asked.

"Absolutely not. I'm still staying out of it. I just can't have you fucking up your marriage because then that puts pressure on me. Uncle tried to hook me up with Mae."

"Interesting," Boogie clicked.

"I suppose."

"Anything else?"

"Yes, stop scaring your wife. It's a miracle she didn't flee Greece after you cut up ole dude."

"She has to get used to it," he huffed, stomping his foot like a petulant toddler.

"Nat she's normal. Normal people don't get used to witnessing murders. If you need to handle something, set up a room and keep it secret. Dre's not like us and you of all people should want her to stay that way."

Andrea and Nat were different in all the ways that mattered. He was rugged and unpolished, she was soft and forgiving. Everybody thought they hated each other but no. They just couldn't see how they were supposed to fit together. Although I had a feeling that had begun to change recently. Because regret flashed in Boogie's eyes, plain and simple. Embarrassment too.

"Ok, ok. I hear you," he sighed with his shoulders slumping.

"Good. Cause last night can't happen again."

"I know."

"Cool."

We settled into a thick, uncomfortable silence since my lecture was over.

This was one of our restaurants and the staff knew our regular orders. I was starving so I was trying to focus on the kitchen, just barely visible from our table, but Boogie's nosey ass was picking me apart.

"Aye man, why the fuck you got your suit buttoned up all high like that? It's hot as hell outside."

The forecast predicted a blistering 102° high and I was in a full wool blend suit with my dress shirt practically sewn to my neck. Honestly I was boiling like a bag of Uncle Ben's Ready Rice, but I couldn't do shit about it until I got out of Boogie's sight.

"Nah, it's cool. I'm comfortable," I said, fixing my collar.

Because the universe had a sense of humor, that was the moment a single bead of sweat rolled down my forehead, and made a show of leisurely dripping off the tip of my nose. It hit the table with an audible plink, just as me and Nat's eyes met.

"Truth," Boogie chuckled.

I knew the nigga hated being lied to but I couldn't tell him my truth. I'd rather be on his shit list.

"Man nigga, unbutton that stuffy ass thing," he said, taking a swipe at my collar.

The ice in our cups rattled like maracas, drawing the attention of other diners as we struggled.

"Cut the shit!" I hissed, trying to dodge him. "We're in public!"

"Yeah and you're acting weird. You got a wire or something? Cause if so we both going down. You stabby, emotionally unstable, bastard!"

"No! Go away! Mind your fucking business."

I ducked too slow and he hemmed me up by my collar like Uncle Nick did when I was still a bad-ass kid. Boogie was like a pitbull. If you let him grab you there was no getting free off of your own strength. Knowing that, I reached for the salt and threw it at his ass. It landed right in his eyes, giving me just enough space to pull away.

"Bitch!" he growled, retreating back to his side. "You wrong for that."

"And you wrong for grabbing my shirt like I stole your loose change!" I fussed back.

"Yeah," he said, blinking out tears.

One of his many talents, Boogie could cry on demand. Which helped in the event of being gassed.

"Cause you're being weird, what- Damn, what the hell happened to your neck?"

I snatched my collar to the side and held it closed with the quickness of an auntie snatching back her purse.

"Nothing," I said quickly.

"Nothing?" Boogie tutted. "Man, them scratches deep as hell! What happened to you?"

Alise Hatchette happened to me, that's what. Do you know how difficult it is to leave hickies on dark skin? I knew how difficult it was, because it was never something I had to worry about before last night. Nor did I have to worry about my cousin finding out who I was fucking.

"I um," I coughed, preparing my throat for the lie. "I got a cat."

"A cat? Really, Truth? You don't even like pets. I bet- Oh my God," Boogie said, suddenly throwing a hand over his mouth.

"What?" I gulped.

"You fucked Alise," he said slamming his free palm on the table.

The rattling sound it made was just obnoxious, which added to my lingering embarrassment.

"That," I started hesitantly. "Is an accusation."

"And I don't hear you denying it."

"How did you even come to that conclusion?"

"Easy. Alise texted Andrea asking if she needed her nails done because she broke one last night. I noticed she could hardly sit at the office, then I saw that she was walking funny when I dropped them off at the salon."

"Fuck, I ain't mean to hurt her," I sighed.

Although technically I didn't hurt her. Her impatient ass did that to herself.

"So you popped her cherry?" Boogie grimaced.

"Unfortunately."

"Ooh wee, you her first and she turned you out. Alise about to run yo ass ragged," he chuckled.

"She ain't turn me out!" I protested.

"Shitttt. You woke up late, missed work, you wearing a preacher's suit to cover up all them whore's marks in 100 degree heat, and you broke ya own rule. She definitely did something to you," he tutted with a dip of his head.

Memories of the previous night flashed in my rioting mind. Memories of her touch, possessive and rough, her teasing kisses, and the sensation of her body leading mine. I got dizzy again thinking about her hand on my throat.

She did something to me alright.

"Can I go with you to pick them up?" I asked while biting my lip. "She ain't say bye this morning."

"Hell naw you can't go with me," Boogie said immediately before adding. "You got crazy eyes."

"Crazy eyes? You worried that I'll kidnap her or something?"

"Honestly, yeah," he exclaimed. "Look, I know exactly how this shit is gonna play out. I love Alise but I know she likes to play games. Too many games. I already know you're not gonna stop fucking her. Y'all are gonna keep this shit up, somebody's gonna get attached, and then she's gone make you lose your fucking mind. I give you a solid 8 months max."

My stomach twisted at my cousin's words. He was reading my life like it was a Tyler Perry script. Then he said it with certainty. Like there was only one possible way for this to end. Like I couldn't control myself.

"You saying this shit like I'm the one nicknamed The Boogie Man," I scoffed.

"Yeah, ok. Y'all keep acting like I don't know what I'm talking about. You got your own lore and Alise's manipulative ass is gonna remind you of it. You like to pretend like you ain't one of us, but ain't nobody above reacting in anger."

I froze at the mention of my past and anxiety swelled in my chest.

Who I used to be no longer served who I planned to become. I couldn't go back. I wouldn't. Not even for a woman who was every bit of perfect.

"I'll talk to Andrea about it," Boogie offered. "If you look at Alise you're as good as done."

"Thanks," I sighed.

I didn't like the looming feeling of finality, but this really was for the best. My instincts told me so.

I had to stop dealing with Alise. Once and for all.

Alise

"You need to soak when you get home," Andrea announced casually. "Stop listening to white women on the internet. Losing your virginity almost always hurts."

I was appalled that she could clock me and I had to scramble to keep my phone from falling in the basin at my feet. This was the exact conversation I wanted to avoid. Did I love my sister? Yes. Was I eager to tell her that I had a bruised vagina from misplaced confidence?

Hell no.

"I'm fine," I said easily.

"Girl, cut it out," she scoffed. "I know that shit hurt. All of the Burry boys got big dicks."

Big wasn't an understatement, but it failed to encompass the reality of Truth's situation.

Substantial was more like it.

Beefy.

"It's just a little soreness," I argued.

"You're walking funny, and you better not let Dex see you. He's gonna have a fucking fit."

"You're not gonna tell him?"

"No. I'm staying out of this. I think it's a bad idea, but you already made up your mind," Dre sighed.

"You've been talking to Mae?" I asked, picking the lint off my skirt.

"I ain't gotta talk to Mae. I know Truth and I know you. The age difference isn't the problem. It's y'all's dynamic."

I swallowed my confidence. Andrea and Boogie were very different and also wildly similar. They were both nosey know-it-alls who spent too much time analyzing people. So I knew her warning had merit even though she didn't know the exact mechanics of what Truth and I had going on.

"Dre, it's not like that. We're just casual."

That felt like a lie despite the fact that it was what we agreed to. I knew the once in a lifetime limit wasn't real the second Truth kissed me, but everything outside of that was unpredictable. I didn't expect him to be so yielding, or hold me so tight. For once in my life, I didn't know what would happen next. But my sister seemed to.

"There is no such thing as causal when it comes to pursuing Burrys," Andrea said gravely. "Think about that before the next time you go and play with that man."

I'd never seen my sister so disapproving of my antics. Her eyes were dark with disappointment and her mouth was drawn tight. Andrea reminded me of Daddy right then. Which was another warning in itself. I could admit that I didn't know everything.

"Ok," I said softly. "I'll end it."

"Thank you my friend," I said to Basma in informal Arabic.

Her family recipe for Kebab Halabi could get me through anything, just like her smile when she served it. She was aptly named which is why I always tipped double.

"Alise, do you have a boyfriend?" Symphony asked as I sat down with our trays.

"Um," I paused.

I promised my Lil Sister that I'd always be honest with her, but all the honest answers were wildly inappropriate. Technically the answer was no. Not definitely, but technically. I was going to end things with Truth on Friday, but really we weren't even dating. I couldn't even say we were fucking because we'd only fucked once. Maybe we were friends? At least until the weekend.

"No," I finished. "I don't have a boyfriend."

"Do you even like boys?" Symphony asked.

Teenagers were a lot like older black women, ruthless and unfiltered. Me and Symphony were only six years apart but somehow I'd forgotten about how direct children were. Her bluntness reminded me of my mama.

"You're the second person to ask me that this month. What about me gives gay?"

"You dress for the female gaze," she shrugged while plucking some food off my plate.

My heart swelled when I noticed Symphony picking at the cubed dragon fruit. Her palate had matured so much in the year I'd known her. Back then it would be a miracle to get her to order anything other than chicken strips, ranch, and cheese fries. Now she was confidentially ordering sushi.

"I didn't think you cared about men because of the way you dress. Pick me's be dressing like depressed librarians," she continued.

Lord have mercy on her teachers. This girl was something else.

"I just have a strong sense of self. I don't live my life for others."

"Is that why you don't have a boyfriend?" she replied.

She also fished for information like my mama.

"Symph, what's this about?" I chuckled.

"I- I like this boy and he asked me out," she asked while tapping the table. "But when I checked with my mama, she said I needed to focus on books, not boys. But I was thinking, you graduated early and you had t have a boyfriend at some point right?"

"Hm." I grunted.

"What does that hm mean? Is that true or is she bullshitting me?"

Symphony was one of the few people who could make me laugh out loud. Most of the time I used laughter the same way I used smiles. Although occasionally it was nice to be reminded what genuine glee felt like. Like when I was dancing with Truth...

"Look, I said I was gonna be honest with you so here's the thing. Mothers want what's best for you. An education, a good job, a future. The problem with boys is that they have the ability to interfere with that."

"How?" Symphony exclaimed. "We're in the same class. He's not grading my essays."

"Well, pregnancy for one," I answered honestly.

"Ew," she grimaced. "I'm tryna kiss. Not be somebody's mama."

"Lord," I laughed. "But that's good to know. A lot of people at your age don't really know themselves and so they end up bending themselves to someone else's wishes."

Symphony quietly processed our conversation, then she nodded before leaning back in her chair with yet another question,

"So is that why you don't have a boyfriend?"

In the past my answer would've been wholeheartedly yes and it still technically should've been. But my stomach flipped when I thought about Truth pulling me close in the kitchen two days ago.

"Yes and no," I sighed.

"What do you mean?" The little nosey auntie-in-training asked.

I knew it was a trap and I still fell for it. The program did a good job assigning us to each other.

"I like a bo- a man. But I don't think it's gonna work out between us," I admitted.

"Damn, why not?" she exclaimed. "If you can't keep a man there's no hope for the rest of us."

"Girl, hush! What the hell do you know about a man or keeping them?"

"My bad," Symphony surrendered, raising her hands. "But as you were saying? Something about a crush."

"You too smooth for your own good," I snickered. "But fine. I gotta crush and he likes me too. Unfortunately we toxic together."

"What you know about being Toxic?" Symphony asked.

I became acutely aware of my own mortality, hearing one of the things I regularly said at that age said back to me. Youth really was fleeting.

"Chile, anyway. We're bad for each other. We might end up leveling each other out, and I don't think I want that for myself."

"Well, if chemistry taught me anything this year, leveling each other out isn't toxic. It's neutralizing. And isn't what grown folks relationships are all about anyway? Keeping each other grounded?"

"Hm," I said again, this time quieter.

Maybe chemistry was on to something.

Truth

Fuck Chemistry.

If some entity was flying around like Cupid shooting arrows of chemistry in folks asses, then they were getting shot out the sky. I wanted their wings mounted on my mantle. I was owed that much after tonight.

"Truth," She moaned.

Makayla waited with airy breath for me to make my next move. Her gaze flicked from my eyes then down to my lips and back again. She was cautiously nudging me toward the inevitable but she never made an outright demand of me.

So I rewarded Makayla's patience with a row of gentle kisses down the slope of her neck. In return, she flowed into me seamlessly, taking whatever I offered without complaint. If I wanted to touch her, she let me. If I wanted to stop, she waited. She was flexible and yielding. Happy to let me lead.

Makayla was exactly what I was used to.

And precisely what I didn't want.

I pulled away again, a final but necessary litmus test. Makayla paused at my silent command. Her hands came to rest on the planes of my chest closest to my shoulders, but they never moved beyond that spot. Her hands never tangled in my hair, or explored my scars, and they certainly never wrapped around my neck. They just rested in perfect lady-like fashion. Nothing sinful about it. Nothing exciting.

Nothing that made me want to track down her location before I went on a date with someone else. What was she doing at work so late, anyway?

It took all of this to realize it was too late for me. I was already intoxicated with Alise's venom and there was no antidote.

"I'm really sorry," I said softly as I took a step back. "But this isn't gonna work."

"Wait, what?" Makayla snapped.

"I said this isn't gonna work out. Please excuse me, I have somewhere to be," I called while rushing back to my truck.

Alise

I couldn't sleep.

That was normal for me. I've always had issues sleeping, but it had gotten worse after Andrea left. I just now realized how crucial Andrea was to my routines. Unfortunately I was too grown to interrupt my sister's night just because I felt some kind of way about change. So I tried to keep busy by alternating between studying and invoice management until I tired myself out.

"Heeeeee," I yawned while stretching overhead.

All my joints popped in rapid succession. It was well past ten and I had been up since 6. The physical effects of my raggedy-ass schedule had long caught up with my body. I was just waiting on my mind.

"Hopefully I'm almost done for the night," I said quietly.

"I hope so too," a deep voice replied.

I spun on the tips of my toes while brandishing my .22 to face the intruder. The offices were usually secure, but you could never be too careful. Especially when it was this late.

"Easy, sweet pea," Truth chuckled. "Ain't no need for all that."

He pressed against my back before bringing his lips to the shell of my ears. The spearmint on his breath tingled against the sensitive skin, and I almost shuddered from a pleasure that was so distinctly Truth.

"I thought you were on a date?" I asked.

"How did you know that?" he gruffed while nipping my earlobe.

"Because I went by your office and the temp told me you were out for the evening," I said with an unsteady breath.

Truth's hands flowed down my back before coming to rest on my hips. His thumbs found purchase in the two small dimples sitting above my tailbone, effectively holding me steady. Which kept me from drowning in his presence, although just barely.

"Hm. Why were you at my office?"

"Because we need to talk, Truth," I whispered.

"Talk about what?"

"Us. We need to end things. We can stay friends, but I don't think we should see each other anymore."

"Oh, ok," Truth hummed.

"So you agree?" I asked with a relieved swallow.

"**No**," he chuckled.

I was turned around manually before I could command my body to do so and Truth placed my hand in the center of his. The office was freezing, but his skin was hot. Hot like we were standing directly under the beating sun. My skin began to horripilate from the breeze coming through the vents and Truth's gaze leisurely fell to my tightening nipples before rejoining mine. But instead of looking at me in simple admiration, he watched me with pure possession. Something sinister was under that suit.

"So I've been thinking," he started.

"Have you really?"

"Oh, yes. I really have. Ever since Monday night then subsequently Tuesday afternoon. I've been thinking about how you fucked with my head. I've been thinking about how you disregarded my rules. And I've been thinking about how you left blood on my couch because you didn't bother telling me you were a virgin."

"I'm sorry," I gasped, feigning sorrow.

Tears began to well in my eyes but instead of relenting, Truth laughed. Then he invaded the sliver of distance between us while picking my chin up to refocus my gaze.

"You're not sorry," he argued. "You're manipulative, you're controlling, and you're downright poisonous. If I had any sense left, then I'd use it to stay away from you. But I don't. In fact I haven't had much of any ever since you kissed me in my office. Then Monday happened and it's gotten worse. I can't even pursue somebody else because I'm thinking of you the entire time. You. A woman I have no business sniffing around."

"All the more reason for us to end it," I said softly, while stroking the thick hair on his forearm.

His eyes briefly left mine while he hissed in a ragged breath. Hopefully one that replenished his brain with enough oxygen to think straight.

Because I certainly wasn't.

"Yeah, naw," he smiled. "That's not happening, sweet pea. Maybe instead you should do whatever you did to me Monday to make me sleep through six alarms."

"Truth," I whispered as I brought my lips to his. "I didn't do anything to you."

"The scratches haven't even healed all the way and yet I want you to scratch me again," he groaned. "All I want right now is for you to make me beg. You did something. What did you do to me, Alise?"

Truth's question was visible on his face. Not curiosity, but astonishment as he leaned in to kiss me for the first time in too long. Old habits die hard, because it didn't take long for my hand to cup his throat while we adjusted to my pace. Not soft and appreciative like he wanted. I wanted it hot, rough, and hungry.

"Aht, stay," I demanded while pulling away.

His nostrils flared out as my hand slid down the length of his body. I could tell he was tempted to look but his eyes never left mine.

I liked that he was a fast learner.

"You said you wanted to beg?" I whispered while spreading his precum over his tip.

I never used more than the bare minimum force and Truth writhed with every light swipe. As if he was being subjected to electrocution. It looked like my assumptions were correct. Tight wound men really were the best.

"On your knees," I said, pushing off of him while withdrawing my touch. He hesitated for just a second too long. So I walked behind my desk and peeled my shirt over my head. Suddenly he scrambled.

"No sir, don't touch," I hissed as I unhooked my bra. "Touching is for good listeners. Are you a good listener?"

"Of course I am," he gulped while I turned to face him.

I slowly pulled one leg out my panties and then the other. They were satin green and made out of the same material as his wedding suit, and they were also soaking wet. I'm sure Truth imagined me wetting his suit that night and now he would know exactly what it would've felt like.

"Then why aren't you on your knees?" I whispered while pumping him.

I lowered him to the ground with his iron-hard dick while his lip trembled from unexpressed pleasure. Not quite a whimper but a little more than a pout.

Just enough to indicate that he knew he was in trouble.

"It's not nice to break into people's offices," I chuckled while switching my grip from his dick to his hair. "What would my bosses think?"

"Hopefully they'd just leave," he smirked.

"I'm glad you got jokes," I chuckled back. "Now open up so I can see what else that mouth do."

This time there was no hesitation. Truth's jaw fell open immediately and his tongue darted out to prepare my seat with a single wet lick. I spread my lips with two fingers to let him see it first, and then I pressed into his handsome face. He instantly brought my clit in between his lips like it was a Lemon head, licking every single sensitive inch with expert precision.

"Fuck, you eat pussy so good," I hissed. "I just know you can fuck up a mango."

I felt his smile against my sex which heightened the pleasure wave I was riding. Something about the visual of his wide grin did it for me, causing my orgasm to rush me like a Georgia State linebacker.

Frustration followed immediately behind my pleasure. I was starting to understand the problem with premature ejaculation.

"It's gone take you some time to build up endurance and decrease your sensitivity," Truth said, kissing my shaking thigh.

Then he brought his hand to my chin while rising to stand.

"Which reminds me, no more rough fucking until you get used to me."

"You must be confused on how this works," I laughed.

"Not at all. But I take care of your person first. You can do whatever you wanna do once you adjust. Until then we do it my way so I don't hurt you. Again."

"I knew she'd run her mouth," I sighed.

"Actually, it was Boogie," Truth corrected while lifting me on the desk.

His tip came to my entrance, but unlike last time, he slipped inside achingly slow.

"Oh, big stretch," he moaned while coming to a seat. "How you feeling, sweet pea?"

"Really full," I answered honestly.

It was a big stretch indeed.

"Well you're handling it so well, baby," he moaned while retreating.

"Fuck, you're exquisite. What colors do you want for your flowers?"

Mae's petty ass voice rang in my head immediately. *You gone be picking out your wedding colors.* I accidentally imagined Truth in his groomsmen tuxedo, then came the thought of marriage. Which coincidentally was less unpleasant than I generally remembered it to be. Possibly due to the fact that his dick was poking me in the heart.

"Flowers for what?" I sighed irritably.

"Our first date," he laughed. "I'm not tryna lock you down yet, sweet pea. I can tell by the way you left my house that you're allergic to serious commitment."

"Don't make assumptions," I said, tugging on his hair. "I just wanted to leave gracefully. That was supposed to be the first and last time."

"It was, wasn't?" Truth sighed huskily.

"Mhm," I nodded while adjusting my grip on his shoulders.

His back flexed with his hips so he could lengthen his strokes. While his thumb gently tapped against my clit. It was already ten times better than the first time and the wild part was that I knew the third time would be ten times better than this. Once was always gonna be impossible.

"Oh well," he shrugged lazily. "We tried."

Fruitful Endeavors

TRUTH- **2** MONTHS LATER

"What are you trying to do?" Liberty asked.

Mama's 60th birthday was in two weeks. She was the only Virgo I could stand and I had every intention of making her milestone birthday memorable. Even if she spent the last five years leading up to it nagging me half to death.

"I hired an event planner. Uncle Nick is letting us host everything at his house since his backyard is filled with Boogie's handiwork. We're doing an elevated garden party."

"I told you he wasn't gone let you throw no party on his compound," Liberty tutted.

"Hush," I grumbled.

My cousin always had a green thumb. Whether it was from necrosis of whoever's hand he cut off that week or from his magic plant whispering touch was debatable, but his skill was undeniable. At first I wanted to hold everything at his house because he had an entire acre dedicated to wild flowers, gladiolas, and dahlias, but his ornery ass shut that down quickly. Luckily he'd done similar work at my uncle's house when he still lived there. So all was not lost.

"Oh, we should try and get some of those glass sculptures!" Liberty suggested. "By Chihuly, I think that's his name."

"He's retired I'm pretty sure, but I'll see what I can do."

"Can you also see what you can do about bringing your girlfriend? Mama wants to meet her."

The sight of my sister's devious little grin made my stomach flip. I didn't know how much information she had, so I needed to proceed with caution.

"I don't have a girlfriend," I said slowly.

"You're a liar," she shot back. "You told Makayla that it wasn't gonna work out, then you rushed off to see some other woman."

"That's not what happened!" I argued.

I didn't rush. I ambled off at an urgent but respectable pace.

"Last week you had lip gloss on your collar," she challenged.

Alise only ever wore sheer, clear, non sticky gloss: An accommodation for her sensory issues. Most days I could hardly tell she wore anything at all so I was confused as hell how Liberty saw it. I didn't know what this power of observation was.

"How the fuck did you even see clear lip gloss?" I scoffed.

"So you admit she wears clear lip gloss!?" Lib exclaimed, pointing her finger in victory.

I didn't know how I kept falling for that shit! I grew up with the nosiest aunties in the world and I still couldn't tell when my sister was fishing for information. It was embarrassing. I felt deep-seeded ancestral shame.

"I'm leaving," I announced while collecting my laptop.

"Aw, come on Truth," Liberty pleaded while shaking my arm. "Why can't we meet her?"

The answer to that question was simple: They already had.

Boogie made it clear in no uncertain terms that I should not pursue Alise and I completely disregarded him. Clearly, I loved pissing off my psychotic cousin. He'd probably bury me alive when he found out. So I was trying real hard to avoid adding any other conflicts to the mix. Such as my mother, once she found out I rejected her romantic candidates due to age difference only to date a woman 14 years my junior.

Yeah, I was super good on that potential conversation.

"There is no one for y'all to meet. I gotta go finish some paperwork. I'll see you Friday for dinner at Justice's."

"Mhm, I'mma figure it out," Liberty promised. "You can't hide her forever."

"It ain't been forever, so toodles for now," I said, chucking up a deuce.

I left my sister to settle the bill because I still had one more nosey nellie to deal with before I could get covered in that signature clear gloss.

The worst of them all.

"Here's our current campaign outline. I've added those stops you wanted in Montgomery too. And we'll have a crew with us registering voters just like you asked," Simon explained.

I looked over the proposed route and relief flooded my system. It was a short tour, but it was maximized for impact. Even if I didn't win the election, the people would still benefit.

"This looks great. I'm happy with this," I nodded.

"Amazing! We'll finalize all the plans, but real quick while I have you. Your mother mentioned that you were seeing someone seriously?" Simon coughed.

"Yes, I am," I smiled coyly. "I'm currently seeing my right hand, but it's a late-night/weekend situation."

"You know what, I deserved that," Simon chuckled. "But seriously, are you in a relationship? Because if so and it comes out before we can get ahead of it, that can jeopardize the election."

Shit.

I honestly hadn't thought of that. I hadn't thought of much really when it came to Alise. Except for her breathtaking smile. Senator Thompson had his own team who was doing the same work, with the addition of grave digging. So now I had to think about how I wanted my dirt to come out.

"I wouldn't say it's serious," I lied. "It's just a summer fling."

Was it a summer fling?

Fuck naw.

I'd be flinging Alise's panties regardless of the season if I had things my way, but that wasn't something to casually announce. Sure, I had changed my mind after the very first night but Alise was very clearly not looking for anything serious, and her being investigated by my happy-go-lucky campaign manager was not a good way for her to find out that I was.

"Okayyy, I'll hold off for now," Simon said hesitantly. "But let me know if anything changes."

"Will do," I said, knowing I absolutely would not be doing anything of the sort.

Alise

"How was your visit with Symphony?" Truth asked, while pecking my cheek.

Kissing me was the first thing he did despite the bags in his hand and his half-hung suit jacket and I loved that. I also loved that he never asked how I'd gotten into his apartment. He offered me a key a while back but I politely declined, letting him know that breaking into his house was my version of an enrichment activity. I needed to keep my skills sharp.

"I still hate driving to the city, but it was good. We talked about homecoming outfits. She's got a secret boyfriend too," I giggled.

"Lis! You're encouraging that?" Truth gasped.

"No, of course not. I think she should tell her mom, but I can't be a hypocrite. You smile in my parent's face once a week only to knock the quarters out of my coin purse behind closed doors."

"Well when you put it like that..."

"Exactly."

"Speaking of hypocrisy," Truth sighed. "I thought you said we needed to spend less time together?"

"I did," I nodded while slicing us an apple.

"So what are you doing here on a random Wednesday, sweet pea?"

Honestly, I missed him. We hung out Saturday, and I told him I wanted space Sunday Morning, but by Monday night I was over it. There weren't enough stolen college sweatshirts in the world to replace his warmth. Or that goofy, know-it-all smile.

"I wanted something to eat but I don't wanna cook it myself," I shrugged.

"Mhm, and yet here you are, making us a snack plate."

I was starting to understand Andrea's preferences for himbos. Smart men were irritating.

"God forbid I enjoy your company from time to time! Yes, I know what I said, but I didn't say we had to start immediately," I scoffed.

"You know, everybody talks about golden retriever boyfriends, but I hardly hear any smoke for black cat girlfriends."

Truth snaked his arms around my waist as he stood before placing the world's gentlest kiss on my temple. The satisfied hum he released after made me realize why I had started wearing my hair off my face more.

I was unfortunately beginning to fall in love.

"Who said I was your girlfriend?" I tutted as he began to rock us across the kitchen tile.

I really did hate to prove men right, but just like a cat, I had to test the limits given to me by knocking shit over. However, Truth was simply unimpressed. His entire body shook with a bone-deep laugh in response.

"Alise, stop fucking playing with me before I show you what my last name could've been. We go together. Real bad too."

"Not you using youngster lingo," I teased.

"Girl, bye. I was gonna take you to get a sushi boat since I only got one docket tomorrow, but you ruined it. Look at you."

"Nooo, wait I'm sorry," I pleaded. "I cut us fruit."

"Mhm," he tutted. "I'll think about it."

"We should get another dragon roll," I smiled.

"I knew you'd say that. I put the order in 5 minutes ago."

My heart swelled in my chest. Truth was so many good wonderful things. Patient, funny, loving. I wanted him to know that I adored him.

"I wanna ride your face when we go home."

As it turns out, that was the closest I could get to telling him how I felt without imploding.

Next time then.

"I'd be honored to be your seat, sweet pea. But I need you to do something for me," he said cautiously.

My heart raced from a strange mixture of excitement and fear. His tone was grave, as if he was about to ask me to help hide a body. Unfortunately, I knew Truth would never approve of me getting my hands dirty.

"What is it?"

"I want you to spend the night. We can have a late breakfast and then I'll take you back to the burbs before work so you don't have to drive in the city."

After we fucked on my desk, we had a conversation. Truth still had his rules, and unlike the age thing, they were truly non-negotiable. We were exclusive for one. For two, I was never to leave his house without notice ever again. My rules were less simple and also less rigid. In the beginning I refused to spend the night. I wanted to maintain some sort of casualness despite the exclusivity clause that came with his dick. Spending the night felt like a sure-fire way to end up serious. The problem now though was that breakfast with Truth didn't sound so bad. It sounded comforting.

"I'll think about it," I shrugged.

And I really would. He made a mean-ass omelette and surprisingly delicious biscuits. All those baking shows paid off.

"Ok, but just in case you were concerned, I got you the exact same toothbrush, the same toiletries, edge control, and several scarves."

He then showed me the picture on his phone for proof. Miniatures of all my favorite brands were arranged in neat rows of fours on his dresser, as if he was expecting this to become a regular occurrence. The consideration was wonderful, but we never discussed what I liked or even went shopping together. Yet I also noticed several pairs of my favorite panties in a basket nearby. It was like a shrine to my routine.

"Honey, I thought I was supposed to be the crazy one?"

Truth hardly ever scared me, but something about his smile at that moment was downright terrifying. Men were generally simple creatures, yet mine was complex. He liked blues, but jazz sparingly. He voluntarily lived in suits, yet he didn't own a single pair of cotton sheets because they were too rough on his skin. He hated chaos, but he looked at me as if I was his rising sun, and chaos was all I could ever be. I knew all that and yet there was still so much for me to learn about him. I guess it was part of the adventure.

"Truth, are you secretly insane?" I whispered.

"No, of course not, sweet pea," he chuckled. "Come on. You know me."

I knew there was more to Truth than suits and rules and I started to argue as much, but I put a pin in it since our dragon roll was arriving. Blowing up his spot over dinner wouldn't further my goal to ride him into midnight. Plus even if he was an undercover nutcase, Andrea and Boogie's marriage contract acted as an insurance policy. So it's not like he could steal me or anything. At least not without consequences.

"We'll talk more about this later," I sighed.

"Sure we will, darling," he shrugged.

I knew right then and there that we definitely would not.

Truth

I wasn't sure who was more deluded, me or Alise. I knew there would be no talking once we made it home, but she was determined to try anyway. She wanted to talk about my temperament, my secrets, and how it all affected our relationship. I wasn't interested in that right then. Those were things we could discuss over breakfast. Luckily for me, Alise was right. I could buss down a mango. Especially the dark, summer-ripe cherry mangoes that practically fell into your lap when the wind blew.

"Fuck. You're such a perfect whore," she moaned.

For you, I thought to myself while her hips bucked against my face. And for her only.

Alise was smart to be wary of my request to spend the night. I was becoming more and more possessive by the minute. Which scared me because it wasn't something I could control. Oftentimes when asked about my reluctance to take a wife, I'd picture Alise. Her hand in mine, our bodies pressed tight, and the possibility of a thousand wonderful futures between us. I constantly dreamed of belonging to her even though that was currently impossible. She had unfortunately been born a decade and a half after me and she had her own life to live that didn't include being married to, "A secret crazo." So if I couldn't have her by my side every day, then I needed her in my arms almost every night.

Because I was falling in love with her.

Alise flexed her telepathy again when she asked me,

"Shit, Truth. Why are you eating me so good? You love me or something?"

I wanted so desperately to say yes, but I knew that would abruptly end my night. So instead I tried to suck her heart out of her pretty pussy. Sometimes it felt like that was the only way I could have it anyway.

"Truthhhhh," she hissed. "Too much."

Sweet pea could fuck me back now, but she was still sensitive. I didn't take much to push her over the edge. I knew that, and yet I didn't relent when she asked me to. I knew what would happen afterward too.

One thing I didn't know was how many licks it took to get to the center of a Tootsie pop, but we both found out together.

Turns out the answer was about 300 good ones.

"Look at that. You're a squirter, baby," I laughed while licking my lips clean.

I grabbed a cum rag from our stack and Alise blinked twice, likely trying to clear the astonishment from her expression. I didn't catch her off guard often, but when I did I cherished it. Even if her face did twist up something stank afterwards.

"You mad at me?" I asked, trailing kisses down her thigh.

She was stunned motionless but I needed her to move, cuss, or do something. Because if she sat still any longer I was gonna attempt to lick her toes.

"No," she whispered. "I think I'm embarrassed."

"For what?"

"I peed on you."

"Ha," I snickered. "You ain't pee on me darling. You simply busted in my mouth. But it's nice to know you care," I teased, rising from the floor.

"Now what gave you that silly idea?" she scoffed while tangling her fingers through my hair.

Her nails scratched underneath my new growth as our lips met for a bruising kiss. Then she grabbed me by the nuts with her free hand and pushed my length inside. Breathing was already made difficult by the way her walls fluttered around me, but then her hand crept up my side and snatched around my throat. The mental noise quieted with a gentle squeeze.

"Alise," I whimpered. "Please."

"Hush," she chided. "Air flow is for moaning, not begging."

Yeah, I was moaning alright. My hips met hers with friction so satisfying that it devastated me when I had to pull away. We fell into an effortless rhythm that had to have been practiced over several lifetimes, a thousand different versions of us. I knew this wasn't the first time I fell for that smart mouth and those musing brown eyes and it certainly wouldn't be the last. I would seek her out no matter what.

I knew for certain I was in love and there was nothing I could do about it.

"You ok?" Lis asked as I flopped face down into the bed.

"I'm fine," I sighed with a shaky voice.

I really was fine. I was just gelatinous. Gelatinous and hungry.

That sushi didn't do shit but piss me off after a night of rough fucking.

I turned off the towel steamer and pushed our cum rag into the laundry bin. Raw sex was fun but I forgot how messy it was. I was also reminded of how crazy it made folks as Alise got dressed to leave. I knew it was wrong, but that pussy was so good I started to question just how long it would take me to disable her engine...

Maybe that was just the post sex haze talking though.

"Hey," Alise cooed.

My eyes fluttered open to a hazy vision of a brown-skinned goddess. At first I thought I was hallucinating but then I realized I dozed off and woke back up. Alise was really there, and she had a tray in her hand with two neatly cut grilled cheese sandwiches, and two mugs of steaming hot tea. With her bare face, cozy socks, and meticulously wrapped braids. She was all ready for bed.

"Are you spending the night!?" I exclaimed, shooting out of the sheets.

"Down boy," Alise chuckled while steadying the mugs. "I just really want an omelette tomorrow."

"I'll make you ten," I promised.

After snacks were done, asses were washed, and teeth were brushed, Alise gingerly climbed back into bed with me. I watched her lay smack in the middle of a pillow then pat the covers down around her delicately. She could choke me and call me her favorite whore until we were both blue in the face, but somehow cuddling made her nervous. I scooped her into my arms immediately after she seemed to settle, then pulled her leg over mine. The high pitched squeak she made when I squeezed her could only be described as adorable. Just like her sleepy yawn.

She stroked my hair with gentle swipes while we talked about everything from perfect sunsets to alien theories. We laughed right up until she began to deliriously ramble about the downfall of public wishing fountains.

The state of public water works was a dire one in her opinion.

Then with one soft kiss to her temple, she fell asleep in my arms.

Alise

Two months.

Two months, five days, 16 hours, and 43 minutes. That's how long it took me to abandon all my rules. I didn't really care about maintaining mystery, or the optics, or keeping Truth at arm's length.

Because on the morning of the 66th day, I awoke to a room filled with daisies, and a counter full of food, and a heart full of love.

Plus a big ass omelette.

"Good morning, sweet pea," Truth cooed.

His long legs conquered the steps in no time.\, sending his freshly washed locs swishing over his broad, sun-kissed shoulders. Then he rounded the bed and presented me with last night's tray filled with a beautiful breakfast spread. Big fluffy biscuits, crispy potatoes, a veggie omelette, and the world's prettiest fruit.

"Did you cut that fruit into shapes?" I exclaimed.

I picked up a heart-shaped melon cube that answered my question for me: Of course he did. Then the fruit had the nerve to be ripe and sugar-sweet too, with a single bite sending fruit juice dribbling down my chin.

Truth's pupils blew as wide as a hunting cat's, watching the juice stream reach my chest. Then he started to lean in to lick it off me.

"Sir! Let me finish my damn food," I fussed while shielding myself with a napkin. "I wanna eat my eggs before they get cold."

He sucked his teeth as he retreated, then he outright scowled when I wiped the mess with a paper towel. However, I still got to eat in peace. He brought his platter up shortly after with an assortment of jams he'd spread on my biscuits every few bites that made me want to swing my feet. All while we talked about my sleepy rant from last night. He agreed that the artistry of fountains was declining and swore to me it would be on his agenda as senator. All of which made me think:

Maybe belonging to someone wasn't so bad.

"Let me help you put this food up," I offered.

Truth had to be at work in two and a half hours, which seemed like plenty of time at first until you factored in the 25 minute drive back to my house. That alone would add an hour to his commute. I felt awful about that, but he wouldn't let me take myself home. He had made a promise.

"You want me to make you a fruit bowl?" Truth asked.

The entire kitchen had been cleaned except for the butcher's block that could put any self-respecting Southern hostesses fruit platter to shame. I was plucking slices and bites off of it the entire time I helped. Fresh cut fruit was a love language, and no one could convince me otherwise.

"Just let me get a couple more strawberries and then you can put it up. Mama's too nosey for me to take this cute ass shit home," I explained.

I ate the first two quickly, but the third one was humongous, juicy, and bright red almost like a painted rendering of summer time. I approached it cautiously, scooping it into my palm in order to get a good bite. It was sensational. Sweet like an entire sugar cube, with just enough tartness to curl my toes. Then the juice ran down my face, chin, and chest like I tipped a beverage cup forward a little too fast.

I relished the world's most perfect strawberry with my eyes closed, but when they opened again, Truth was directly in front of me. His pupils were dark and dilated again and this time there was no telling him to wait. He pushed me onto the counter then dragged his tongue down every afflicted inch of me. I normally loved being in control but my dumb girl brain was delighted by his gentle dominance. It was like getting dessert after eating a rich bourguignon.

"You get turned on by the strangest things," I sighed, as he licked between my breasts.

"I get turned on when you sneeze," he grunted. "I'm obsessed with you, Alise."

Truth was smart to quiet me with a kiss because Lord knows I had plenty of questions. What did he mean by that? Did he feel the same way about me as I felt about him? Was this just my inexperience talking or did we actually have something here?

"Can I have you?" he asked while breaking our kiss.

I pressed our lips together and Truth's hands came to my sides to explore the peaks of my curves while my fingers traced the length of his massive arms. The restraint in our respective touches fueled the fire burning between us with each soft, seeking kiss.

"I suppose that's alright," I nodded.

My gown was gathered at the apex of my hips while Truth discarded his sweats. Then he entered me with urgency, like he was delivering for one of those companies that promised you'd get your order in 30 minutes or less.

"Big stretch," I whimpered.

We fell into perfect harmony with breathless kisses and rough morning fucking.

"Fuck, sweet pea," Truth groaned while sucking my bottom lip. "You taste so good."

"Is that why you cut up all that fruit?" I panted. "Just so you could lick it off me later?"

"Naw, maybe I just wanted to do this," he hissed before dangling a bunch of grapes over my open mouth.

I caught one between my lips and Truth grinned with the most nefarious little chuckle.

"Just like a Renaissance painting, baby," he grunted. "God, you're so fucking beautiful."

We all know what being fed and fucked usually implied, but never in all of my wildest, delusional dreams did I expect to be offered grapes, strawberries, and honey-dipped melon while getting stroked down on the kitchen counter. I couldn't tell whether it was my sugar high or my impending orgasm that made my whole body shake. I also couldn't breathe deep enough to catch what Truth was giving me. I just had to take it and hope I didn't lose my grip on his shoulders. This confirmed for me what everyone had already been saying:

Burry boys were demons in designer suits.

"Cum for me, sweet pea," he whispered after pushing another strawberry in my mouth with his nimble tongue. "Wet up your dick, darling."

He ain't have to tell me but once. Between the rhythm in his hips and the sugar lingering on his lips I was soaring. I was the luckiest woman in all of the South, if not the world. Nothing could be better than being in Truth's arms. Nothing felt better than his skin on mine. Not even dancing under starlight could compare to watching his smile outshine the sun as our bodies joined together to create one entity made of shared bliss and...

And love.

I was breathless from the heady combination of realization and good dick. I was in love with Truth Greene. Pleasure bloomed in my belly while the words formed on my tongue.

"Truth, I-"

I choked on my confession as he drove deeper inside of me. Who could talk like this? He was fucking me so hard that I could barely think. It was like his tip was poking my skull.

"What's wrong, Lis? You got something you wanna say, baby?"

Like I said, smart men came with the unfortunate side effect of being irritating. But even his habitual snark couldn't deter me.

"Hush, dammit! I'm tryna to tell you something."

"I'm sorry, sweet pea. I'm listening," he said, in that soft voice he reserved just for me.

It made me realize that love between us really was inevitable, and suddenly I didn't feel so scared of the future anymore.

"Truth, I l-"

Truth

"I cannot believe this shit!" she yelled.

I winced at the sound of my sister's voice. Partly because she was too fucking loud, and partly because I was more than certain that she could see my bare ass.

"First off, I knew it! I knew you were seeing someone. And second off, really nigga? On the counter? It's not even 10 in the morning!"

"Liberty!" I hissed. "What the fuck do you want?"

She tried to side step me and I hunched to crowd out her view of my dick lodged in Alise's pussy.

"Well first, I want you to put your dick away. Then I want you to introduce me to your little lady friend."

"Liberty!" I hollered. "Why are you in my house?"

"Well I needed to borrow your foot massager and I thought you'd be at work," she shrugged.

God, I hated being the oldest. Younger siblings were worse than snot-nosed chirren who proclaimed the snack you were eating to be their favorite, while simultaneously asking if you had games on your phone.

"That's not what the fuck an emergency key is for," I growled.

"Truth, honey," Alise whispered. "Please unsheathe yourself. This is no way to have a conversation."

Every part of me knew she was right, except for my dick. My dick was in no mood for an eviction after a morning of watching her eat strawberries like a 90s video vixen.

"Now, Truth!" she hissed after sensing my hesitation.

Liberty's head snapped toward us furiously.

"Now I know that ain't who the fuck I think it is," she exclaimed.

"Hi Liberty," Alise waved from behind my arm.

"Turn around before you see my nuts!" I hollered.

"Ew. Damn ok, I'm turning."

Since Liberty refused to take the hint, me and Alise scrambled into decency. I mourned the loss of her warmth silently and with a scowl.

"Wow, you dumping Makayla makes perfect sense. How long has this been going on?" my sister asked.

"About two months, technically three if you wanna count that time Truth tried to impale me in his office."

"Alise!" I chided.

"What? I count it," she shrugged. "Which is why your little fondue date with Makayla hurt my feelings."

I don't know why when I busted up in Alise's office to have her for dessert, but sure.

"Pick another topic of conversation please," I hissed.

"Oh, I got plenty of questions," Lib chuckled. "Are you two exclusive or?"

"Exclusive," I gritted.

It was probably just Liberty's simple curiosity but the question left a putrid taste in my mouth. I was never the sharing type and I'd straight up murder a nigga over Alise.

"Touchy on that subject I see..." she whispered. "Anyway, are you gonna tell Mama or?"

"Or what? Mind my business and move at my own pace?"

Unsatisfied with my answer, my sister turned to harass my girlfriend.

"What about you Alise? Are you gonna tell your parents? Because I'm sure they're trying to find a husband for you as we speak."

Alise winced ever so slightly at the word husband. Which wasn't surprising but it did hurt. Part of me was still holding out hope that she'd change her mind. That part died a bit when she started to look for her keys.

"I have to go," she whispered, taking a step back.

"Wait, no. I'm still taking you home."

"Truth, it's fine. We already burned up thirty minutes."

"Alise, I promised. Just let me get dressed," I said, trying to catch her arm.

Alise shook my hold with a light-footed spin, then I was face down on the floor before I could blink.

"Lis, I-"

"Hush and stay put!" she roared.

My mind whitened, and the world around me blurred. I couldn't focus on anything except the hammering of my heart. I remained on the floor just like she directed.

"Tr-"

"Truth."

"Truth! Are you ok?" Liberty hollered.

I snapped from my trance in a blur of emotions, but the woman responsible for most of them was gone. There was no need to check behind the furniture this time. I was sure.

Alise put me in subspace and left.

I gave Alise three rules. Three truly non-negotiables.

Don't think you're about to be fucking someone else while you're fucking me.

Don't lie to me about where you are or how you're feeling.

And finally, don't leave my house without telling me.

"FUCK!" I yelled.

My anger numbed the sting of my scraped skin when I pulled my fist back from the drywall. Then it numbed the lung-burning intensity of the laughter that followed. It was funny because I hadn't caused property damage in almost ten years, but two months dealing with Alise and I was right back to old habits. Right back to square one. I needed-

"You need to talk to Boogie," Liberty whispered, supposedly reading my mind.

Unfortunately, she was right.

How To Break Rules

A**LISE**

I had 33 missed calls by the time I made it home. I was afraid to check my text messages but I knew they were well into the upper 50s.

Truth had given me three absolutes. One of which was not to leave without him knowing.

I was wrong.

Again, I had developed enough introspection to admit that. Yet I was too frightened to admit it right then. Having your boyfriend's sister catch you in the act was one thing, but her reminding you that you might be married off to someone else in the event that your relationship went sour was something totally different. I didn't even know if I wanted to be married, but when the thought crossed my mind, all I could picture was Truth. So I freaked out and I left. Truth and I hadn't gotten around to that discussion yet, and I didn't want to have it then with his sister.

"Mama! Daddy! I need to talk to you!" I screamed, kicking off my shoes.

The wind from my movement hit my nose and I realized I still smelled like sex, so I had to stand back by the door. Andrea was right about the necessity that car perfume was.

"Alise, what's going on, sugar plum?" Mama asked.

Daddy stood behind her with the same concern. They hadn't seen me in over 24 hours but I came into the house hollering. I was never the type to make a scene but this was different.

"Are you looking for me a husband?" I asked.

My parents looked everywhere else but where I was. The floor, the ceiling, the hall. Hell, even the wall calendar which they almost never checked. I often felt like I bought it for my own health.

"Well, are you?" I snapped after enduring a long, awkward silence.

"I mean, we're not not looking for you a husband," Mama answered. "No one is expecting you to walk down the aisle tomorrow."

"But you have to understand, these things take time," Daddy finished.

"Oh ok," I nodded. "Well you can feel free to reclaim your time, because I'm not going for an arranged marriage."

"Alise, arranged is such a strong word," Mama sighed. "Matched is much better."

"So is single. Or better yet, so is the phrase, married for love."

Daddy grimaced at the suggestion. As if love wasn't the reason he married Mama.

"Alise, I'm not saying there's anything wrong with that, marrying for love. But you have the chance to do something different. After all, marriage is a contract," Daddy explained.

My lungs filled slowly and completely. The air was crisp and cold because Mama preferred the house to be arctic and daddy always let her have her way.

Because he loved her.

"I'll only say this once. If you think you will marry me off to the highest bidder like you did Dre, I will burn down the altar and fall off the face of this planet. Do you understand me?"

"Now Al-"

"DO YOU UNDERSTAND ME!?" I screamed.

I hated driving to the city, but I hated driving out to dead man's land more. My only solace was all the pretty flowers Boogie maintained. Unfortunately it was still too hot to enjoy the gardens. Which is why I was glad Andrea answered the door on the second knock.

"Word on the block is that you cussed them people out," she laughed.

"Where's your husband?"

"He's not here right now, but best believe we'll be talking about this."

"Talk about what? There's nothing to talk about," I insisted.

My sister sauntered through her foyer with her wide hips switching, pushing bouquets back into place, straightening pictures, and finally, handing me a wine glass.

"Play with somebody else, Lis. We can dance, cry, and complain together. But play with somebody else."

My face twisted with the idea of an argument, but I immediately backed off when I saw Andrea's eyebrows shot high.

"I love you," I sighed. "What are we ordering for lunch?"

I had forgotten that rideshares and other delivery services couldn't come onto the property. So Mister Nick was happy to drop us off a sizeable lunch from Marbella's, a burger bar with deliciously greasy smash burgers and sourdough buns. A meal that could only be washed down with an ice-cold coke and good gossip.

"So she caught you?" Dre laughed. "On the counter?"

"Unfortunately."

"Then she asked you if y'all we're getting married?"

"No! She asked if I planned on telling Mama and Daddy because they were probably planning on marrying off."

"Well, she's not wrong," Dre sighed with a head tilt.

"That's what bothered me the most," I admitted.

I didn't want to marry anyone, but the more I thought of marriage, the more I thought of Truth. Visions of white weren't complete without midnight skin draped in emerald green. I wanted to get lost in that daydream but my sister wouldn't let me sulk. The last of the wine was split unevenly between the two of us, with myself getting the larger pour. Something I suspected Andrea did on purpose.

"So," she sighed. "Trixxie's?"

"Trixxie's," I nodded.

Despite what she preferred to call it, Andrea wasn't allowed to frequent certain places anymore. She didn't like the word "allowed" because she was a grown woman who could do whatever she wanted. However, Boogie often reminded her that should she **want** to fuck around she could certainly find out. So we stuck to the rivers and the streams we were used to, I.E. what the boys owned. Trixxie's was bought out by the Burry's back in 16'. That meant our drinks were free, and since Andrea could immediately be linked to Boogie via the rock on her finger, the men were avoidant.

"I forgot how much I loved dancing," she huffed as we ambled back to the bar.

Vinnie, the club's manager, saw us come in. She's always been close with Andrea and she had absolutely no problem switching up the playlist to old school hip-hop so that Andrea could sweat her lace off. I still don't know how she dealt with wigs in this Alabama heat, but it was impressive.

"How is your glue not lifting?"

"Magic," she giggled. "Which reminds me, I need a quick refresh. Wanna come with?"

"No, you go. I'm waiting on the drinks. I need a nice cold lemon drop to soothe the pain."

"Lord," she sighed. "Ok, I'll be right back. Order us a plate of fries too."

Andrea and carbs, a tale as old as time. Luckily, I had already put the order for two sides of fries in with our drinks. So now all there was left to do was sit back and-

"I need to talk to you," Liberty announced.

Talk I suppose.

She didn't bother waiting for my reply before she scooched into the seat next to me. Liberty was also the baby out of her siblings, and we were a lot alike despite our age difference. We were both pushy, clingy, and truthfully spoiled. Only I wasn't as extroverted.

"Would you prefer signing?" I asked quickly, freeing up my hands.

Liberty had a cochlear implant, but I knew clubs could become over-whelming when you weren't used to constant noise. Her nosey ass may have ruined my nut that morning, but I still felt like being considerate.

"You can sign?" she audibly exclaimed.

"I speak 7 languages. I'm a polyglot."

"You're much smarter than you allow people to believe," she signed back. "The smart ones are always trouble."

"I'm not trouble," I argued with the wave of my hand.

"Bullshit!" she hit back. "You break all of Truth's rules. Which is prob-lematic enough on its own, but the crazier part is that he allows you to."

"I know," I admitted with a sigh.

If the last two months had taught me anything, they taught me that Truth was unusually complex. He had a temper, but he wasn't quick to show it. There wasn't anything deep breathing and a walk couldn't fix. He was also adaptable, although he didn't prefer to be. Him and Boogie had that much in common. They were selective in their compromises. Only ever with the women they-

"Do you even like my brother?" Liberty signed, interrupting my train of thought.

"Of course I do," I frowned.

The suggestion that I didn't angered me in a way I didn't know was possible. Was that what possession felt like? I didn't know for sure, but I didn't appreciate it either.

"Then why did you leave earlier?" she asked.

I also didn't appreciate this conversation.

"You were being nosey. I'm not having a conversation about the direc-tion of my relationship for the first time with an audience. I don't even want to have a wedding."

"I don't like your answer," Liberty admitted. "But I respect it. I'm not really great at boundaries-"

"I can tell," I interjected.

"Hush. As I was saying, I'm not great at boundaries when it comes to my immediate family, and I suppose I already see you as an extension of us. So I just skipped the formalities and started asking questions."

"Is this an apology?" I asked before picking up my lemon drop.

Liberty groaned like I was stabbing her. I've always hated the rumor that the youngest siblings were dramatic, but I was beginning to see that it had merit.

"Yes, I'm sorry for butting in. Now will you stop avoiding Truth before he punches another hole in the wall?"

"He punched a hole in the wall?" I grimaced.

"Yes, because I'm assuming you broke yet another one of his rules," Liberty nodded. "You know, I'm starting to question if you're as smart as you think you are."

"Excuse me?" I scoffed.

"I'm just saying," she shrugged, throwing her hands into the air. "There are some rules you can only break once. I suggest you figure those out quickly."

Liberty left me before I could reply. Although there was nothing I could say. All those missed calls told me she was probably right. Some things were impossible to come back from.

Truth

"What are you looking at?" Justice asked.

It was Friday night dinner and my oldest two brothers were responsible for the meal. The only problem was that they couldn't cook worth a damn. So I was still hungry after takeout soup, salad, and pizza.

"Hello? I know you heard me," Justice snapped. "You watching porn or something?"

I didn't respond, I just slowly lowered my phone back beneath the table before slipping it into my pocket. Panicking would only make suspicions grow, and my week had been bad enough.

"Emails," I shrugged. "For the campaign."

"He's checking her location," Liberty supplied.

"Her? Who is her?" "Freedom choked.

As soon as she said that, here came my other two brothers with their two cents.

"You got a girlfriend, nigga?" Harmony asked. "Since when?"

"See what you started?" I scoffed at Liberty.

She sat quiet and unremorseful after practically bombing my night, enjoying her second helping of soup. If we were still kids I probably would've tipped her bowl over, or worse, thrown a sock in it.

"Nah, nah, nah," my brothers laughed. "Leave Lib out of it. Whose location are you checking and why? I thought you outgrew crazy?"

"He didn't," Justice scoffed. "Please don't let the smooth taste fool you. This nigga was grandpa's runner up if Boogie didn't take the job. Don't forget."

Oh how I wished they would. I hadn't been that person for almost a decade. I was a firm believer that people could grow beyond the limitations of their upbringing.

I certainly had.

"She's avoiding him, so he's keeping tabs on her," Liberty added.

Mostly.

Liberty was definitely a menace, but a liar she was not. Alise was avoiding me, and I was keeping tabs on her. It started after she left. I found out she was at Trixxie's and I put a bounty out for any man who bothered to even look at her. I bugged her phone the week after she first kissed me, and although I told myself it was for her security in case she somehow got linked to me, deep down I knew it wasn't. Knowledge was power, and I wanted the power to pop up whenever I deemed it necessary since I always knew where she was.

"Damn Liberty, you know who it is? Tell us!" Freedom exclaimed.

Liberty shot me a quick, dirty scowl and then shook her head.

"I can't do that," she sighed. "I'm the reason they're not talking to begin with."

"Did she tell you that?" I asked.

"Yeah, kinda. I overstepped and I apologized for it."

"Lord, Miss Mystery Lady got Lib to apologize? Truth, I think that's your soulmate," Harmony laughed.

Air seeped into my lungs quickly with a deep, belly-filling breath. Soulmates always sounded like a bunch of bullshit to me. I was supposed to believe that everyone has exactly one person who makes everything click? Regardless of what you had going on in your life or what was happening in theirs? No matter the difference in your distance, class, or upbringing? Naw I ain't believe that for one second.

But that didn't start my heart from tripping up every time I thought of Alise in the same context.

Alise

"Buenos Noches, Yadira," I waved.

Yadira shot me a big cheesy grin before sprinting to her car in a fit of giggles. That was slightly uncharacteristic considering most days she threatened to pour scalding-hot coffee on men who harassed her waitresses, but I figured she was still just a girl. Maybe she was a girl had a really good day. Or maybe they were sharing tips and she was excited because she knew I was about to order one of everything on the menu. Either way I loved that for her.

I knew fatphobia was real very early on. Andrea had Mama's shape. She was plump and short with curves that dipped like valleys and soared like mountains and a belly that matched. Because of that, people automatically assumed she ate like shit. Even though my sister was the type of person to *always* order brown rice and pay for extra veggies.

Me on the other hand? I ate like fat meat wasn't greasy. A meal wasn't complete without meat and I met my daily fiber requirement via fruit and divine miracles. I was sure I'd get around to liking veggies eventually, but not right then. Right then I needed a good greasy burger to stop my heart from hurting.

I needed a Marbella's burger.

The door swung open easily but the dining area was dark and mostly empty. I saw Henry in the kitchen rushing around, but there were no customers, and no hostesses. Friday was Marbella's busiest day of the week, topped only by Sunday brunch. The lack of customers and reduced staff flooded me with suspicion.

Then I heard him.

"Alise," he cooed.

His voice was gentle, endearing even, and as usual, smooth like Guinness.

"Truth," I gulped. "Are you following me?"

Silence followed my question just briefly before heavy footsteps filled them. He was pressed against my back no more than four paces later. His scent smothered my anxiety.

"Of course," he chuckled while kissing my neck. "All planets orbit their stars."

"It's been two days and that ego has already gotten out of control," I scoffed.

"Why? Because of the planet comment?"

"Definitely because of the planet comment," I nodded.

His ringing laughter dominated my senses while his mint-heavy breath teased the sensitive skin of my collarbone. My nerves reacted as if someone was sliding an ice cube down my spine. I started to reach for him when I felt him retreat, but as if he could read my mind, he placed a kiss where I needed it the most.

"Can you really blame me? I've had no mistress to keep it in check for most of the week."

"It's been two days, drama king."

"Two days too long," he whispered before spinning me around.

He was dressed in a suit, which was classic Truth. However, the novelty was in his presentation. He looked resolute and unhesitant. Like if I smiled at him and tried to take it back, he'd steal me away.

"What are you doing here?" I asked softly.

I just barely resisted tangling my fingers in his free-flowing hair as he moved closer.

"Having dinner with you. Is that ok?"

"Yes, but-"

"But what?"

"Aren't we in a fight?" I pouted.

I found the reminder upsetting, regardless of the fact that it was mostly my fault. Time away from people usually refreshed me, but space between me and Truth felt like someone was starving me of sunlight.

"No, sweet pea," he chuckled while kissing my forehead. "We aren't in a fight. We need to have a conversation about what happened, but that's all."

"That sounds like a potential fight."

"Nah, not tonight. Unless you plan on pinning me down again?" he grinned.

Truth's smile was an eager dare. A guarantee that I could get it any time, any place. Even in the middle of my favorite burger joint.

"I'm hungry," I said quickly, remembering that we were still in public.

That wasn't much of a deterrent, but Marbella's was Dexter's favorite restaurant too. What would I do if we came to Brunch next week only to be sat at one of the tables I fucked Truth on?

Because I honestly believed it would be multiple...

"Come on," Truth laughed, looping my arm in his. "Our table is over here."

He guided me to a set table near the fountain surrounded by beautiful pillar candles. Warm light danced off an intricate lace tablecloth and against the stunning gold cutlery, and of course, an ice-cold lemon drop as well.

"This is gorgeous, and also right on time," I said, tipping my lemon drop as he grabbed my chair. "But where is everyone?"

"At home eating Whataburger since they couldn't afford to buy out Marbella's," he shrugged.

My chair was swiftly pushed in, then he took the one opposite of me, all while grinning like a cheshire cat. Like he didn't just say what he said.

"You bought out Marbella's for the night?"

"Yes, that's correct."

"Why?"

"Because I wanted to have dinner with you."

"Ok, I get that, but you could've bought out anywhere else for I'm sure, a third of the cost. So why Marbella's?"

Fed up with my questions, Truth pushed his hair back from his eyes and sucked in a sharp breath.

"You're right," he said slowly. "I could've reserved Chateau De Orange, Cutlass, or Fisher's Wharf for much cheaper. But Marbella's is your favorite restaurant. So now we're here. Is this alright?"

My body warmed all over once my brain realized that Truth actually knew me. We were having a candle-lit burger dinner. Not some small plate bone marrow course with locally harvested lawn garnish and decent ambiance.

"It's more than alright," I managed to whisper.

"Good," he smiled. "So about Wednesday."

"I'm sorry," I exclaimed. "I didn't mean to put you in subspace and I shouldn't have left."

The words rushed out before he could even finish his sentence. I had wanted to tell him how sorry I was for the last two days but I couldn't bear to do it over text, and calling him back seemed like it would be worse than getting it over with face to face. Hearing his disappointment without getting his embrace afterwards would break me.

"Thank you for that, but I also owe you an apology," Truth sighed.

"For what?" I sneered. "You didn't leave me face down, drooling on the floor."

It was an accurate assessment of the events that occurred, nevertheless, Truth was not pleased to hear them recounted that way.

"Hush, woman," he hissed. "I want to apologize for the way you were questioned. It wasn't right for Liberty to put you under that kind of pressure and I should've stopped it immediately. Regardless of how this all works out in the end, it will always be my job to protect you. Will you forgive me for fucking that up this time?"

"Of course," I smiled before looking over my shoulder. "You hear that?"

"Hear what?" Truth asked, leaning in close.

"The sound of my pussy purring," I giggled.

"Bye, Alise. Let's eat something so Henry can go home," he laughed.

Truth

Life was so strange.

One minute you could be eating nasty ass iceberg salad with your annoying siblings, and then your knees could be touching your shoulders the next.

"What's wrong, Tru baby?" Alise giggled. "You like that?"

My imaginary camera slowly panned to my dick, where it lay sticky and glistening in her palm before she swallowed it again. Then her thumb traced the sensitive ridges of my ass. If I hadn't popped the tags on her pussy myself two months back, I'd be questioning her experience. This was veteran-level throat. Alise was sucking my shit so good that I was about to send Senior a belated Father's Day gift.

"I asked you a question," she said, freeing me from the jaws of life.

I writhed in her grip as she flexed her hands around me, milking me without giving me the satisfaction of friction. Just pressure and slight pain.

"Yes, sweet pea," I whimpered. "I love that shit."

Alise gave my tip a sweet kiss before she moved to mount me, using my extended legs as leverage.

"Even more than this?" she moaned, as she slid down my length.

Her ass came down hard on my balls as she bounced again with her pussy squeezing me the entire time. I said a small prayer that if God should take me off the Earth anytime soon, that this was how I wanted to go. With a fine-ass stallion busting my shit in Amazon position.

"No, not more than this," I choked.

She was fucking me so good that I almost wanted to cry, but I knew I didn't have permission to weep.

At least not yet.

"I missed you," she whined while kissing me. "And this perfect, fat dick."

"I missed you more," I admitted.

Her walls massaged my dignity away with every rhythmic bounce and I began to pout every time she retreated. I wasn't the one doing the fucking so there was nothing I could do about her prolonged absence. I just had to take it like her good boy.

"Aw, look at your handsome face," she teased. "Are you upset you can't live inside me?"

"Yes," I groaned. "Life is unfair."

I had to work instead of being this perfect woman's fuck toy 24/7, and even if I was unemployed, she still had her own shit going on. She couldn't just fuck me until we blacked out.

No matter how much I begged for it.

Speaking of begging, that's exactly what I did when I realized that I was one excited bounce away from unleashing a science fair volcano inside her.

"Alise, please baby. Please, I can't take it. I don't wanna nut so soon," I sobbed while trying to hold her hips still.

She swatted my hands away and then lost trust in me. So they ended up pinned over my head.

"Nobody asked what you wanted, baby," she hissed. "This is my show."

"Please," I whimpered. "I'm gonna make a mess."

"Then make a mess, Truth," Alise whispered as her lips pressed against mine.

My moans became a consistent song with Alise's every movement. A deep, sinful, unsettling song. I grew up in a family that made wanting impossible. I never had to want for anything. Everything was mine if I just asked for it, but this was different.

Because I needed Alise.

My orgasm came on hot and violent. I clung to every inch of her body like raindrops on a blade of grass. I let her signature scent drive me crazy to the point of seeing stars, and I let her have the air out of my lungs.

I had given my all to Alise Hatchette.

We caught our breath in silence for a few moments before Alise got brave enough to assess the damage. Her slight dismount revealed what appeared to be copious amounts of uncured resin to the untrained eye. Or a big ole cum puddle for reliable freaks.

"Wow, Truth," she murmured. "That is a really big mess."

"I told you," I whined as she pushed me out.

Losing her warmth once again disturbed my spirit. Suddenly I had cuss words for everything that had gone wrong that day. Including busting too fast.

"It's ok," she cooed. "We can clean it up."

When I heard, *clean it up*, I pictured a shower with two kinds of soap and practically boiling water. However, it quickly became clear that Alise had something else in mind. She gingerly straddled my chest, giving me the most perfect view of her ass, right before she sucked my spent dick into her wet mouth.

I didn't hesitate to do the same. She tasted like the best possible mixture of lust. So I licked every inch of her clean and I only stopped because she made me. Her arms shook from post-pleasure tremors while she turned to face me, her nipples taut and stiff.

"Round two?" she asked while wrapping my locs around her fist.

My scalp tingled and the sensation rushed to my dick, turning my third leg into stone like some sort of twisted Medusa retelling.

"Yes please," I choked.

Alise

"I'm about to call the police," he grumbled.

Then he shot me the stankest side eye. Disappointing as it was, I had to unhand his dick. It looked like five rounds was his absolute limit.

"See, I knew I should've gotten a YN. Yo old ass needs a rest and shit," I teased.

"Yeah ok," Truth scoffed. "Gone get you some of that weak ass skinny jean, gas station-honey pack dick. Most young men barely wash they nuts. Yo coochie gone be tore up."

"You'd probably kill them before we could even get to that point," I laughed.

"Yeah, probably," he admitted.

I laughed but he didn't, and I quickly realized that we were no longer joking. Fright was the victor of my heart at that moment. Because politics and perception aside, Truth was fully capable of that sort of destruction.

"Alise, I really like you," he said after a while.

"I know," I nodded. "I like you too."

Truth's fingertips traced the hair on my forearm in soft circles while his eyes worked to catalog my expression as if he was looking for something. Whatever it was, it was something I didn't know how to conceal, because he smiled after a bit.

"So I've been thinking," he whispered while pecking my temples.

"You seem to do that a lot," I giggled.

"Yeah, being a justice and all," he shrugged. "But listen, I know you ain't looking for a husband and I'm not trying to change your mind."

Well it was a little too late for that. My heart raced every time he said husband. My brain just had to get with the program.

"However, I do think it would be beneficial to both parties if we started to allude to our relationship in certain social circles. Your parents would be last of course. Because let's be real, neither one of us has the band-width to handle Mama Hatchette right now."

"Truth, are you trying to soft launch our relationship?" I giggled.

"Yes, absolutely. I don't want there to be any confusion."

"You mean you don't want men bothering me."

"Yeah, that too. I was very upfront about being possessive. I feel like you don't be listening," he huffed.

Then the monster rolled me on my side to tickle me.

"Stop itttt," I howled.

"You gone start listening?"

"Yes, yes! I'm listening."

"Alright," he said, slightly withdrawing before lunging at me again. "I'll let you off with a warning... This time."

"Well thank you, your honor," I giggled.

My legs stretched across the cool sheets before tangling with Truth's, then I collapsed against his chest with a content hum. His heartbeat was steady and slow, indicative of his exhaustion, but it was still my favorite song. Just like his smooth voice.

"Alise?" he said softly as he kneaded my shoulders.

"Hm?"

"I know you like trying folks for fun, but please don't ever again try me. Wednesday was the first and last time that you could break one of my rules and then avoid me. Ok?"

My eyes flickered open in disbelief. His tone was so grave but his heart beat remained the same slow, steady song. His skin didn't sweat, his breaths didn't quicken, and his muscles remained relaxed. His body didn't react to the anger in his voice. He was in complete control and I was not.

"Understood," I whispered.

Skeletons

ALISE

"You look so pretty," Drea cooed.

I spun around in the velveteen gown. It was strapless with a high split, and the color of a rich midsummer eggplant.

Truth's favorite color.

It was my pick paid for by no other than the man himself for his upcoming Alumni ball. Several of his law school friends would be in attendance, some now the board members of prestigious universities, some professors. So besides looking pretty, I also had a chance to network for my upcoming program.

"Thank you. I really like it," I cheesed.

"You should," Andrea said, flicking her wrists to fluff my train.

I noticed she had a new bracelet on, likely a gift from her husband. It seemed like they had been getting along well. She mentioned their upcoming trip to spend Thanksgiving with his Mom's side almost every time we talked. Mama was devastated, but I knew this would be good for them. They needed time away from all of this.

"Mhm, it's too bad y'all couldn't come."

"Mhm."

"When are y'all leaving again?"

"You want me to do your makeup don't you?" Dre sighed.

"Yes please, sissy. I found somebody to install my wig but I couldn't find a makeup artist in time. It's the holidays."

"It's two weeks before Thanksgiving, but sure. I got you. I leave at 3. So you have to come over by ten if you want a beat."

"Thank youuuuu," I cheered, throwing my arms around her. "I love youuuuu."

"Yeah, yeah. Sure you do," she scoffed.

"I do," I affirmed. "I just really need to get out of the dress before I'm late."

I had 40 minutes to make it to the courthouse before his break. Truth had a very busy week with the upcoming holiday season. I thought the cold would encourage folks to stay home and out of trouble, but it turned out it was actually the perfect encouragement for theft, larceny, and coercion. That left him with a whole bunch of cases and a teaspoon of time. So I started eating with him during his lunch hour to make sure we still had quality time together.

"I never thought I'd see you domesticated," Dre chuckled.

She was still under the impression that I broke up with Truth. So she was operating under the assumption that I was doing all of this for another man. Which honestly made my supposed domestication even more unbelievable.

"Hush," I chided. "You cook mac and cheese for Boogie once a week. He can practically smell it through the phone. He's like a fat bloodhound."

I knew I did too much with the last part about her husband, especially since I was in her face, asking for favors. Dre wouldn't admit it, but she was sensitive about Boogie.

"Rude," she scowled. "Actually, I need to double check our flight times."

"No! I'm just joking. But I love you, I'll see you later. Next Friday, at 9:30. With coffee!"

"Yuhuh!" she hollered behind me.

I just barely had time to blow Dre a kiss before I sped off in the direction of downtown. I wouldn't admit it out loud, but I actually enjoyed cosplaying the domestic life.

Truth

"No, don't squeeze anything else on my calendar. Tell him not today," I hissed.

Simon could reschedule. I didn't have the bandwidth to sit and listen to anyone else talk. At least not for the next hour. The holiday season was beating my ass.

"Oops. Wait!" Mariah yelled.

It was too late. By the time she said something, I had already opened my door to find my office occupied. She was right to warn me because I started to cuss. Mother fucker was sliding off the tip of my tongue until I smelled the sweet, spicy, and rich perfume that haunted my dreams.

"Hi Tru," Alise cooed. "I brought us lunch."

She held out a picnic basket that matched her cottage-fairy aesthetic. It was decorated in mushrooms, frogs, and plants I didn't know the name of. Whatever was in it smelled delicious, and *warm*.

"Lis, did you actually cook?" I gasped.

I couldn't tie back the astonishment in my voice. Alise was capable of cooking, of course, but I never expected her to do it. This situation felt like folklore in the making.

"Don't sound so surprised," she giggled. "I told you I cook occasionally."

"It smells like meat though."

"I was armed with plum wine and black gloves. So I was able to tackle a steak."

She shrugged it off like it was no big deal, but my heart was exploding. I was a sucker for not-so-grand gestures, and Alise cooking me a steak at 12 in the afternoon was basically a proposal. The words, *I love you* almost plopped out of my ass like cow shit.

Luckily I caught it though.

"Thank you, sweet pea," I sighed, squeezing her tight. "I really appreciate it."

There was no amount of inference in the world to prepare me for how delicious Alise's cooking was. Mama Hatchette was an excellent cook and so was Andrea. However their food tasted like home. It was good, it was comforting, it definitely got the job done with no complaints.

But Alise's steak sandwich? Shit, it reminded me that people could become world-famous chefs.

"You sure you wanna be a lawyer?" I asked, scraping the seasonings off my plate.

"Yes, I'm sure," she giggled.

"Ok, I guess. I feel selfish being one of the only few people to witness this greatness, but if you're sure, then fuck them folks."

"Thank you for your support, baby."

"Speaking of support," I said, throwing my eyebrows into the air. "Are you still looking at Jackson Marks for Law school?"

Alise had a very thorough five year plan that included scenarios and possible pathways for each one of the universities she was interested in. If she got into Harvard, she planned to minor in business and go the political route. If she went to Howard, she would lean more into community service and activism. Jackson Marks, though, had so many possibilities that it had its own page. Safe to say it was her top choice.

"Is the sky blue?" she smirked.

"And sometimes gray," I chuckled. "But listen. A little birdie told me that the new Dean is going to be in attendance at the Alumni Ball. I also have it on good authority that she's screening for prospectives this weekend."

"Are you serious? Do you think I'll be able to talk with her?"

"I know you will," I laughed. "Me and Kerry go way back. She owes me one."

My back was on the ground before I could blink and I was being peppered in excitable kisses.

"Truth, thank you. Thank you, thank you, thank you," she exclaimed.

Alise was so happy that you would've thought someone brought her a unicorn. Her happiness had that L word wiggling around in my mouth again. I had regular practice keeping it at bay, but it was getting difficult. How long was a nigga supposed to pretend to be nonchalant? It was a lie and I didn't like lying to her. Besides everyone knew I was very chalant when it came to her.

"Of course, darling," I chuckled. "It's the least I can do since you drain my balls so well."

"Ugh. Men ruin everything," she scoffed while pushing off my chest.

"You ruin my underwear," I shrugged.

"Speaking of ruining underwear," she smiled. "What time is your next docket?"

"In forty minutes."

"It's in this building?"

"Yeah. I don't have to do too much today."

"Good!" she exclaimed before rounding my desk. "Then we have time."

"Time for what?" I asked stupidly.

She showed me better than she could tell me. With a nimble wrist and a smirk twisting her lips, she flicked open the buttons on my slacks and freed my dick. Which surprise, surprise, was hard.

"Sweet pea," I groaned.

Alise made a perfect circle with her fist, wet my tip with hot spit, and then dragged her hand down my length at a pace that made me hallucinate. Then she pumped back up quicker than the first time, but with a slightly looser grip. Which produced the nastiest suction sound I've ever heard.

"Fuck, I knew you'd be terrible," I admitted with a breathy moan. "What are you doing to me?"

"Just some quick stress relief, handsome."

Alise whispered her reply in my ear so that she could nip me and inject me with that poison she called passion. A drug that had finished me a long time ago.

My thumbs found her nipples, hard and hot underneath the thin cotton sundress she had on. I was grateful that she hated bras even if I despised the way other men dared to look at her. Because at least I got to enjoy her like this.

Scandalous and free.

"Stop thinking so much," she demanded. "Relax."

Relaxing sounded nice, but my eyebrows pushed together instead. Thinking was my primary function, and right then I was thinking about slipping her perfect tits out of that dress.

I didn't listen so it shouldn't have surprised me when Alise flexed her dominance by tipping my chin up and locking it in place. She was kind enough to move closer for me to reach her chest, but I quickly figured out that was a choice made for my torture.

"Look at you," Alise whispered, pressing her lips against mine. "So eager and wet."

I tried to look down at the precum she was now smearing over me, but she wouldn't let me. Instead I was made to kiss her soft lips over and over again until my brain threatened to black out from the lack of blood flow and the lack of air.

"Alise, please. Baby wait," I pleaded.

My mind was white with pleasure which was quickly becoming too much for me to handle.

"I can't do that. We only have 29 minutes left," she grinned.

Then Alise opened her mouth to let a single stream of drool coat my angry dick. Her speed didn't change, but the pressure did. She was doing her best to emulate how good her pussy squeezed me. Meanwhile I was thinking about cuts, bands, and colors, and the way her nipples fit perfectly in my mouth. We both knew I would've long pulled her into my lap if she hadn't restrained me. That fantasy turned out to be my undoing, and I came against my stomach with a struggling whimper.

"Good job, Tru," Alise cooed. "You did so much for me, baby."

I glanced down at the evidence. It looked like a full pint of milk spilled onto my stomach, covering everything from my thighs to my navel.

"Fuck, I gotta go to work like this," I groaned.

This wasn't the first time Alise had ruined my work clothes, but I hadn't refilled my backups since the last time. I had clean robes so it wasn't that big of a deal, but I wasn't looking forward to the possibility of my neighbors seeing me with nut stains on my shirt when I got home.

"No you don't," she chuckled. "I got you."

Alise was on her knees in front of me before I could think to protest, swiping her tongue up and down my sticky belly.

I lost track of time watching her which led to me having to run down the hall 25 minutes later with my shirt half-buttoned.

But at least I was clean.

There were definitely upsides to having a beautician as a sister, but there were also downsides.

"Hey, cuz! How the kids doing?" I waved.

Downsides like mini family reunions every time you wanted your hair done. My cousin with the six bad-ass kids was at Liberty's, likely getting her crumb-snatchers hair done for Thanksgiving. Two were hanging off the trellis in the yard while the other four were god knows where. My sister was a saint because there was no way I'd let that many people in my house **and** give them a discount while they finger-printed up all my stainless steel and glass, but Liberty had always loved kids. Unlike myself.

It wasn't that I disliked kids, I was just painfully aware that they were people. I felt like most people wanted to have *babies*, not raise kids, and those were two different things. Once you were aware of the difference, anything over three to four children felt excessive. I personally only wanted two, and I still had a few years before I got bored enough to do that.

"They doing good," Janessa smiled. "The boys getting big. Maybe they can come with you for a weekend sometime."

"Hold up," I said, raising my palm. "I think I hear my sister calling me."

Liberty didn't even know I had pulled up, but best believe I used every excuse to get out of that conversation. I didn't even have a proper bath tub. There was no way I was keeping 4 Wild Thornberry boys for a whole weekend.

"Slow down, Slime," Liberty chuckled. "Janessa don't know where you live."

"Shit you never know these days," I sighed. "I went and got a late-night milkshake one time and Boogie found my whole address."

I sought independence from my family during college. So I moved out of the dorms during my sophomore year without telling anyone. That lasted a good month before The Hound found me.

"Speaking of Boogie," Lib started.

"Speak of the devil and he shall appear," Boogie finished while prancing in the room like an expensive show dog. "Come here. Let me talk to you."

I shuffled back before he could lunge at me, all too aware of how this would work out if I was slow. Niggas never wanted to just "*talk.*"

"Don't bust none of my shit up," Liberty hissed before trotting off to sanitize combs.

"You know I'm good for writing a check," Boogie called.

Then he spun around and pointed at me. "Speaking of writing checks, you went and wrote one you couldn't cash."

"You can't tell me who I can and can't fuck," I hissed, raising my fist to swing.

Boogie caught my first jab but luckily I was quick enough to recover and crash against his ribs with a speedy left.

"I can when it comes to that family," he gritted. "Especially since you're in love with her."

My fists dropped to my side in painful defeat while my mind scanned through four months of memories. Alise's smile and the sweet melody of her laughter was abundant amongst those. Visions of her consumed my every thought. So much so that I didn't even see the fist flying straight at my mouth.

My lip split with a bright burst of blood that wasted no time staining the collar of my shirt. The wound burned just like my temper.

"Bitch," I hissed, spitting the excess blood on the ground. "You gone pay for that, Booger."

Grandpa taught all of us how to fight. Fighting wasn't a skill exclusive to Nat, and neither was winning. I kissed my chain before tossing my jacket and shirt aside. The first rule of fighting was to get comfortable. You couldn't throw good punches if your clothes were restricting.

"Oh, so now you mad. Now we get Slime back," Boogie chuckled while circling me.

"Fuck naw, Slime ain't back. But you ain't finna whoop on me like I'm a hoe-ass nigga either."

He got too cocky and too close and I tripped his ass, unfortunately he caught himself and came right back at me.

"I wouldn't have to whoop yo ass if you would've just listened," he hissed.

He swung at my right shoulder and I ducked with just enough time to tag him in the thigh.

"You don't run me. You run the business!"

"This shit affects the business," he spat.

Boogie's big ass ran for me. I swung, he ducked, and somehow we ended up locked together on the floor, with his arms around my neck.

"We got a contract, Truth! You know that."

"You have a contract," I grumbled while trying to lower my metabolic rate.

Anyone else would've panicked, but I knew that I had the best odds of getting out of his grasp with a clear mind. Everyone had an achille's heel. I just had to find Boogie's.

"Don't be fucking stupid, nigga," he scoffed. "My contract affects all of us. We're not the only ones with expensive lawyers. They have loopholes just like we do. You're gonna break that girl's heart and it's gonna ruin my marriage."

I had bitten him twice while he was talking and even punched his rib. Nothing was working and I was running out of air. The last thing I needed was for Boogie to think he did something just because I passed out.

Luckily, I remembered something.

"And you- Hehehhee! Truth, what the fuck?" he laughed.

Nat was deathly ticklish. Under his armpits and by his hips especially.

That gave me just enough leverage to shake his grip and fill my lungs.

"Did you just fucking tickle me during a fight?" he scoffed. "That's cheating!"

"It's not cheating when you were about to choke me out! Worried about my relationship when you need to be worried about regulating your nervous system."

"Maybe I'd have time to regulate my nervous system if you stopped doing stupid shit! I told you to leave that girl alone."

"I tried," I admitted. "It doesn't work like that."

"Make it work!" he hollered. "Your ran-through ass ain't had no problem breaking off no woman before. You get one taste of brand-new pussy and now all of the sudden you're noble. No."

"Shut the fuck up! Alise is more to me than sex. Everybody isn't you. We don't all treat women like breeding stock."

Nat's shoulder's lowered to his side while a single, hot tear rolled down the side of his cheek. I struck a nerve somehow, and I almost expected him to drop the fight, but he only sniffled once before charging at me. We toppled to the ground with a rumble, sending gel containers, black rubber bands, and braiding hair flying.

"YOU RUIN MY FUCKING LIFE!" he roared. "YOU'RE JUST PLAIN SELF-ISH. YOU COULD GET ANYBODY. WHY DOES IT NEED TO BE MY WIFE'S SISTER?"

"I DON'T WANT ANYBODY!" I yelled back while spraying spritz on his face.

He couldn't close both eyes fast enough, and now his right eyelid was damn near stuck to his forehead.

"This isn't ideal, but I didn't get to choose. We just click. We work. I don't know why!"

"You're so full of shit. You always had to do everything I did. Including fucking a Hatchette."

I blinked and my vision switched from vivid color to rage red. Then Boogie was being held over my head until I had enough leverage to toss him into the furniture.

"I know they let you think that the sun rises and sets on the crack of your ass," I hissed, throwing him to the ground. "But everything is not about you! Nobody gives a fuck about violating *your* contract except you! You're projecting because you think Andrea's gone get sick of your evil ass and figure out how to leave. You don't actually think I'm gonna hurt Alise. You think you're gonna hurt Dre."

Fire blazed in my cousin's eyes and I knew I hit the nail on the head. He'd probably kill me if we weren't related. Which was something I respected, but not feared.

"I-" he started while flicking braiding hair off his forehead.

"I told you thick-skulled simpletons not to bust up none of my shit!" Liberty hollered.

Her voice was wobbly and strained. That snapped me out of my rage, and I grimaced upon realizing how far we'd taken it. We broke her styling chair, a hair accordion thing, a TV, and even a supply shelf.

"Liberty, I'll pay for everything," Boogie offered remorsefully. "Don't worry."

"Ha! You damn fucking skippy you gone pay for everything," Liberty chuckled. "But that doesn't change the fact that I got 7 heads to do today and no chair. I'm about to make some lunch, and when I get back I want my shit put back together. There's a toolbox in the hall closet."

"But-" Boogie attempted.

"Fix it!" she hissed. "Now, damnit!"

"You got any extra screws over there?" Boogie grumbled.

"Yeah, I got a short and a long."

"Toss me a short."

"Alright."

That was the first time we'd talked in forty minutes. Usually you couldn't shut us up once we got in a room together. Now it was deathly silent, like a practicing temple.

"Y'all almost done?" Liberty asked, peeking around the door frame.

"Yes," we sighed simultaneously.

"Good, it's some beef stew in there when y'all finish. Just make sure y'all sweep up all the rubber bands first."

She left and we returned to silence. Until I heard Boogie's stomach rumble. His shit sounded like a wounded horse. It was just loud and obnoxious.

"You think she made cornbread?" he asked.

"Probably," I shrugged.

Liberty would eat cornbread with every meal given the chance, so I'm sure she made some for her beef stew.

"I hope she used red potatoes," I whispered.

"I think she did. She got a ten pound bag last time she visited my house," he replied.

The room went quiet again. I fixed Lib's supply rack back to the wall, then started picking up hair clips.

"You almost done with the chair?" I asked.

"Yeah, I'm just tightening the adjuster."

"Coo. I'm about to sweep so we can eat."

Ten minutes later, the chair was back in place, the supplies were organized, and the floors were swept and spot mopped. It looked better than it did two hours ago.

"Damn, Liberty got y'all cleaning up in here?" Malcolm asked, swinging around the corner.

Malcolm was Liberty's first husband. They were still married and there were no mentions of divorce so far, but I didn't like that nigga and neither did Boogie. We both had a feeling he wouldn't be around long-term. So he was her starter husband in our eyes.

"We were just fixing what we broke," Boogie replied coolly. "Come on, Truth. Let's go eat."

"Y'all feel better now that you ate?" Liberty asked. "Are you capable of talking to each other instead of body slamming like neanderthals?"

Because we loved to be lectured, we both grunted in response. Liberty was clearly fed up with our bullshit so she snatched her drink off the counter and dipped. Leaving us in the wordless symphony of eating and drinking.

"I'm sorry," Boogie said after a while. "I know I got some stuff to iron out with Dre, and your relationship with Alise felt like an extension of that."

"I understand," I shrugged. "But you don't have to worry about me. If anything, Alise is gonna break my heart."

Boogie immediately grimaced,

"That is the worst possible outcome for this situation. You gone snap out. Hell, you just body slammed me for bringing it up."

"That's different. I've been whooping your ass since we were boys. I know how to conduct myself otherwise."

Was that true?

Mostly.

There were times when I questioned my restraint. Especially that week we didn't talk, but I didn't think my internal doubt was noticeable to the public.

"Sure you do," Boogie gruffed, throwing his eyebrow high.

A clear sign that he believed I was speaking the universal language of bullshit.

"I do," I affirmed, trying to convince myself more than anything.

My faith was definitely the size of a mustard seed, but I hoped I could walk the talk if it came down to it.

For my sake and hers.

Alise

"You gone make it on time?" Dre asked.

I sat in my car with my phone on speaker outside of Liberty's house. My appointment was at 8 but I always ran 15 minutes ahead of time. I was trying not to wake her if I was too early, but her lights and music were already on when I pulled up.

"Yeah, I'm getting my wig installed now," I yawned. "Mama did my braids last night so it shouldn't take long."

"Ok, let me know when you're on the way. I'll have Boogie save you a plate."

"Love you," I sighed. "Let me get in here."

I sent a quick text letting Liberty know I was outside and the door swung open 30 seconds later. She was dressed in a pair of black sweats with her long locs tied back into a bun. You could tell she was Truth's sister when her face was bare. Everything from her nose, to her brows, and her ears was copy-paste from him.

"Good morning," she signed.

"Good morning," I rolled back. "Thank you for doing this for me."

"Your money is green ain't it? Come on, get in here. It's freezing."

Liberty's house was a lot like Burry estate, with plenty of old money charm seeping from the furniture and the decorations. I could tell she had an affinity for gold by the details on the intricate picture frames. I could also tell that she loved her family by the same picture frames. There was an entire gallery wall dedicated to her brothers and Boogie, the honorary 6th. Her initial reaction to me made a lot more sense. She was protective of them.

We passed by a completed nursery on the way to the salon and I almost said congratulations until she hastily shut the door. The poor thing was near tears, so I offered nothing except a pat on the shoulder and understanding silence. I had learned long ago that sorry was a word overused, and I wasn't about to contribute to her probably endless and mostly meaningless condolences.

Her salon was at the end of the hall on the first floor, and I was pleasantly surprised to see it had its own mini fridge, snack bar, and bathroom. Liberty was a creative just like an artist of any other media, and it was clear she had invested in her work.

"Alright, what we doing?" she asked, clicking her nails together.

I quickly produced my phone and showed her the pictures. I wasn't a regular wig-wearer so I just dug around on Pinterest for styles I thought were cute and suitable for a black-tie formal event.

Liberty did not seem impressed.

"You want it exactly like this?"

"Um, I think so," I nodded.

"With these big ass bang-baby hairs?" she frowned.

"Isn't that the style nowadays?"

"For some people, but we won't be doing that. That's gone look crazy around your widow's peak."

"Ok, then. What do you think we should do?"

"Oh, I'm so glad you asked," she signed quickly. "Take off your bonnet. Let's get started."

"Turn your head to the side," she instructed.

I was getting framing layers cut before she roller set me. As a braid loyalist I had no idea what any of those words meant, but I trusted Liberty.

"This is gonna be so fire," she mumbled. "I need to ask Truth for pictures."

"I can send you pictures."

"Oh, ok."

Liberty suddenly stopped cutting and the room went completely quiet. Then I heard the scissors close. I didn't think she'd stab me but I still jumped back on instinct. You never knew where people's minds were.

"Relax, I'm not gonna cut you up," she laughed. "I'm actually a pacifist. Which the boys find hilarious."

"It is pretty hilarious," I snickered. "I don't know you can be peaceful around all those brothers. Dex is 15 years older than me and I still have to occasionally punch him in the head."

"That's actually the whole reason why I'm a pacifist," Liberty explained. Them niggas got on my nerves from age 6 to 16. I didn't know how my momma was surviving until one day I peeped that she ignored them 60% of the time. If they couldn't get a reaction out of her, they moved to their next target. Which was me until I mastered the ancestral art of being unbothered and minding my black business."

"I need to master that art," I scoffed.

"What do you mean? Are you not unbothered?"

"No, I'm regularly perturbed," I explained. "I just have a great poker face. And probably undiagnosed behavioral health issues."

"You know what, fair. I always knew it would take someone a lil crazy to keep Truth entertained. No offense."

"Oh, none taken. I know who I am."

Silence returned again, although this time it was less uncomfortable. Maybe that was because I was no longer afraid to be stabbed with a pair of hair shears. I could just relax into my thoughts.

"Do you actually like Truth?" Liberty asked. "I know I've asked that before, but humor me again. I just get worried for him sometimes."

Her voice wobbled with vulnerability, like the thought of romantic misfortune befalling her brother might be the last straw. I don't know why but my heart pulled for Liberty. Her vulnerability prompted the same in me.

"I'm in love with your brother," I answered honestly. "Which is really unfortunate because I had a plan."

"You make a plan and God laughs," she shrugged. "Especially when it comes to love."

Something about Liberty's statement soured my stomach. Because it made the warning feeling I pushed down months ago resurface. It was the same feeling I got as a little girl when I would pick at a hangnail despite knowing better and then seeing it bleed.

"Excuse me for a second," I said, sliding out of the chair.

I went back down the hall and right out the front door into the crisp autumn morning air. Then I took a belly-deep breath in just to push it out as a deafening scream. I screamed so loud that the birds roosting at the top of the nearby oak fled the scene, and once that was done I cried. I allowed myself to cry for three whole uninterrupted minutes, and when my time was up, I dried my eyes, wiped my nose, and headed back to the salon. Liberty was waiting on me with the world's most puzzled expression.

"Did you hear someone screaming out there?" she signed.

"Yes," I replied curtly.

Then I sat back down with my head cocked to my right side so she could finish cutting my layers.

Aphrodite

TRUTH

   I didn't know what to expect out of the night. I mean, I knew what to expect. I'd done alumni balls before. The networking, the dancing, the laughing at corny ass Caucasian jokes, and sneaking Lawry's onto the baked chicken dishes, but I'd never done it with Alise by my side. Or anyone for that matter. Historically, I wasn't eager to be linked to women. However, if the last few months taught me anything, they taught me there was a first time for everything.

   I was excited for once. Alise was adamant about waiting to reveal her dress until the night of, so all I had was a fabric sample to coordinate my tie. That left so much to my imagination. I spent weeks dreaming about how it fit against her body, and how the crushed velvet complimented her creamy brown complexion. Then most importantly, how it would feel when I held her in my arms. I couldn't wait to have Alise in my arms. I just had to get through the thirty minute drive to Hatchette Estate.

   What Alise told her parents to make them comfortable with the idea of us spending time alone together, I'm not sure. However, when I expressed the desire to pick her up, she insisted it wouldn't be a problem. She said she could handle her parents. I wasn't concerned because Dexter was who I really had to worry about anyway. Somehow he'd been positioned as the keeper of the Hatchette women, but not in a, *"I'll shoot your prom date"* way. He was more like a sheepdog protecting his herd. Keeping them safe from the encroaching wolves and happy when their parents weren't around to do it.

If only he knew what Alise was up to...

Thoughts of my girlfriend's overprotective brother should've been the last thing on my mind, but I couldn't help it. I was starting to realize that I wanted Alise to be a permanent fixture in my life. So Dexter was a bridge I would need to cross eventually. Especially if I wanted her to be my wife.

Wife.

Liberty would have a fucking field day if she knew I was thinking like that. Mostly because of my past disinterest in matrimony, but also because we both knew Mama and Uncle Nick would be two more problems to solve. Crossing bridges and paying tolls seemed to be the theme lately. Especially on a night like tonight.

"Hey, I'm on the porch. Do you want me to knock?" I asked, pulling my phone to my ear.

My palms were slick with anxious sweat, making the phone slip like a cartoon banana a few times before I finally got my shit together.

"No, I'm coming down. Give me a second," she answered.

Alise hung up before I could say anything else, but that was probably a good thing because that pesky L word was once again on the tip of my tongue. Cupid was constantly taunting me, and he was shooting my black ass with 40 caliber bullets now instead of arrows. It was becoming a problem.

That problem was unresolvable once the doors swung open. Alise stood in the center of the foyer with the prettiest purple train flowing behind her. Recognizable purple velvet made up the skirt of her dress and the majority of the bodice, with soft layers of lavender mesh visible down the center of the top. Of course, flowers were sewn into the trim. Because it wouldn't be Alise without flowers.

"You look beautiful," I grinned.

I almost added on some extras to my compliment but her mama was right beside her, so beautiful would have to do.

"You're not too bad yourself, Mister Greene. You clean up well," she giggled.

If we were anywhere else, I would've showed her just how well I could clean up. Unfortunately we weren't, and her Mama was looking right at me, grinning. That woman reminded me of a happy nun. A nun on Xanax.

"Thanks so much for letting Alise network with you tonight. She's serious about law school. Have you seen the five year plan?" Mama Hatchette asked.

"I have," I confirmed. "She's got it down to the color of her socks."

"Oh, you know then! I'm so glad you two became friends! I told Senior that you'd be the perfect mentor. You're just as ambitious as she is."

I gave Alise an amused half-grin. She told her folks I was her mentor. The only thing I was molding was her pussy to my d–

"Did she tell you that she strong-armed me into it?" I laughed.

Alise cut her eyes at me disapprovingly before her mother checked her expression for confirmation. Which she found in the form of a sly smile.

"I believe it. Everyone thinks Alise is some shy angel but she's actually quite the bully. Ha, one night I got up to get some water and she had Dexter in the dining room playing tea party. It was eleven at night and all he could say was that she made him. He was 18 at the time, she was three."

My heart swelled imagining tiny, bossy Alise forcing the crashout otherwise known as Dexter Hatchette to participate in a late-night tea party. It seemed that she was always a force to be reckoned with.

"So her bullying me was just inevitable then?" I smiled.

"Of course," Alise replied. "Now let's take these pictures for Mama so I can find a lemon drop before this wig gets too hot."

She moved to my side, adjusted me like always, and then snuggled in close. The house was full of focal points, but I was staring at the lace on her scalp for whatever reason.

"You look gorgeous in anything, but I miss your braids," I admitted with a whisper.

"Don't worry, you can pull this too," she replied with a quiet laugh.

Then she dragged her nimble fingers across my chest, causing my nervous system riot.

I struggled to maintain a smile while my dick crept down the leg of my pants. Agitation built in my belly with every shutter click. There were so many poses to model and none of them involved me bending her over the entryway table.

I never hated taking pictures more than in that moment.

Alise

Truth was being quite the gentleman. Not one dirty joke was cracked the entire thirty minute drive to the city center. He even resisted my ass being in his face when we climbed the sprawling stairs to the Birmingham Museum and Art Gallery.

"You're tame tonight," I said as we crossed the bridge. "Everything alright?"

Truth sucked in a sharp, steadying breath then subtly craned to look at my ass.

"I'm trying my best to be civil. Because if I don't, I'm gonna forget my table manners and tear your fancy dress up like tissue paper," he replied.

Rushing blood warmed my cheeks from the sultriness of his drawl. Which was something I was disastrously addicted to. Sometimes I listened to recordings of his rulings to masturbate. It was almost as good as the real thing.

Almost.

"Tru-"

"Hush, woman. Save whatever it is for later. I can't be drooling like a rabid dog in front of these white folks. We need to get your pretty behind into law school."

That was exactly what I needed to hear. As much as I loved bouncing on dick, I had other things to do. So I needed to focus for the time being. At least until the last few songs played.

I never noticed how similar Truth and Boogie were before tonight. They grew up together, so it made perfect sense, but it was unexpected at times. For example, Truth didn't seek people out. He was always the person of interest. It didn't matter what he was talking about. There was a crowd hovering wherever we went, and they even formed perfect queues when the space surrounding him ran out. Truth Greene had his own nosebleed section. It was entertaining to witness, but exhausting to experience. My goodness, white men could talk. I had four lemon drops in an hour once the probate attorneys got a hold of him.

I never dreamed that people could be so talkative and yet so damn boring.

"Excuse me, gentleman," Truth announced shortly after the sixth introduction. "I need to grab my gorgeous date a bite to eat."

Then he pulled me away from the crowd.

"You didn't have to do that," I protested. "I was fine."

"You were smiling but you were not fine. You were bored, then once you started getting hungry, you were agitated."

I stopped moving at once. The hem of my gown swished around my feet like flowing grass, indicating the abrupt change of pace I was feeling both physically and mentally. My heart quickened but my mind slowed to a crawl.

"But l was smiling," I whispered.

"Come on, darling," Truth rasped while picking up my chin. "We both know I'm smarter than that."

"I honestly think that's the most annoying thing about you," I sighed while cupping his hand. "Felicity's husband can't even read."

"Ah, the burden of intellectual equality. It must be so heavy on your back. Come sit and rest a while."

"It is, thank you for noticing."

"Of course," he chuckled. "I notice everything about you."

He said it like it was nothing. But that couldn't have been true because my heart stilled in my chest until my brain remembered that I was alive. Then it screamed at me to breathe. Air couldn't fill my lungs fast enough, and so I drowned in Truth's presence.

Dinner wouldn't be served until 7, so Truth made me a small plate of fruit, cheese, and classic boiled peanuts to tide me over. He had his own snacks, so we listened to the orchestra in silence for a bit until he caught me watching two women have a heated exchange about their husbands.

"You really can't help yourself can you?" he chuckled.

I snapped away from the outside conversation I was engrossed in, back to the sparkling eyes of my handsome date. He was waiting patiently, lips already curled into a teasing smile. As if I could do no wrong even while actively doing wrong. Something told me Truth didn't care about that though. He seemed like he was just happy to be there.

That was undeniably refreshing.

"So you never get curious?" I giggled.

"Not like that, no," he said with a shake of his head.

Normally I'd call him a liar. However the past few months of dealing with Truth had taught me otherwise. He was quite content minding his own business. Unlike most of his fellow gender, he really did enjoy peace.

"Well you're missing out," I tutted.

"How so?"

I was never much of a talker, and that hadn't changed even though the idea of spending eternity talking with Truth made my heart jump.

"Dance with me?" I asked softly.

Far too softly in my opinion.

"Of course, Sweet Pea," he smiled as his hand stretched for mine.

We glided to the center of the ballroom hand-in-hand, unrushed and resolute. Then Truth pressed me into him with one hand to the small of my back. My arms came to his shoulders while Truth's took a leisurely journey to my waist, squeezing my curves as he went.

Yeah, I was resolute in my decision to fuck the shit out of him later on. I didn't care if he ripped the dress. He could turn it into confetti if it made him happy.

"You see the woman in red who just laughed?" I asked softly.

"Mrs. Letz? Who's sitting next to the lady in green?"

"Mhm."

"Yeah, what about her?"

"Well, she's about to leave her husband," I whispered, letting my lips tickle the shell of his ear.

Truth's heart thumped against the abundant cotton and silk of his suit. His hands tightened around my waist instinctively, just like they always did when we were fucking. I loved how well mannered he was in public, because I knew he'd be anything but once we were in private.

"How do you know?" he finally asked, his drawl slow and dripping with lust.

"Because I can read lips so I know she's secretly tired," I answered honestly. "And while she does smile when he comes by, she leans away from him every time. Sometimes she even looks at his mistress."

"Now I'm curious. Who's the mistress?"

"Anna Mae Clarke," I laughed, subtly eyeing the bubbly brunette. "She's young and naive enough for him to get away with it. She thinks he's gonna be the one to leave. Even though men don't leave their wives."

"A sad but true statement," Truth sighed. "Although I do understand. I wouldn't leave mine either."

An air of finality clung to his words, and the sentiment only intensified when he stepped back to look at me. The passion simmering in his eyes told me everything he wouldn't dare say out loud. Every plot, plan, and missed opportunity so far.

Truth Greene loved me, and he had every intention of making me his wife.

Truth

I was supposed to be showing Alise my favorite painting. It was a neo-impressionist painting of a black woman eating an orange by a sunny window. Her feet were bare and her hair was tied back in a scarf. The unexaggerated joy of the subject reminded me of Alise, and when I missed her something terrible, I would sit in my office and stare at the canvas print of that painting to soothe the sting of our distance. So I wanted to show it to her.

That was the plan.

Instead, I was hoisting her onto the foot of a marble statue older than my bloodline, and gathering her dress at her hips.

"Where are your fucking panties, Lis?" I hissed while dragging my thumb between her folds.

"Well, I couldn't find any to match my pretty dress so I figured going commando was better than clashing," she cooed innocently.

I leaned forward with a sigh and let her scent flood my nose like burning incense. She smelled spicy and rich like always, but behind that was the undeniable scent of desire. Sweet, hot, wet desire.

"You're a liar," I growled before capturing her mouth with my own. "A beautiful, intelligent, nasty little liar."

It didn't take long for me to become unsatisfied with the brazen action of simply touching her. Alise was overwhelming as usual, overwhelming in a way that dared me to melt into her. Soon I was craving the taste of her sex, and with one kiss too many, I bent onto my knees and placed a kiss on her lower set of lips.

"Truth," she moaned. "This is a bad idea even for me. Anyone could catch us."

"Not if you're quiet, sweet pea," I laughed. "Everybody's on their way to being inebriated and if they're not drunk, then they're kissing ass. I don't kiss nobody's ass but my woman's, so if I want to do as the Romans do while in Rome, then I need you to be the best girl and hush up with all that fussing and whimpering."

"Ok," she whined before biting her bottom lip. "But you will pay for this."

She guided me back to my rightful place by the crown of my head, and while I'd usually create a hard time for her, I could tell she needed this. We'd had such a busy month, I hardly got to eat her out at her desk anymore.

Alise rode my face like I was a trained battle horse, capable of handling any act of God she threw my way, and now that she had got over her discomfort of squirting, I very well could. Her bud grew stiff and throbbed between my lips, and she drowned me so well that I forgot I was on solid ground. Instead I was out at sea, merrily rolling on the tops of waves while the water carried me where she pleased. Eventually Alise's cries brought me back to reality when they synced to the melody of the orchestra.

"Truth, stick your dick in me," she commanded with a heavy, desperate breath.

"You could at least say please," I grinned.

"Fuck me before I start knocking this shit over," she hissed before softly adding, "Please."

"Look at you being nice," I chuckled while standing.

I released my belt with a quick one-handed tug then let my slacks settle low on my hips. One advantage of being a frequent flier here was becoming familiar with the museum's blind spots. This particular installation took up nearly an entire wall, which limited a potential passerby's ability to see exactly what I was doing. From a distance, I'd just look drunk and disheveled. Which wasn't too far off from the truth.

Alise was dopamine to my system, and we both knew I'd always fall apart for her.

"My pretty sweet pea," I moaned as I slipped inside her. "Do you know what you do to me?"

Alise knew. I could tell because she smiled when my teeth pierced my bottom lip, and she held my chin tight in her palms so I had no choice but to look at her while she ruined me. Hell was probably just as warm and welcoming as Alise at first. Then it swallowed you up once you got comfortable. The light in the museum wing was just bright enough so that I could watch my soul become trapped in the brown of her shining eyes. Every coordinated stroke brought me closer to my goal of dissolving into her, even though I knew it could only be for a little while. I was in a sterile, chilly museum at an obnoxious party, but here and now with her I was home.

"Fuck," I hissed.

Unfortunately I wasn't a man who could make it last forever. Most days I would nut if Alise smiled at me, and that's exactly what happened. She grinned wide, showing off all her bright white teeth when I got a little too active on her clit, and she took me down right with her. I thought I'd have a little more self control since we were hunching on priceless art, but I guess not. I just hoped we didn't break anything.

"Truth Greene!" Alise chided. "Did you rip my dress?"

I looked down at the torn fabric in my hand. The lining of her dress had been split all the way up to just under her ribs. It looked bad, but it was repairable.

"I turned you into a Twinkie and you worried about a minor rip?"

"That's nothing new," she scoffed. "But this dress is. Vickie is gonna kill me when she sees this!"

"Vickie is on my payroll. Which means she's the best in the business, which means she can fix it. Don't worry your pretty little head about the gown right now. Right now I need you to go get cleaned up."

"Why? You don't want folks to know you fucked me at the feet of Aphrodite?"

"Is that who this is?" I queried while looking up.

The plaque was mounted on the wall behind us, detailing The Goddess Aphrodite's preparation for her ritual bath. What most people considered a bath back in those times though was more akin to what most Southern women would consider a hoe bath. Which is exactly what I was about to send Alise to go do. Everything about the moment was ironic and hilarious.

"She just like you for real."

"Hush! And you go clean up yourself. We'll meet back in the ballroom by the drinks in ten. Alright?"

"I done fucked you so good you need a lemon drop?" I teased.

I dipped to steal a kiss and Alise retaliated by nipping me. She had sharp little canines, which made sense because her diet was 75% meat. She was basically a velociraptor in human form.

"Alright, darling," I chuckled while helping her down. "See you soon."

Alise skittered off before I could get another joke in, and I stood there watching her instead of handling what I needed to handle. It didn't matter that she was wrapped in a football field's worth of fabric. I could still see those long legs strutting and switching beneath her gown. The same legs I'd been dreaming about for months on end.

It was funny.

At one point I really believed Alise was someone I'd be able to get out of my system. It was unlikely from the very beginning, but still I held out hope that we'd somehow grow bored of each other and move on amicably. Now I knew for certain that was impossible, because the phantom of her presence kept me in that exhibit for far longer than I realized.

Amicable was out of reach.

"Hey, I didn't know you were attending tonight Mister Senator," Simon exclaimed while tightening his belt.

I caught his eyes in the mirror when I looked up from washing my hands. He had a big grin as usual, and he was dressed in a classic, but safe, black tuxedo. A black tuxedo that matched the black pumps tapping impatiently in the stall he came out of. Black pumps that were too impractical for his wife. Simon kind of reminded me of Giancarlo Esposito if Giancarlo was a bit greasier and less mysterious. Still I understood his allure. He took care of himself, he was generally cheerful and fun to be around, and he looked good at his age.

There was something about him I didn't quite like though.

"Yes, I'm doing a favor for a friend," I replied with an easy shrug. "She's trying for Jackson Marks."

"Uhuh," Simon said while pumping soap on his hands. "Is that the same friend you were admiring Aphrodite with?"

Red clouded my vision again as my movement slowly came to a halt. Implications were one thing, detailed accounts were a whole other ball game. I could take the hit on my reputation, it wasn't that big of a deal for me.

But Alise?

"Relax, soldier," Simon chuckled while raising his hands in surrender. "If you go down, I go down. I've already spent my advance, so I can't have that. I just wanted to ask because I thought you said it wasn't serious."

"It's not."

"Isn't her father Andre Hatchette?"

"Yes, but–"

"Oh, it's beyond serious then," Simon tutted with a headshake. "Your cousin is married to her sister. Your families are already intertwined. I imagine your uncle is ecstatic."

"They don't know," I sighed, bringing my hand to my forehead.

"They don't know? Really? Would that by chance have something to do with her age?"

I remained quiet. Alise's age was a problem, but not in the way most people expected. I was in my thirties. I knew exactly who I was, the good, the bad, and especially the ugly. Alise hadn't gotten to discover those parts of herself yet, and if she had, it wasn't nearly as in depth. Youth could be a wonderful thing, but it was also a time for discovery. I wanted her to learn, and grow, and be sure of herself even if I couldn't always be a part of that journey. If our families knew that we were dealing with each other, she would be holding my hand at an altar by next summer. It wasn't that urgent for me.

I would wait for her to be ready.

"If you say anything-" I gritted, my hands twitching with the urge to wring his neck.

I was more than my past. I was sure of that most days.

But sometimes Slime whispered in my ear like Venom.

Carnage was occasionally delightful.

"Oh believe me, snitching on a Burry boy is the furthest thing from my mind. I make my jokes, but I'm no jester. However, I do want to remind you that we discussed what happens when you have skeletons. Truth, this is a problem."

"It's not. I got it under control."

"Truth, I've known you since you were yay-high to a horsefly, and given that you're now well over six feet, that's a very long time. You don't do drama, you don't do secrets, and I've never seen you do what you just did in that exhibit. You do not have this under control!" Simon argued.

I had another argument in true attorney fashion, but it became moot when my phone buzzed with a simple text.

"*Where are you?*"

My ten minutes were up and regardless of how leaving would make me look right now, I had to go.

"Listen, I'm sorry. We can talk about this later, but I have standing plans."

"Truth!" Simon hissed as I ran out to the ballroom.

"I'll talk to you on Monday!" I called.

I found Alise nursing a lemon drop as expected. Sugar from the rim of the departing glass clung to her upper lip and I wanted so badly to lick it away, but instead I settled for handing her a napkin. We had watching eyes and I had already been too reckless.

"Where'd you go?" she asked, gently dabbing her lip.

"I ran into Simon in the bathroom," I confessed.

Alise quickly became unsettled, and her eyes darted around the room until she found Simon. She watched him for a moment, but her expression remained neutral. I had no way to gauge what she was thinking until she looked up at me, with the tiniest frown forming on her lips.

"What happened? Is everything alright?" she asked.

Something begged me to be honest with her about the conversation I just had, but the other part, the part that knew I would freak her out and blow up our whole night, told me to shut my fucking mouth.

"It was nothing, sweet pea. He's just fussing at me about upcoming deadlines like usual," I supplied.

For whatever reason or another, Alise accepted my answer. She relaxed against my chest as we came together for a dance, and lying began to feel especially wrong. Did I really want to ruin her trust in me over something like this?

"Alise," I said softly while picking up her chin. "I got something to talk to you about."

She looked at me with those big analytic cougar eyes before a soft smile stretched across her beautiful place.

"Wait, me first," she said. "I feel like you'll be less cynical if I go first. You know you like to overthink things."

"Wait, overthink what things?"

"Us."

"What about us?" I gulped.

"See there you go overthinking," Alise sighed while bringing her palm to my cheek. "Although I find it more enduring than I'd care to admit. Truth listen, I l-"

"I've been looking everywhere for you!" yet another familiar voice interjected.

Kerry Donovan and her wife both greeted me with warm hugs. We all met back in grad school when I still had a little too much dip on my chip, and while that had changed, our friendship hadn't. However, I wasn't the person of interest tonight. Tonight Kerry wanted to meet the multilingual avid volunteer with a business degree.

"And you must be Miss Hatchette. We are so pleased to meet you!"

"It's lovely to meet you as well," Alise waved before turning to Yuri, Kerry's wife. "Hajimemashite," she said warmly with a slight bow.

I knew enough to know Alise had done a very nice greeting in Japanese. Yuri beamed with pride. If you didn't know any better, you'd think she was the one trying to recruit Alise. I was also proud, but for a different reason. My girlfriend could speak 7 languages. I couldn't believe that my dumb ass had gotten so lucky.

"That never gets less impressive," Yuri said softly. "Your pronunciation is perfect. You have a gift."

"Thank you," Alise smiled.

"I will say, I don't think I've ever seen you wear color to one of these. Not in the decade that we've been in attendance." Kerry said while eyeing my suit.

My suit was classic black with a white dress shirt, but it was customized with purple velvet trim on the inside of my cuffs and a bowtie to match.

"Ah," I laughed, looking down at my tie. "It was at Alise's request. She enjoys coordinating."

"A visionary and a leader. You have a great future ahead of you," Kerry laughed. "Mind if I steal you away from Grumpy Greene for a little bit so we can talk more about it?"

"Go on," I said as she looked back at me for confirmation. "I'm not going anywhere."

She nodded and walked off with the Dean of her dream college, and even though I knew this was the beginning of her next chapter, I really did mean what I said.

I wasn't going anywhere. I'd wait until I was really old and gray if I had to.

The Problem With Fairytales

ALISE

"I can't believe it's almost Christmas," I murmured.

The South was notorious for slinging up red, green, and gold as soon as the temperatures dropped below 50, but it almost felt like that made Christmas arrive quicker. Once those trees went up it was a wrap. I was prepared to be stressed for the next three to five weeks.

"Shit, I can," Truth grumbled. "This year has been long. I just wanna rot in bed for the next ten days."

"We can do that," I cooed.

The courts were closed except for urgent cases. Nothing civil was scheduled until the beginning of next year. Symphony was on a trip to see her family in Kansas, and despite Boogie being out of town, there wasn't much to do at HQ besides the routine end-of-year paperwork. We were free of all other obligations except each other.

"Maybe," Truth sighed, pulling me close.

I thought I was close enough since our noses were just barely touching, but Truth wanted to be chest to chest and belly to belly. Most nights it felt like he wouldn't be satisfied until we shared skin. Not that I was opposed.

"I'm hopeful but not naive. Every time we try to relax, someone either busts in here or has an emergency."

"Aht, Aht! Don't say that," I chided. "You gone jinx us."

"My bad," he groaned before rapping his fist against his nightstand. "There, problem solved."

"I don't know," I whispered. "Maybe I should knock on your wood just to be safe."

"I'm so sorry, sweet pea," Truth groaned while forcing his eyes open. "I know it makes me old but I'm too tired. Today was long. I had to manage cleanup at the farm, Dre almost shot me.The wood works are temporarily closed."

"That's ok. I'm good with this too," I cooed. "You're warm."

Truth emitted the kind of heat you'd find in a vintage quilt, hand stitched with love and made possible by cuss words. He also was cozy, especially when he traced small circles on my back and arms.

"You're never beating the black cat allegations," Truth smiled while running his palm along my spine. "Never ever."

Lo and behold, that man was right about us not getting peace.

My phone rang in the wee hours of the morning despite it being on DND. There were only a handful of people that I excluded from my DND list. Out of those few individuals, there was only one who'd be up and ready to talk at 8 am. I swiped right without looking at my screen.

"Lis?" Andrea whispered.

"Yes, Dre?" I grumbled drowsily.

"Where are you?"

"Uh," I said, shuffling through the covers to find my discarded clothes. "Home, why?"

"There's a box on my desk."

My mind immediately jumped to the worst possibility. Anthrax, body parts, or a bomb. Boogie was out of town on "business" and most people knew that. My sister was a target because of her husband, and it didn't help that she was greener than sugar cane. I was texting S&D before she could finish explaining. Truth was already awake and just as concerned.

"What? What kind of a box?" I asked while pulling on my shirt.

Truth threw me a new pair of panties and a pair of pants, while I tossed him fresh socks.

"I don't know," Andrea said hesitantly. "It's wrapped like a gift. I'm sending you a picture."

The picture came through almost immediately. It was a perfectly square box wrapped in ornate green paper. It was pretty, but it reminded me of poison. Whatever was in it couldn't be good.

"Don't touch it," I said firmly, in case she got curious. "We're on our way."

"We? Who is we?" she asked.

It was rude, but I hung up on her ass. She was focused on the wrong thing. There was possibly a bomb in her office and she wanted to be nosey. That's sisters for you I guess.

"What's going on here?" Andrea asked when her eyes landed on the man trailing behind me.

I guess Boogie didn't tell her that we were still messing around. Even though he beat Truth's ass for it. I wasn't in the business of having other people in my business, so I was happy to let her think whatever she wanted. Truth however,

"Uh."

His honest ass was gonna be the death of me.

"Nothing," I smiled. "You know Truth is an upstanding citizen. He was kind enough to give me a ride home from the bar last night."

Andrea remained skeptical. She looked between us and when she couldn't get a reaction out of me, she focused on Truth.

"Anyway, did you open it?" I asked, changing the subject.

"No, you told me not to."

"Right, good. Let's make sure it's not a bomb first. I've already called S&D's explosive manager."

"Since when do you know the explosive manager?" Andrea shrieked. "Wait, how do you even know about S&D!?"

To answer her question, I knew about S&D before I knew about period cramps. I just recently started meeting everyone though. Truth introduced me to the explosives manager after we bumped into them at a cocktail hour one night. Felix was great. His wife, and I went out for coffee occasionally and sometimes he and Truth would join us. But that little detail wasn't important right now.

"Let's go get a cheddar bacon bagel. We'll think better on a full stomach," I said, carting her off.

"So, are y'all fucking again?" Andrea asked while stabbing a few mini hash browns.

The cafeteria didn't even serve mini hash brown, but Boogie stocked the kitchen with 5 pound bags one a week specifically for Dre. She was spoiled, and honestly, a little rotten. She knew it too.

"We never stopped," I admitted with a sigh.

"I thought you broke up when you left his house without telling him."

"He forgave me."

"Oh, bwahaha. Is that what you think? You think Truth is being Christ-like?"

"Andrea."

"Ok, I'mma leave it alone for now," she sighed. "But I want you to know that he let you off with a warning."

You're saying this like I'm the one married to the leader of an international cartel."

"No, I'm saying this like you're dealing with the runner up of the same organization. You may be grown now, but I-"

Andrea's lecture ceased when we heard footsteps coming around the corner. Truth entered the cafeteria with a grimace, likely because he heard us. I felt awful about that, because his expression was one of remorse.

"Sorry to interrupt this seemingly very tense discussion, but Felix is done," Truth announced.

It was time to see what was in the box.

"A pair of panties?" I sighed while sinking into my office chair. "That wasn't on my bingo card. I thought for sure it'd be a hand or something."

"Somebody's probably fucking with Dre," Truth shrugged. "Trying to make her think her husband's cheating."

"Well, is he?" I asked, with just enough of a serious tone to earn a mean side eye.

"Alise, please be so fucking for real right now."

"Ok, my bad. You're right. Should we be concerned though?"

"Meh. It's on my radar. I'll do my part to keep Dre safe, but I don't involve myself with the family business anymore. It's too much."

"That's fair," I admitted.

I wasn't sure what happened to make Truth so adamant about keeping separate from the more unsavory side of things, but I respected it. He experienced things that I wasn't privy to and might never be. That just came with the territory of having an age gap with your partner.

"You know what we need?" Truth sighed.

"Hm?"

"We need a weekend getaway. No phones, no laptops. Just quiet, a stocked fridge, and a soft bed."

"I hope to high heavens that you aren't suggesting we go camping."

"Ew no," he frowned. "I don't do mosquitoes and I'm not waking up stiff from sleeping on the ground. I'm talking about renting a cabin or something."

"That actually does sound nice. One with a hot tub?"

"Alise, hot tubs are disgusting."

"Well damn! At least a soaker. These old bones are tired."

"Girl I- Ok Alise," he chuckled.

Truth rounded my desk with grace and pulled me into the safety of his arms, where I allowed myself to find peace. Being the youngest of three, I got to watch everyone else's mistakes and learn from them. Dre taught me that if you were gonna lie, then you needed to tell a little bit of truth to make it believable. Dexter taught me that life wasn't always what it seemed. Lots of people lived in smoke and mirrors. And they both taught me that vulnerability was an emotion that could be twisted up and used to cut you like glass. So I wasn't vulnerable often. But today I could be.

"It's hard keeping everyone together, huh?"

"I'm worried that something is gonna happen to her," I cried.

"No she's fine, darling. Boogie won't let anything happen to Dre, and at the very least, she has Uncle Nick looking after her too."

"Ok," I sighed, sniffing back up my tears. "Let's take that trip this weekend."

"Are you sure? We can always wait, sweet pea."

"I'm sure," I nodded. "Or else we'll never get time al-"

I was interrupted by a loud, rhythmic knock on the door. Dre stood in the threshold with a stack of paperwork, a pen tucked between her lips, and a pair of readers sliding down her nose. I gave her a gentle smile like always even though she was interrupting my cry.

"My bad, I just need to borrow your white out," she said, rushing to my desk. "Wait, did y'all fuck on this?"

My smile remained but my eye twitched just slightly. I needed caffeine, quiet, and maybe even a blunt after a day like this.

"I'm booking the cabin now," Truth chuckled with a robust head shake.

"Where are you going again?" Dex asked.

He was chewing on a chunk of sugarcane with vigor, keeping his eyes focused on mine. It was Thursday night and I was taking a five hour road trip with Truth in the morning. I tried to leave late, once everyone was in the bed to minimize the questions, but I didn't count on Dexter being awake downstairs. Apparently he had taken up bird watching, and he was hoping to spot a Swamp Owl. Now my keys were under his palm while he interrogated me.

"I'm just taking a little trip to The Smoky Mountains with a few friends," I answered.

"Right before Christmas?"

"Yes, they have a wonderful holiday display. Is that ok with you?"

"I guess. Who are the friends? I didn't know you had friends."

He sat down his sugarcane on a nearby saucer, and then brought his chair closer so he could stare directly in my face.

"Unless you're lying?"

"I have no reason to lie," I countered with a smile. "I'm going with Mae and-"

"Mae ain't a friend. That's an alibi."

"Hush, Mae and Sydney."

"Who is Sydney?"

"We met at the alumni ball."

"Interesting. Is that the one Truth accompanied you to?"

When I said I learned from my siblings wisdom and mistakes, that included Dexter. You see, over the years he figured out the best way to learn about what was happening around you was to appear too stupid to comprehend it. Because of that, he had enough dirt to start a potato farm. So I knew he was asking me about Truth because he heard something. Hopefully it wasn't anything substantial.

"Yes, but he left me to my own devices. You know Truth isn't one for socializing with the younger crowd."

"Do I know that? I mean sure, but I also know that you're spiritually 32. You own custom thimbles."

"That doesn't make me old, that makes me sensible. Sensible enough not to get myself in any trouble, might I add."

"Mhm, I guess. I'll leave it alone for now."

"Thank you. I'll keep Mama off your back about getting remarried for now," I said, finally picking my keys up from the table. "See you Monday."

"What took you so long? I thought something happened to you!" Truth exclaimed while helping me out of the car.

I sent him a text as soon as I hit the foyer since he liked to meet me, but I didn't count on being asked twenty-one questions.

"Dexter intercepted me. He had questions," I chuckled.

"I really need to go talk to him," Truth sighed, with a lour.

He looked guilty, as if I wasn't willingly lying to my family. I didn't like to be bothered and that's exactly what would happen once Mama caught wind of us. We'd be paraded around like English royalty. Made to wave at old people and kiss babies. Hell, we might even be put on a float.

"Tru honey, it's not that big of a deal. We can enjoy ourselves without the intervention of our families for a little longer. At least until after this weekend."

"Why, what's going on this weekend?" he teased while spinning me by my waist.

"I know you better have ordered eggs for breakfast on Saturday," I giggled.

"Of course, I know how sacred your omelettes are."

I made myself comfortable while Truth handled my bags. Well, bag. I was bringing myself and one large Telfar. A oxblood Telfar since a bitch was trying to get in the Christmas spirit.

"You're just bringing one purse? Are you sure you won't need anything else?"

"I'm pretty sure. If I do, we can always go shopping."

"I guess. What's in here anyway?

"The usual. Toiletries, hair scarves, vitamins. Oh, and undies. Since you got mad at me for not wearing any last time."

Truth's smile faded and was replaced with a predatory glare. Wide, focused pupils and a set jaw reminded me that we were all just animals. Especially when we were on the hunt.

"Oh, so it's just panties?" he said while drawing his tongue between his lips.

"I didn't say that. However, you should know that I like to travel light."

"Mhm, ok. You like to travel light. Does your undergarment inventory include the ones you're wearing now?"

"I never claimed to be wearing any now," I smiled, spreading my legs just slightly.

I had a long-sleeved sweater dress on, but it was just short enough to draw interest at the right angles. Angles only Truth was privy to.

"We're about to go to bed anyway," I teased with a fake yawn.

I stretched my arms overhead slowly, allowing him to enjoy how my hard nipples poked through the ribs of the knit fabric covering me.

"Yeah, we sure are about to go to bed," he grinned.

"Truth."

"Sweet pea."

"You know, I was thinking."

"You seem to do that a lot. Especially after we have sex," he groaned.

The bed depressed slightly as he rolled over to face me and I finally realized just how huge he was. His arms were the size of my head. I understood why he preferred them tall and why his mattress was custom. This was a lot of man.

"Whatchu thinking about?"

"Well now I'm thinking about how meaty you are," I whispered while squeezing his pec.

"Focus, niggette!" he chided, swatting my hand away.

"Ok, my bad. But seriously, what are we doing for your birthday?"

"Lis, my birthday is in April."

"Yes, and it's December now. You know I'm a planner. We could take another trip."

"I don't know," Truth huffed while staring at the ceiling. "Next year is gonna be so busy. Plus you have your official Jackson Marks interview that week and I want you to focus on that. I kind of just want to have a small get together at Burry Estate."

"Oh," I whispered. "I'm sure that'll be fun."

It would be. Burry Estate was huge and the gardens were beyond green. There were so many plants there thanks to Nat that it needed its own national botanical designation. It would be postcard perfect.

"Why you saying that like you ain't gone be there?"

He snatched his whole upper body back like I had nothing but audacity for thinking logically.

"We're not public, Tru," I reminded him gently. "I can't just show up and-"

"Sweet pea, hush. That's enough of that. I'm not celebrating my birthday without you by my side. Yo Mama and brother ain't that scary."

"Are you sure? I don't wanna put you in a tough spot during your campaign."

"Why cause I'm a creepy old man who likes em young?"

"Yes exactly," I nodded.

"Hush woman," he chided. "We'll be fine."

I was rolled flat on my back and peppered in kisses. So many kisses that I could hardly catch my breath. Truth was never beating the golden retriever allegations.

"Truth, down boy!" I giggled.

He froze immediately, like an over-competitive kid during a field-length game of red-light-green-light, then collapsed to my side with a pout.

"I'm sorry. It's been a long week. I missed you," he confessed, still kissing my cheek repeatedly. "I'm only a man, Alise."

"You're a big baby, is what you are."

"Your big baby."

"As long as you know," I whispered while stroking the soft hair covering his shoulder blades.

As my fingertips traced circles in his warm skin, my tongue once again itched with a confession. Nothing had changed in the last month. My heart still raced at the thought of forever with him so I figured it was only fair to tell him.

"Tru, I l-"

His phone vibrated against the nightstand so vigorously that it nearly fell off it. He was quick to swipe down, only for it to start again.

"You've got to be fucking kidding me," I hissed.

"It's fine, I'll make it quick," he huffed.

My irritation only increased when he answered the phone and Dexter was on the other end.

"Aye, who is Sydney?" my brother asked immediately.

Truth looked at me with a question visible in his eyebrows, and I looked back with a silent answer. Chin down and eyes big.

"Some girl Alise met at the Alumni Ball," Truth answered seamlessly. "I think she attends Jackson Marks."

The way we synced to the same page tickled me something serious, and Truth had to leave the room so that my laughter wouldn't blow up our spot.

Yeah, that confirmed it.

I loved that man.

Morning came quietly and quickly, unlike night. Truth woke me gently when the day was still blue and dewy, with restraint in his touch and a hot tea in his hand.

"The car is already packed and warmed up, sweet pea. Get dressed and you can go back to sleep once we leave," he said.

He made it easy. My clothes were already laid out on the recliner and my shoes were in reach. I washed my face, brushed my teeth, slid into my travel pants, and then followed Truth out to the truck. Where a toasty blanket was waiting for me.

"Wake me up at the halfway point?" I asked. "I want you to get a break too."

"Ok," he nodded. "But for now, close your eyes."

When I woke up the sky was bright and the hum of the city was gone. I could hear the power of the engine, soft 90s R&B, and the occasional crunch of a dislodged pebble. We were driving through the mountains, and waterfalls surrounded us on both sides.

"Wait, where are we?" I asked, stretching my stiff joints.

"Nantahala. About an hour out," Truth answered with a grin.

"An hour out!? Truth, we were supposed to switch halfway!"

"You were resting," he shrugged. "Besides, I had it. Plus now you get to enjoy all this."

He motioned to the world rushing by around us. To tall, wintery pines, snow capped mountains with cascading waterfalls, and persistent evergreens peaking through it all. I saw a bird pass between two outstretched branches of the overhead trees and my heart leapt.

"It is really pretty," I admitted quietly.

"It sure is," he whispered while stealing a quick glance at me.

Truth was incapable of simplicity. At least not when it came to dwellings. We rolled up a steep hill into the driveway of a private treehouse, covered in windows, and strung up with lanterns. The steps were wide and carved instead of constructed, which really lent to the fairytale of it all.

"What do you think, sweet pea?" he asked with an anxious grin.

What did I think? I thought that soulmates were real and God sent me one. That's what I thought.

"It's beautiful, Tru," I sighed wistfully.

"The Fairy princess approves. Just wait to you see the inside."

The inside fiercely rivaled the majesty of the outside. The cabin was open except for the toilet and bedroom. So in the center of the space next to the wood burning stove, there was a large, deep barrel soaker. I thought I would be the most excited for that since I couldn't stretch out in most tubs, but then I saw the balcony. It was sparsely decorated save for a swing and two lounge chairs seated in front of a chiminea, however the view was phenomenal. We were overlooking The Roaring Fork and the Appalachian mountain tops. I felt like I was in a National Geographic documentary.

"Ok, seriously. You did such a good job."

"Well thank you, darling. I take my duties as yo sugar daddy seriously."

"Shutup," I giggled while pushing his shoulder.

He let me get my lick off before pulling me into a perfect kiss. A kiss that reignited all the roiling flames I felt yesterday.

"Truth, I-"

"Call from Simon."

"You've got to be fucking kidding me," I huffed, throwing my head backwards.

Truth once again declined it, but for whatever reason Southern men were incapable of taking a hint, and Simon called back just seconds later.

"Just answer and then put your phone on DND," I sighed. "It's fine."

"I'm sorry, sweet pea," he loured. "I'll make it quick."

Truth knew I hated hearing Simon talk so he stationed himself in the bedroom with the door cracked for the duration of his phone call. I was hungry so I started to make us a little bit of Brunch so we didn't have to plan out the rest of our day on empty stomachs, and I was grateful that Truth stayed true to his word and stocked the fridge. There was everything from fresh cut fruit, to avocados, to feta crumbles, and fancy ham in there. It was like he downloaded a list of all my cravings straight from my brain.

"Hey Tru," I called before realizing he was on the phone.

I stopped myself before he could answer, as technically I wasn't a variable that Simon knew about at the moment, and instead took my question to him.

"I thought you said it's not that serious, Truth!" I heard Simon hiss. "You're on vacation with the girl in another state. It sounds serious to me."

"Simon, relax," Truth sighed. "We're just having a little fun. This ain't nothing to worry about."

"So what, is this another conquest for you? You're just getting her out of your system then?"

"Yes, exactly," Truth confirmed with a soft grin. "We'll be done with this before election season. I promise."

I didn't hear what was said after that because my heart was pounding in my ears. All this time I thought this was love, when in reality I was just succumbing to the naivety of my youth. Truth didn't take me seriously. I was just something to pass the time. A novelty. I softened my gait and backed away from the door, leaving him to his conversation.

And his weekend.

Truth

It took twenty minutes of sweet talking to get Simon off my phone. I hated having to placate the fears of grown men, but I'd do it if it meant finally getting some quality time with Alise. I wanted a weekend alone with her for so long and I wasn't going to ruin it with business. The senate seat was important to me, sure, but politics and optic plans weren't my life.

"My bad, Lis. He's been real paranoid recently," I explained while swinging the door open.

Except I explained it to no one because Alise wasn't in the main cabin.

"Lis?" I called, knocking on the bathroom door. "Are you blowing that muhfucka up?"

I knew something was wrong when I got absolutely no response. Not even a quiet, "Boy, *fuck you.*"

I ran outside, hoping to disprove my anxious mind, but what I found did nothing of the sort, because Alise had disappeared. All that was left of her was haunting quiet, and a note written in glitter ink taped to my windshield.

"*I had a great time. See you around.*"

Storm Clouds

I had in fact not seen her around, and it bothered me every single day.

Everything had been going so good, and then suddenly she was gone. Like fleeting sunshine during a week of thunderstorms. Now waking up was starting to feel like a hassle. Safe to say I was fucked up about it.

"Truth, this is getting ridiculous," Liberty signed.

She was silent, but she still had a chastising tone. Especially when she motioned to my living room. Even I couldn't deny that my living space was... haggard. There were dishes stacked on the floor near the couch, clothes piled up everywhere, and questionable stains on my most frequented soft surfaces. Still I couldn't find the motivation to care.

"And you're getting fat," Harmony added with a scowl.

I also didn't give a fuck about limiting my winter sweets. They helped me keep it together. I could work on my A1C later.

"Please get the fuck out," I sighed, and then signed for Liberty. "You two are on my nerves."

"No, you're on our nerves!" Harmony fussed back. "You doing all of this over a regular ass breakup?"

I stared at the ceiling and then rubbed my palms over my face to chase the intrusive thoughts away. I could fix this if I really wanted to, but I wasn't that person anymore. I couldn't be.

"If it's a regular breakup," I started. "How come no one knows where Alise is?"

Both my siblings went quiet.

Yes, Alise had broken up with me, and she had also fled the state, if not the country. I wasn't sure which one, and while I could've found out where she was if I really wanted to, I refrained. Not tracking her down was the last bit of self-control and humanity I had left for this situation, and I was holding on to it for dear life. If her parents and her siblings didn't know where she was, she didn't want to be found. I had to respect that.

I guess...

"Listen, Truth. We're not saying that you can't feel the way you feel. I for one know you loved Alise," Liberty explained.

Despite being ghosted, I was still actively in love with her. However, I wasn't about to make that confession now. Boogie was already in the nut house. Somebody had to have their act together.

"But, you can't just rot in your feelings. Get up, clean the loft, take a shower, and please come get a retwist. You look like you have a half kinky wig sitting on your locs."

"Ugh," I sighed. "If I get a retwist tomorrow, will you leave me alone for a few days?"

"That's a start, so sure," Liberty relented. "We'll let you get cleaned up. These dishes better be done tomorrow though or I'm calling mama and telling her everything."

"Yeah, yeah," I scoffed, waving her out.

I was feigning indifference, but that threat lit a fire under my ass. I ain't have time to be dealing with Aster Greene and her questions and concerns.

Once I finished with the dishes, I decided that maybe Liberty was right about some fresh air doing me some good. So I found a decent fitting pair of jeans and a tee shirt then went to visit Boogie. He was currently hospitalized for a suicide attempt. That news also didn't help my mental state, but at least his wife was on her shit. She was reorganizing everything to keep her husband safe.

"How's it going, schizo?" I teased.

Schizophrenia was a hereditary disease, and unfortunately it ran in the family. We had record of it going back almost five generations. The gene was usually only expressed after exposure to severe stress and trauma. Making Boogie's neurotic ass the perfect vessel. Luckily his symptoms were mild enough to be treated with a single shot in the ass once a month. He was relieved when he got the news. He wanted to be present and functional for his baby.

"What's up, fatso?" Boogie countered. "Alise still not talking to you?"

I don't know why I played these reindeer games with his ass. Meds or not, you couldn't fix asshole.

"Aye, fuck you," I laughed. "If you would've died, Harmony would've been raising your baby."

"Eugh," he grimaced. "I'd be haunting everybody."

We talked about everything else for a few minutes while Boogie meticulously cleaned his room. Housekeeping usually came in once a day while patients were in therapy or being seen, but they didn't meet his standards. I still didn't know how he was cohabitating with Dre. She liked her spaces to look *lived* in.

"So what's up with you and Alise? Are you ready to tell me what you did?" he asked.

I knew he could tell I'd been trying to avoid the topic of me and Alise every time I visited, but I thought he'd let me harbor my secrets a little longer.

"I honestly don't know what I did. Maybe I got too clingy or something," I shrugged. "It ain't like she left me a detailed rejection letter."

"I don't know," Boogie sighed. "Doms don't get scared by clingy."

How he knew who was doing the bending, I'm not sure, but the accuracy of his statement unnerved me.

"Aye, we close, but I'm not talking about my sex life with you."

"I'm just saying. She was definitely fucking you, not the other way around."

"Is there a point to this?" I scoffed.

"Yeah, my point is something happened. She ain't just up and leave her life just because. This was a fight or flight situation and she chose flight."

Damn Boogie's smart, insightful ass. I never thought about it like that before. He was right. Alise had a plan, and by God she was sticking to it. Something had to happen to make her abandon her plan, her sister, and her community. She wouldn't leave all of that behind just to fuck with me. She was more rounded than that.

"I guess," I sighed, not wanting to give him credit. "You might be right."

I wasn't gonna feed his ego. He didn't need any more compliments. It was bad enough Andrea decided to give his ass a baby. We'd never hear the end of that.

"Ain't you glad I ain't kill myself?" he chuckled derisively.

Boogie was joking because that's what we all did when we were uncomfortable, but joke or not, I'd never deny it.

"Every day," I agreed with a sniffle. "I'm glad you're still here, bruh."

Then I brought him in for a hug. Because a week ago, the opportunity to hug almost left us.

"Look at you all clean and deodorized," Liberty teased as I plopped down in her styling chair.

After seeing Boogie the day previous, I went home, cleaned up the rest of my mess, and gave my scalp a good scrub. That was partly because I caught a glimpse of my reflection in the hospital windows, and partly because Boogie exclaimed that it was snowing on his shoulder when he broke out of our hug. Unfortunately Liberty was right. I was sad, but it was time.

"I'm so proud of you. Wait, did you do them dishes?"

"Yes," I groaned while showing her my picture proof. "So you and your brother can leave me alone."

"Mhm, for now," she replied while poking at my overgrown parts with a rattail comb. "Let's get this under control."

Liberty passed me a hand mirror three hours later. My hair was tucked into neat squares, styled in barrel twists, and finished with thick, minty oil.

"It look good, this shit kind of tingles though."

"Yeah, you need it cause it was hella white girls partying on your scalp. If it was anybody else, I would've thought they were rolling in baking powder," she snorted. "Pure cocaina."

Liberty was laughing so hard that it was scaring the birds outside the window. She was laughing so hard that she was about to knock herself over. Hell, she damn near did. She was sliding down the chair in slow motion.

"I hate yo country ass," I scoffed.

It took her a while, but she finally caught her breath after farting mid chuckle. I guess that was too much for even her.

"Whew ok, just let me do a boomerang for IG and then you can go," she chuckled.

"Sure, whatever."

I didn't consider myself old per say, but I could admit that I had old nigga traits. For one, I hated VR googles. They just looked stupid. For two, I didn't understand the IG stylists' obsessions with looping videos. I felt like a picture could get the job done just as efficiently, and I hated when Liberty greased me up specifically for said looping video.

"Oh my God, you could at least smile. Damn. You looking like I'm holding you here against your will."

She kinda was, but if it was bad enough, I'd let her retake it. I was finally taking Simon's optic lectures seriously. Looking mean wouldn't get me points in the approval ratings. It would get me stereotyped though.

"Ugh, fine. Let me see it first," I sighed.

She damn near threw her phone in my hand, and just like she said, I looked mean and unconsenting. After watching for five seconds, I was ready to agree to a reshoot. But before I could hand my sister her phone back, my thumb slipped.

And guess whose story was up next?

Why, Alise Asasi Hatchette, of course.

She was in Europe.

I could tell because of the architecture surrounding her. The background was full of antique stone, grand pillars, and cobbled streets. If I had to guess specifics based on the pretty flowers growing in pots at her feet, I'd say she was in the South of France. Oleander was prolific in Provence. She didn't look much different besides having a slightly slimmer waist and a paler complexion, but that was only if you weren't looking at her hands.

"Truth, give me my phone back, nigga! What are you even looking at?" Liberty squeaked.

She was prepared to snatch it back, and I was prepared to fight her over it, but she stopped when she saw whose pictures I was looking through. Especially when I landed back on the first one.

"Oh my Goodness," she gulped, covering her mouth.

I could hear the fear in my sister's wobbly voice, but I wasn't going to be the one to assuage it. At least not right now. I didn't know if Alise was being careless or funny by posting this shit, knowing she was friends with my sister but we'd find out soon.

"Excuse me, Lele," I sighed with a laugh. "I got a plane to catch."

Alise

France was beautiful, in a magazine perfect farmhouse sort of way. I could see the charm, especially in day-to-day life, but it wasn't for me long-term. I missed home. I missed humidity, consistent sun, and seasoning salt. Not just generic seasoning salt, I missed Lawry's. I was grateful that Dexter picked somewhere quiet though. I don't think I could've pulled myself together without it.

When I left Truth, the first thing I did was cry to my big brother. I suspected Andrea was pregnant and I didn't want to drag her into my mess, plus she'd hit me with a resounding I told you so. Dexter would be mad, but he'd be understanding, and he'd support what I wanted to do. Even if that meant impulsively fleeing the country and leaving my life behind. You know, just girly things.

"Babe, are you almost ready? We have to be at the airport by 1."

My fiancé stood in the door dressed in a linen polo and a pair of jeans. The outfit hugged his perfect, statuesque body nicely, but something was still missing. Perhaps a chain?

"I'm coming, I'm just trying to pick out a dress," I replied.

"A dress for what? We're not going to meet the Queen, Alise. It's just my brother. A pair of pants and a blouse will do fine."

"Mm, do you have any suggestions?"

"No. You know I don't do all of that," Terrance sighed before pecking me. "Just pick something. I'm sure it'll be fine."

He left the room before I could respond, yet his absence was unmoving. My smile remained.

Meeting up with Terrance in France was a complete accident. When I first came over, I did so with the intention of scoping out the country and the schools. I'd give Birmingham a decade or two and visit on occasion, but I knew better than to go straight back even when the tears dried up. Truth had broken my heart, but I had broken his rules. That wasn't an excuse for him being a chauvinistic ass bitch, however, I knew enough about who I was dealing with to know that I couldn't just parade around in the same city as him and not face some sort of consequence.

So I left with the intention of relocating permanently, and I ran into Terrance Holmes who was floating the same idea. He was starting a winery that cultivated its own signature cheeses. A duo that was meant to fit into the charcuterie trends with ease. He knew I had a business degree so we became friendly, and eventually that friendliness led to some late night-walks and chaste kisses. He thought I was still a virgin so he never pressured me, and I was good with that. Sex caused too many emotions. Feelings were a horrible byproduct when you just wanted to get your nut off. So I removed all of that and focused on the business aspect of our blossoming relationship.

Just like my daddy suggested.

Yesterday's proposal was beautiful. It was in a garden during noon and all eyes were on us. There were so many pictures taken that it felt like a movie when I flipped through them.

Now we were engaged and I was happy.

So wonderfully happy.

"About time," Terrance sighed while bringing his hands together for a celebratory clap. "But you look beautiful, Lis."

"Thank you," I beamed.

I didn't feel beautiful. I felt bloated and these jeans were pinching, but I was ready on time and that's what mostly mattered. I could hide in my tower of mumus later.

"This will be super quick and we'll be back to real life in no time," Terrance affirmed.

Something ancestral told me that he was not lying, even if I did feel a bit uneasy at the moment.

"No time at all," I agreed.

Agreed stupidly, might I add.

Arrival and check in was quick since France didn't do the same security theatrics as America, and because the Holmes had their own fleet of private charter jets, boarding would be even quicker. I had a flute of champagne in my hand for approximately twenty minutes before Terrance announced that the plane was ready. In and out. We were flying to London, meeting Tyrell, then flying back home. After that I'd be locked in my tower and left to my own devices. It was the perfect day.

In theory.

The small passenger plane gleamed in the distance, and the crew was waiting with bright smiles and freshly pressed uniforms. The tarmac was recently powerwashed, the sun was shining, warm spring air surrounded us, and not one hair was out of place. Yet something felt amiss, and my suspicions were confirmed when I heard a frantic announcement in perfect French that all international flights were temporarily grounded. Planes began rolling back to their gates almost immediately.

I thought it was because of the changing weather at first. The sky had gone from bright blue to hazy, ominous gray in a matter of minutes. Maybe rain was coming. Or maybe it was a storm.

I turned out to be right, it was a storm brewing. I knew it the moment I heard that buttery-smooth Southern drawl that haunted both my dreams and nightmares alike.

"Where you think you going, sweet pea?" he chuckled.

I spun around on my heels like a windstorm, nearly knocking myself and Terrence over. The devil himself stood 15 feet back in front of his own plane, the once-retired Baphomet II. He was dressed in an all black suit with black sunglasses except for the lace oxblood-colored hanky in his breast pocket, and even his blunt was color coordinated.

"Truth," I whispered. "What are you doing here?"

He smiled.

It was wide, and white, and it damn near felt like poison, but that smile faded when he looked down at the ring on my hand.

"That's a damn good question, Alise," he chuckled. "But I got a better one for you. Did you really think that I would let you marry someone else?"

The irritation in his voice was undeniable and while I was generally confident, I wasn't delusional enough to think I could talk my way out of this. Especially with Terrence here.

"Alise, what the fuck you got going on with Slime Ball Burry?" he asked with a gulp. "Do you owe him money or something?"

"I hope to high heaven that you ain't fuck this bitch ass nigga," Truth hissed. "But back to my question."

"Aye!" Terrance shouted. "Who the fuck are you talking to?"

A man's pride was more foolish than helpful.

I didn't realize it until it happened, but I never heard anyone outside of family yell at Truth before. That was a mistake though because guns were drawn immediately. Terrance had security, but it wasn't a fifth of the power Truth had. He had a team of at least 12. That was the Burry standard.

"Clearly I'm not talking to you," Truth laughed. "Is your name Alise?"

"Obviously not, but you see this ring on her finger. Burry or not, you're not talking to my wife 1-"

"Wife?" Truth scoffed while tossing his blunt at his feet.

One foot extinguished the flame while the other one pushed him forward across the gravel. All the distance I had worked so hard to put between us was gone in a matter of seconds, swallowed up by the coolness of his imposing shadow.

"Nah, she ain't your wife," he said calmly while looking over his glasses. "Matter of fact, you can hand him that Ringpop ass shit back. Go ahead, sweet pea."

"Truth," I pleaded. "We can talk about this like adults."

"You mean like you did when you left that note on my windshield?" he laughed while pulling out a Smith & Wesson.

His expression then morphed to one of pure, unbridled anger and un-compromising intent as he fired a single round into the leg of Terrence's bodyguard.

"Give it back, Alise. Or else I'm lighting this whole mother fucking plane up."

My senses dulled as I began to slide the jewelry off my finger. Terrence's voice was dampened, becoming nothing more than background noise as I did what I was told. I knew Truth wasn't bluffing. He was exactly what kind of monster I feared him to be.

I placed the ring in my opposite palm and thrust it forward wordlessly.

"Alise," Terrence exclaimed while shaking my arm. "You don't have to do this."

"Terrence, please take your ring," I said calmly. "He's not joking. He will shoot up your entire plane. You're already one man down."

"You better listen," Truth chuckled. "Alise is highly intelligent. She was smart enough to leave the country, but yo stupid, publicity-seeking ass blew up her spot. Oh what could've been. Damn. Anyway, let's go, sweet pea."

"Truth," I begged, this time with tears streaming down my face. "Please, just wait."

Actual tears.

It was enough to make him pause, and when he pulled his hanky out his pocket to dry my face, I saw a flash of softness. A glimpse of the golden retriever who'd make me omelets on Saturdays. However, that man was back in hiding as soon as I reached out to touch him.

"Stop all that crying and get your ass on the plane, Alise," he said firmly. "We got deadlines to meet."

I hesitated to move and Terrence saw that as his last chance to try to convince me to stay.

As if either of us really had a choice.

"This is kidnapping! You can't just force a woman onto a plane without her consent!" Terrance argued.

Truth lit another blunt and took a big draw before once again smiling.

"I bet yo daddy know all about doing shit to women without their consent," he countered.

And Terrence Holmes paled.

"Exactly. You can talk all you want, you can even spread the news of what happened here today. However, all that shit got consequences that extend beyond your pride. So stay in your motherfucking lane, mind yo business, and maybe if I'm feeling generous, I'll refund her bride price for the inconvenience."

"My bride price? Excuse me?" I balked.

"Oh come on now, darling. You knew your daddy wasn't giving yo ass up for the free. Look at how much your sister cost. Y'all Hatchette women are expensive. Terrence here probably paid what, about 15 mil?"

"12," Terence mumbled.

"Wow, that would've been an absolute steal," Truth laughed. "Unfortunately I'm about to hit yo ass with a 5 finger discount. Toodles, bitch nigga."

I was directed to walk up the stairs while Truth followed behind me. The doors closed on my quiet, provincial life, then the engine roared with all the power of the forthcoming chaos. Every one of the anxious pangs I had nearly a year ago resurfaced. I finally realized just how bad of an idea pursuing Truth Greene had been.

"Did you enjoy your little intermission?" he asked while spinning my seat around to face him.

His jaw was clenched tight just like the fist he had digging into the arm rest of my chair. Silence became my best friend, because there was nothing I could say to him that he wouldn't run wild with. Truth was hurt, and he was pissed.

"Oh, so you wanna play the quiet game? I mean that's fine," he shrugged. "I got plenty to talk about, and about five hours to do it."

"How'd you find me?" I whispered. "I destroyed my other phone."

"Phone logs from Dre, the style of the architecture, the plants. The dress you were wearing in yesterday's pictures was an exclusive only available in store at La Belle's Voir. Your skin started to pale from the lack of sunlight."

"I blocked you and Boogie."

"You forgot about Liberty," he chuckled while extending his pointer finger. "Although I do love that you're a girl's girl. That'll make this next part about ten times easier."

"This next part?"

"You'll see, darling. I got grand plans for you and I."

The man wasn't a liar, he talked the whole five hours. Apparently I had missed a lot in just three in a half months. Boogie's expedition, Andrea's beginning stages of pregnancy, and various parties, balls, and lunches. I didn't care about that part so much, however Truth wanted me to know that my name was being spoken in high places. My plan was working even when I left it on autopilot. He almost sounded proud, but every time I looked at him, all I saw was cold, calculating anger. That didn't get any better when we landed back in Birmingham.

"Where are we going?" I asked while watching a blacked out Escalade pull up to the plane.

Truth was busy texting someone but when I asked the question, he gave a resolute response.

"Home," he grinned.

Forty minutes later we pulled into the Sterling Acres subdivision. I could see the roof of my parent's house from the top of the hill. I had been internationally intercepted, forced to give an engagement ring back at gunpoint, and kidnapped to an entirely different country, yet I didn't sweat once.

But the idea of facing my parents?

"Hell no!" I screamed, while banging on the partition. "Stop this fucking car."

"You can cut all that hollering and carrying on out," Truth snapped. "They don't work for you yet, sweet pea."

"Yet?"

I hoped the next words out his mouth would be a thorough explanation. Instead I got a smile and a placating pointer finger telling me to hold on while he answered a phone call.

"You already there, Unc?" he asked.

"Already where?" I scoffed.

"Ok, we're up the street. See you in about two minutes."

He looked satisfied after he hung up. Like somebody who won the lottery.

"Truth, what the fuck did you do?" I hissed.

"Oh, this is just the beginning," he smiled. "I ain't did nothing yet."

Anxiety consumed me when we finally rolled onto the pea gravel that lined the driveway of my childhood home. Every resounding crunch sent my heart soaring. I couldn't face them after three months with news like this.

Truth exited first and then rounded the car to open my door. I guess he thought I'd be easy about this, but I wasn't about to tell my mama I was fucking on desks with my chin held high. I wasn't telling her that at all.

"Get out the car, Alise," he growled.

"I'm not doing shit!" I spat back. "You might as well set this motherfucker on fire."

"Here we go with the dramatics," he huffed. "You going in one way or another so you might as well be a lady about it and get out the car."

"Fuck you, Truth!"

"You promise?" he grinned while leaning into the cabin with his head tilted on his shoulder.

"Put me down, you fucking dickhead!" I screamed. "Put me down, damnit!"

I was dizzy from screaming and pounding on his back with all my strength, but it wasn't making an inch of difference. He was still lugging up the steps, and I was still slung over his shoulders like a big catch.

"We both know how to sign, so just know if you bust my eardrum with all that hollering, you still gone have to hear about it," he chuckled.

Everything was funny to him, even when I kicked against his ribs and pulled his hair. The asshole would moan in my ear, then kiss my shoulder.

"I like that rough shit," he'd whisper.

This must've been the migraine guarantee Andrea was talking about when it came to Bothersome Burrys.

Mister Nick was already posted at the door, looking just as concerned as the neighbors down the way did. Hell, he almost looked scared for me.

"Truth, what's going on?" he asked hesitantly while eyeing me. "You called an emergency meeting on a Sunday?"

"That's because it's acquisition day, Unc," Truth chuckled while finally returning me to my feet. "Call legal and tell them to fire up the printers. We got some contracts to sign!"

We sat across from each other in the dining hall, Mister Nick, Truth, and legal sat across from Daddy, Mama, and I. Dexter stood in the door, likely itching to cuss me out for the half-truth I told him months ago, and Boogie was on the line with Andrea. The air vibrated with tension and nobody was smiling. The rain outside didn't help. It came just as quickly and unexpectedly as the rest of this. Nobody knew what was going on.

Except for Truth.

"Nick, what's this about?" Daddy asked. "This is my first time seeing Alise in three months and you brought her here with legal? We didn't even know she was back in the country."

"Honestly, I don't know what's going on," Mister Nick shrugged. "Truth just called me and told me I needed to be here."

"Truth honey?" Mama asked. "What is this about?"

"I apologize for my intrusion, Mama Joy," Truth sighed. "But I'll be honest. I came here to collect my wife."

The entire room gasped like a telenovela soundtrack. I couldn't even believe the words coming out of his mouth. We stopped dealing with each other because he wanted to remain unattached. Marriage was one big ass attachment. What did he mean, his wife? Dexter wasn't cross dressing anymore as far as I knew.

"Alise, is he talking about you?" Daddy asked.

"I guess so," I shrugged softly.

"Oh, come on now, sweet pea," he laughed. "Ain't no need to act so shy about it. You weren't shy when you were kissing up on me in my office."

My eyes snapped shut. I was unwilling to see my father's reaction or Truth's triumphant grin. I couldn't even imagine how Mister Nick's face twisted up. He was an animated man.

"Wait one God damn minute," Nick exclaimed. "You were talking about Alise when you said you were seeing someone serious. Boogie, did you know about this?"

"I beat his ass for it," Boogie sighed into the speaker. "Niggas are hard headed."

Well, that was something we had that in common. Everybody told me to leave this man alone. Stubbornness was once again biting me in the ass.

"That's why you had that fucking limp!" Nick exclaimed into the phone.

It was like someone had dumped out a big puzzle in front of us with the edges finished. Everything was coming together for everyone.

"Listen, I'm not here to stir up conspiracy theories or anything like that," Truth said, redirecting the conversation with a pointed hand. "I wanna talk business. Dre, you give me your daughter today, and I'll repay her original bride price to the Holmes, plus 200% in contingencies because I know this wasn't in the plans. Free shipping and handling included."

"I don't want to marry you," I scoffed. "And I'm not cattle. You can't just bargain for my life."

"Well you can't marry nobody else," he countered with a smile. "If you try, I'll kill them. Terrence Holmes? Dead. The next nigga? Double dead.

You'll be the dictionary definition of a Black widow. Andre, is that what you want for your baby girl?"

"I'm still trying to figure out how we got here," Daddy admitted with a tense brow. "Alise, what did you do?"

He looked at me the same way Mister Nick did earlier, except there was far more fear in his expression. If my life had a soundtrack, dramatic organ tracks foreshadowing the severity of the moment would be blaring by now. There was no answer that could bring satisfaction to this situation, because the truth was I-

"You wanna know what Alise did?" Truth gritted while leaning on the table. "Alise broke every single one of my rules. She tortured me for months, played in my face, and blatantly disrespected my non-negotiables. I do apologize that y'all have to find out because she fucked around, but I'm leaving here with my wife, or I'm gone spend every single second of my free time tearing y'alls lives apart. Starting with this house. What do you wanna see go first, Lis? The kitchen? Your room?"

"Nephew," Nick protested. "We have contracts, you can't just take their women!"

"I don't give a fuck about the current contracts. Write a new one. Like I said, I either leave here with Alise, or I'm tearing all this shit up. Don't forget who makes all this hiding and secrecy possible. S&D is my department. If y'all wanna do y'all dirt and get away with it, you know what to do. Andre, sign my papers."

"We can give up S&D," Daddy said. "I can't make the same mistake twice with my girls. We'll make it work without them."

My stomach soured from the strength of the admission. Of course Truth ran S&D. The only reason he went into law was because he got his start in forensics. I don't know how I didn't piece it together sooner.

"That's right, sweet pea," he chuckled. "The signs were always there. You just didn't pay them no mind because you loved me. You thought I was just the softness I showed you. But that's done with."

"Truth, I'm sorry. Please," I begged. "These are my parents. This is their livelihood. Our home. We can work something out, but I can't marry you."

Truth leaned forward in his seat, making the table creak under the weight of his now planted elbows.

"Sweet pea, look at me," he demanded.

I slowly turned my head to meet his. His eyes were so large and dark that they looked like voids. The warm chocolate that I once loved was long gone, and now they were portals to a world unknown.

"Either you agree to marry me, or I'll become the reason your daddy has a second, and probably final, heart attack," he said easily.

"Aye man, now you getting out of hand!" Dexter shouted. "We don't have to entertain this shit. Alise, stand up!"

Truth immediately drew a gun from each side of his waist.

"Lis, you get out that chair and I'm shooting out both of your brother's knees," Truth hissed. "He'll be a guaranteed double minority. There's only one way you're leaving this room, and that's on my arm."

Fear choked me so remained still. Truth never once lied to me and I doubted he'd start now. It was a horrible time for tears to start, yet I couldn't help it. I was accepting that I didn't have any other choice. No one was coming to save me from my choices. I had to go with him.

"Truth, sugar please," Mama petitioned on my behalf. "I know that Alise isn't innocent here, but she's not ready for this. You've never liked inexperience, and hell she hasn't even laid with anyone yet."

"Oh, she ain't tell you?" Truth laughed, snatching his head back.

"Tell us what?" Mama gulped.

"No wonder everybody thinks I'm losing my mind. But here's the real tea, I was Alise's first fuck, and I might even be her last provided I don't die first."

The room was so quiet that you could hear the cat fart, the trees swaying outside, and even the waking crickets. If this was a TV show, that would be the season finale.

"Alise," Daddy boomed with disappointment etched into his features. "Is that true? Did you give your virginity to Truth?"

This was exactly what I was afraid of. Now all of my business was out in the open. Now I had nothing to hide behind. Not even a smile. Lying was pointless when it came to a man as calloused as Truth so I nodded instead, trying my best to swallow the lump occupying my throat. I watched the fire in my father's eyes die as he processed my answer. The color seemed to drain from his skin as he turned to face Truth and Mister Nick with an answer.

"We agree to your terms," Daddy said plainly. "Draw up the contracts."

"Dad, no!" Dexter shouted. "She can't marry that man!"

He tried to reach for me but Truth's team pinned him to the ground at his silent command.

"Good doing business with you, Hatchette," Truth said while standing to collect me. "The money will be in your account by the morning, but her room is getting cleared out tonight. Get a move on, y'all!" he shouted.

A team of 30 ascended to the living quarters of the home I loved and began packing my room with military precision. Women with crisp white gloves folded every single garment, while men with dollies passed the boxes and furniture down the stairs. It was completely empty 20 minutes later, with not even a speck of paper on the ground.

"Mama Joy, I hope you can find it in your heart to forgive me for being so rude and interrupting Sunday dinner," Truth started. "But if not I understand. However I do want to let you know that you and the girls have a week to get everything planned."

So he coerced me into marriage and he was also rushing me? Mama couldn't even start her protest, because I was in sheer disbelief of his audacity.

"A week!?" I shrieked. "Truth, even Boogie gave us more time than that."

"He did," Truth agreed. "But Andrea ain't try to flee the country, now did she?"

"It wasn't no try, I did leave your ignorant ass," I spat back.

"Ah, there she is," Truth smiled as my parents watched us in disbelief. "My match made in Hell. Come on, sweet pea. We better get a move on if we wanna eat dinner on time. You know how you act when you get hungry."

"I hope you choke," I gritted.

"Yeah, I just bet you do," he countered, stepping close.

I didn't miss nor appreciate the reference to our past.

"Asshole," I tutted.

Once the contracts were signed, I was loaded back into the Escalade, and the moving trucks were queued behind us. It looked like quite a bit more than just my things but I didn't comment on it. I just wanted a moment of quiet after everything that had happened.

"Whatchu thinking about, baby? Dinner? Your wedding dress? Don't worry, you can still wear a white one even though you fucked me half to death. I won't tell nobody."

"I hate you," I whispered.

"No, you hate consequences," he countered with a pointed finger. "Yo sneaky ass ain't get enough whoopings growing up and now look at you. You running around giving your daddy heart palpitations."

"I'm pretty sure that was your fault. And by the way, if you ever threaten my family again, I'll kill you in your sleep."

"Mhm, sure you will," he chuckled. "Whatever brings you peace, sweet pea."

We arrived at a property that could really only be described as a manor about twenty minutes later. Small stone cottages were set back from the main house, while the entirety of the property was surrounded by trees. Rows of big, fluffy hydrangeas sat trimmed neatly in front of the ramped entrance, and gold-accented lanterns were each lit by a single pillar candle. If I wasn't so irritated, I'd be rushing to admit how beautiful it was.

"Where are we?" I asked when he opened the door. "You couldn't even kill me where I was comfortable? Some man you are."

"Girl hush," he scoffed while pulling me from the car. "I know you don't like the city so welcome to Greene Manor. This will be your home."

"Great, and where will you live?"

"In your skin like a botfly if you don't stop playing with me," he grinned. "Come on, dinner should be ready."

Dinner was ready and Truth must've been starving. Because I barely had time to take in the sights around me as we rushed through the foyer, the living room, the parlor, and then finally into the kitchen. However from what I could gather, the house was clean and well organized. It also looked like a bigger replica of the loft. There were earth tones, floor lamps, and impressionist art pieces everywhere.

"Whose house is this?" I asked as Truth pulled out my chair.

"It's mine," he shrugged. "My father left it to me when I turned 18. I just didn't like how much space it was for one person."

"I'm not having any babies to fill this motherfucker up," I hissed.

"Ew, girl what the fuck? I just kidnapped you out of France. Do I seem like someone who should be raising children?"

"Oh," I said, relaxing my shoulders. "Excuse me for assuming."

"It's fine," he shrugged. "Although I wouldn't mind practicing after we work everything out."

"Haven't you had enough of that? Where's the chef bitch you been fucking on?"

"Robert doesn't like boys," Truth laughed. "And even if he did, he's not my type."

Robert came out from the butler's pantry shortly after that to serve us, and while his side eye told me he most certainly heard the conversation prior, he maintained his professionalism.

I was served a gooey double cheese burger and a generous helping of herb fries and fruit salad, while Truth had a meatloaf dinner.

"So you hired a chef so neither one of us has to cook?" I asked while taking a bite of my burger.

Again, if I wasn't pissed, I'd be pounding the table in joy about how good the food was. Robert might have Marbella's beat.

"I want you to be comfortable."

"I'd be comfortable at home."

"I'm sure, but that's simply not gonna happen."

"Truth, why are you doing this?"

"Why are we having dinner? Because I'm hungry, shit. Please don't start acting like you too cute to eat. I've seen that jaw in action."

"No shut up. Why are you trying to force me to marry you?"

Truth slowly lowered his fork, and once again I saw a glimpse of familiar softness. The same softness that shielded me from the city noise when he held me at night.

"I was never going to let you marry anyone else, Alise. I was just giving you time to realize that. But ain't no try. We're getting married next Sunday, or I'm going to spend the rest of my miserable life torturing your family."

"You aren't that cruel," I argued.

"That is fundamentally untrue," he said, sucking the meat from his teeth. "I don't like acting like this but it's my default. Balance and self-control is a lot of work."

"You don't even want a wife," I sighed.

"No, I didn't want a wife previously. But like with most things between us, you're a special case."

"So what, I'm just supposed to give up my dreams and goals to satisfy yours?"

"Who the fuck said that?" he scoffed. "Do you know how much of a brag it is to have a wife who studies law at Jackson Marks? A wife that speaks seven languages?"

"Eight now," I corrected.

"Shit, even better!" he exclaimed. "But the point is, I want you whole. I still want you to pursue all your dreams, aspirations, goals, everything. The world will always be your oyster, it's just in seven days, I'll be your husband."

"Marrying me won't make you happy," I said, trying one final time to dissuade him from what I knew would be a cursed union.

Clearly we were the definition of toxic. There was no need to legally enshrine it.

"New rule," he sighed while refilling my water. "You can lie to everyone else. You can keep your secrets and your walls with anyone else, but you don't do that bullshit with me. I'm tired of it. Do you understand?"

"Truth, I-"

"Alise Asasi Hatchette, do you understand me?" he barked. "It's a yes or no question!"

His voice was so impactful that it rattled the pictures on the walls, and I feared the house of cards I'd been carefully rebuilding would come crashing down around me if he raised his voice at me again. I was strong, but not strong enough for that.

"Yes," I said, after calming my roaring heart. "I understand."

Wedding Bells

TRUTH

"The Preacher is here," Boogie whispered. "And Auntie Aster is-"

Aster was bursting into the room as we spoke. Her feet were moving so fast that I didn't know how her sharp ass heels weren't burning a hole in the hardwood. Old houses really were built to last.

"Come on in," I scoffed. "It's not like I could have my dick out or anything."

"Boy, shut up!" she hollered. "I spent five years cleaning that thing and you got the nerve. That's how I know you've lost the fucking plot."

"This is what every man wants to hear on his wedding day," I nodded. "His mama talking about his dick."

"Truth, I swear to God you better shut your mouth! I came in here to try to talk some sense in you, and you acting like you ain't got no home training. That's why we're in this situation now. You cannot marry Alise Hatchette!"

"I don't know what you're talking about," I shrugged. "In case you missed it, I can. The Officiant just got here about five minutes ago. Besides, I thought you liked Alise."

"Everyone likes Alise, but that's not the point. Truth, she's too young! Think about how this will look!" Mama begged.

"Mama, I did think about it," I confessed. "Which is why I switched the linens to sky blue. They look much better with the baby's breath and amaranth."

"She's gone stab yo ass and I'mma watch," Boogie whispered before finding a seat.

"My God, why did I have all these fucking hard-headed boys?" she mumbled. "Son, you are running for senate. Your wife would be 21 while you'd be 36 in two weeks. You will look like a kid-diddler!"

"You mean not unlike the current politicians, who are being charged with actual sex crimes? Look Mama, I appreciate the concern for my image, but I simply don't care. Alise is not a child, she's a young woman with a potty mouth and a mean streak. She's a willing-ish participant."

"Ok, but how would your constituents know that?" Mama argued.

"I got the text messages to prove it," I shrugged. "Want me to show you the one where she threatened to hang me by my nipples?"

I made it to the altar, but I could still feel the sting of Mama's slap on my cheek.

In hindsight, that wasn't the safest way to get my point across, but it was efficient. I didn't have time for anything else. That's why we were getting married so soon. Sure part of it was spite, but the other contributor was the pressure of events forthcoming. We needed to tie the knot before my tour started, and before Alise got accepted into school. Otherwise the news outlets would have a field day.

"Did you remember to position guards at all the exits?" I whispered to Boogie.

"She ain't gone run, Slime," he sighed. "You know she doesn't like publicity stunts."

I thought that too once upon a time but then I found her ass in France after a Paris proposal.

"Shit, you can never be too cautious," I shrugged.

Just as soon as I said that, the organs started and the talking ceased. I got a bit of deja vu recalling Boogie's wedding to Dre last year. Especially when the doors opened and the sun shined a spotlight on the apples of Alise's cheeks. She was stunning always, but the off white gown complimented her perfect complexion in a way that made every second feel divine. The flowers on the hem of her skirt reminded me that she was always my dream. The crowd was noticeably smaller and the air outside was still cool, but this was still a day for the history books.

Which meant it was the perfect time for my anxiety to act up.

Alise must have sensed it too because the grace in her gait warped just slightly when we made eye contact. However, her smile and poise returned once she remembered where we were. I really did love my little manipulator.

"Thank you, sir," I whispered once she reached the altar with Senior. "I promise to take care of her."

"Eugh," he scoffed while shaking my hand for the crowd. "I'm not worried about Alise. She's a wild card. I'm just glad I don't have any more kids for your evil bastards to claim."

Then he rejoined the crowd with an equally off putting smile. Funny enough he forgot about Dexter, but I wasn't going to remind him of that. I didn't want to do too much today. This was exhausting enough.

The ceremony began with a sermon like always, and I tried to use the familiarity of the words to ground my anxiety. Unfortunately it didn't work because three months was just long enough for me to become sensitive to Alise's touch again.

"What's wrong?" Alise whispered with a grin. "Are you having second thoughts?"

"Never that," I chuckled softly before admitting the truth. "I'm anxious."

"Why?" she asked with tenderness in her tone.

"It's part of my BPD."

I closed my eyes when I said the last part, mostly out of fear that her reaction would make me have second thoughts. Petulant Borderline Personality Disorder wasn't a bag easily unpacked, and it was a big bright red flag to a lot of people. Hell, if the shoe was on the other foot I'd probably feel the same way.

Which is why I was surprised when Alise's gloved hand cupped my cheek. I jumped at first but once I caught a whiff of the familiar perfume clinging to her wrists, I leaned into her touch with a relieved pout.

"It's ok," she said softly. "You're ok. Just breathe."

"This is so embarrassing," I mumbled.

"You'll let me spit in your ass but this is embarrassing?" she countered.

She said that a little too loud because when I finally looked up, I noticed that Pastor Jackson's eyes were about to pop out of their sockets. It was a good thing he was on payroll too.

"Hey, I have to draw the line somewhere."

"An anxiety attack during your wedding is crossing the line?"

"Exactly," I nodded.

Luckily I was feeling better, because it was time for our vowels. I started to disassociate a bit when the pastor read the petition of promises, but I was ready when it came time for me to say,

"I do."

From there it was smooth sailing, because I didn't have to do much other than focus on Alise's lips.

"And do you, Alise Asasi Hatchette, take this man to be your lawfully wedded husband? For rich or for poor, in sickness and in health, as long as you both shall live?" Pastor Jackson asked.

Silence swallowed the altar for a brief, yet intense moment, and what a wicked temptress my almost-wife was, because she unraveled me with a mischievous smile before giving me her word.

"I do," she declared loudly.

Pastor Jackson's shoulders slumped in relief then he married us with a resounding clap.

"Then by the power vested in me by the Great State of Alabama, I now pronounce you man and wife."

I really did try, but once her lips folded into mine, reality was a wrap. I had some memories of walking back down the aisle and accepting congratulations. However, I was surprised that the day ended by the time when we started to head home.

"It really was a beautiful wedding," Alise sighed, as I helped her into the car.

"It was," I agreed.

I buckled her in carefully, making sure not to snag the lace on her dress. Then once she was secure, I climbed to the other side.

"You don't remember a single thing about it after our vowels do you?" she asked.

"Nope," I admitted while closing my eyes to search through my recent memories. "I mean except for our kiss. That shit was hot. Everything else was very overwhelming."

"Truth, why did we even have a wedding?" she groaned.

"Because I figured you'd enjoy some of the traditions. Plus it makes this look less like a hostage situation."

"That's exactly what this is," she frowned.

"Yeah, I know."

We spent the remaining ride in silence. Both of us were in recovery from the busyness of the week, so I didn't mind it as much. I just wanted to hold her. I was still mad that she left, but it was hard to maintain distance. My moods were swinging all over the place and right now I was elated that she was officially mine. Even though she didn't want anything to do with me. She made that clear by running off as soon as we got home. Then I probably made it worse by merging our rooms. I forgot I did that.

"Truth, where the fuck is my bed?" she hollered.

Her voice traveled two stories down to where I sat on the couch, and it was still sharp enough to send goosebumps across my arms.

"I sent it to storage," I sighed.

I wasn't fooled by the silence that followed that admission, and it was a good thing too because Alise rushed down the steps in her bridal lingerie with a look that could kill a less formidable man.

"What the hell do you mean you sent it to storage? Where am I supposed to sleep!?" she shrieked.

"You know," I yawned. "At first I had a grand speech planned out that talked about how you are now my wife, and how we were now a unit, and how we need to move like one."

I couldn't finish my explanation without interrupting myself with yet another yawn and this one seemed to go on for miles.

"But honestly, now that I've come down from whatever that was, I just feel like an asshole. I'm sorry. I'll sleep on the couch and you can have the bed."

I was somewhere in between wake and sleep, but I was still conscious enough to notice Alise's posture softened. Hopefully that meant she wouldn't stab me when I did pass out because I didn't have it in me to fight her off. Being murdered by my wife on my wedding night would be a hell of a way to go out.

However, after a while, Alise sat on the cushion next to the arm where I had propped up my legs. Then she peeled my shoes off.

"I forgot about those," I chuckled with another yawn.

"I really hate that you told me about your BPD," she scoffed while taking my watch off. "Because now I know why you act like you do. That's still not an excuse though."

"I know," I admitted with a gulp. "Thanks for marrying me anyway."

"Shut up," she grumbled as she moved on to my tie. "It's not like you gave me much of a choice. Besides, feelings don't go away just because a man kidnaps you."

"They don't go away when a woman abandons you in the woods either," I countered.

My tie was undone and soon she was on to my cuff links. She almost started on my belt, but she hesitated just long enough to dissuade herself.

Bummer.

"I didn't abandon you, Truth. I just didn't want to be lied to anymore," she sniffed.

"Who lied to you?" I asked, nearly knocking myself off the couch. "I never once lied to you."

I was sure of that until I thought about the Alumni Ball.

"Not about anything serious at least."

"Truth, it's been a long day, an equally long week, and my feet hurt. I don't have the bandwidth to talk about this now. Can we please just go to bed?"

"Go ahead, Alise. I'm good down here. There's a throw in the ottoman."

"Truth, get up and come to bed with me. I'm asking you to come to bed with me," she groaned.

I blinked once, then twice, and one more time for good measure until I was certain that we were both in reality.

"I think I'm tripping," I yawned. "Because I almost thought you asked me to come to bed with you."

"I did," Alise hissed while pulling me off the couch. "Come on."

After I brushed my teeth and washed the day off, I sat in the bathroom watching my wife. Her routine wasn't really complicated but it was thorough, and witnessing it felt soothingly normal. Eventually she was tying a scarf around her edges and securing it with a clip. Bed time was officially here once that happened. My body started to shut down for the day as soon as I saw the lip oil wand glide over her lips.

"Are we gonna cuddle or are you going to make a little pillow wall like you did the first time?" I asked.

"Get in bed, Truth," she sighed. "It's two in the morning."

I must've been God's luckiest bastard because despite all her fussing, Alise did wrap her arms around me. I didn't take the gesture for granted so I quickly pulled her onto my chest before she changed her mind, and luckily she allowed it. All was right in the world at that moment, and I finally felt normal after months of pretending. Right until her hand slid into the waistband of my PJs.

"Whoa! What are you doing?" I shrieked, pulling her hand out.

She sat up instantly, like I was the one on the offense. Meanwhile she was trying to make gravy out of my giblets.

"I'm so confused," she whispered. "Why are you freaking out? All I did was touch you."

"Yeah, that's the problem. You're not about to be touching on me."

"Truth," she chuckled before her voice turned serious. "I'm your wife! We're married! Married people fuck!"

"Oh, that's not what this is. We married, but we won't be fucking," I scoffed while gathering the sheets by my neck. "Fucking you is the whole reason I'm in this mess."

"Wait, what do you mean? What do you mean, we're not fucking?" she gasped.

"I mean that my body and your body will not be joining. There will be no joining of the flesh. I'm keeping my dick to myself, thank you very much."

"Truth, you cannot be serious!"

"Oh, I'm deadly serious. Why should I sex you? So you can put me in subspace and try to dip again. No. You broke my rules, and these are the consequences. We. Are. Not. Hunching."

The State Of Things

ALISE

I had been married for two months, and my husband still wouldn't fuck me. Most days I spent hours scouring the internet for advice on how to change his mind. Sometimes I'd be blessed with the view of his half-chub poking through his sweats for my efforts, but for the most part I was cooked. Even when I got my official Jackson Marks acceptance two weeks ago. Achievements always put me in the mood, but his ornery ass refused to relieve me. We celebrated with family, but when I tried to mount him later at home, he tucked his dick between his ass cheeks. After that he threatened to buy a chastity belt and melt down the key.

"I'm gonna run away," I whispered into my empty champagne flute.

I was at brunch with my girls, because hobbies and socialization were the only way I could stay sane. But these bottomless mimosas were just reminding me that I was also bottomless.

"Terrible idea," Andrea replied.

"Zero out of ten," Mae added.

"Seriously, don't say that again," Liberty signed. "He probably has your bra bugged with a mic."

"I don't care!" I whined. "I'm horny and my husband won't fuck me. This has to count as some sort of abuse. I wonder if I could get an annulment."

"Girl, where is Truth right now?" Mae laughed. "Ain't no judge gone sign off on that. Especially since he has dirt on all of them. No fault divorces don't exist when it comes to men like that. Which is why you should've left him alone a year ago when we told you the first time."

"Ugh," I scoffed, disliking how bitter being wrong tasted on my tongue. "I hate it here."

"Wild idea," Liberty signed with an eyeroll. "But have you tried talking to him? Truth is mad because you left. Telling him why would probably help."

I thought back to that frosty December morning with a pout. Everything was so perfect and wonderful. Right until Simon called.

"No, I'm not doing that," I frowned while pushing down the memory. "Ooh, I know. I'll just pay him a visit. He's about to go on lunch."

The table groaned because they all knew this would be another fruitless endeavor. Yet I was determined to get my way, and too drunk to realize just how bad of an idea bothering him at work was. Thank God Muver existed to enable my bad decisions though.

I could smell his cologne lingering in the elevator when I arrived, which meant I just missed him. The familiarity of his scent dredged up so many memories. Including some of the ones I cherished the most, namely our first kiss. The ride up to the 12th floor was too long, and my patience was too short. I was practically feral. He didn't even have to fuck me at this point, I'd be happy with anything beyond a quick peck.

"Mrs. Greene!" Mariah exclaimed, once I strutted off the elevator. "Truth is in a meeting. He told me to let you know that-"

"Hush, Mariah. I don't care about his meeting," I said with a wave. "Go get yourself some lunch. I'll cover for you."

Mariah was a smart woman so she fled the scene of the crime as soon as I took off my hoops to pick the lock on my husband's office door. Part of me wondered if he did all of this just to limit my access to him, but a more vulnerable part of me wondered about the possibility of another woman being behind his door. Plenty of people would say that was a valid explanation for why he was denying me sex, and so I hesitated for a moment, too scared to face that potential reality.

Fortunately and unfortunately I heard Simon's laugh soon after the thought crossed my mind.

Truth wasn't a cheater, he just knew me too well.

"Simon!" I greeted in that weird faux transatlantic voice he did. "Nice to see you again. Can I please have a moment alone with my husband?"

"Mrs. Greene," he sighed. "What a lovely surprise. What brings you in this afternoon? Perhaps too much to drink?"

"Cut the shit, Simon," I scoffed. "We both know you don't like me. Luckily I don't have to pretend to care. You work for my husband. Which reminds me, get out. I want to talk to him about something private."

"Truth?" Simon asked, sending one eyebrow high.

"Can you give us just a moment?" Truth sighed while clipping his paperwork. "I'll send you a message once we're done chatting."

"No need," Simon said, rising from his chair. "I think we've reached a good stopping point. I'll email you a summary and you can reach out if you have any questions."

"Sounds good. Thanks for stopping by," Truth nodded.

"Where's Mariah?" Truth asked once I locked the door.

"I don't know. She must have grabbed lunch."

"Alise, you can't keep bullying my staff," he chided. "That was incredibly rude."

"It was, wasn't it?" I agreed while sliding into his lap. "Maybe you could teach me some manners?"

For whatever reason, Truth allowed me to kiss him, and he didn't even pull away when I stuck my tongue in his mouth.

"I'm still not fucking you, sweet pea," he mumbled, placing his lips against my throat. "Although I will admit that this is tempting."

That wasn't the answer I was hoping for, but it had potential.

I never begged, but I could absolutely put on a show. Which is exactly what I did when I slid onto his desk and pulled my panties around my ankles.

"Are you sure I can't tempt you some more?" I asked, while spreading my lips for him.

Truth remained silent, but his eyes tracked the movement of my fingers as I stretched my entrance open. It didn't feel nearly as good as he would've, but it was good enough to make me moan. I guess that moan was enough to push Truth over the edge. He stood so fast that he nearly knocked me off the desk, but he caught me just as quick. Then his thumb slid over my mound and settled onto my clit. He settled for simply swiping my bud at first, but he quickly became dissatisfied with that limit. His greedy fingers replaced my own while his other hand locked around my throat. Suddenly interrupting him at work was a great idea.

"Is this what you want, Alise?" Truth grunted in between kisses. "You want me to fill you up and stretch you out?"

I pushed my hypothesis even further by dragging my recently freed hand down the length of his body, and when I reached his zipper I found an abundance of evidence in my favor.

"Yes, Tru," I panted. "I want you to fill me up."

"Uhuh, you miss this fat dick don't you?" he grinned. "You miss all these veins and midnight slow strokes? Do you miss the way my nuts slap against your ass? And the way I kiss you when I can't take it anymore?"

The picture he was painting was so accurate that I nearly sobbed. I missed all of that, but I also missed this. Touching him, holding him, having his bare skin against mine. I missed who we were five months ago. I missed our trust more than all of that.

"Yes, baby," I whined. "I miss it more than anything."

"I know, sweet pea. I can tell by the way you're leaking all over my desk. I miss being in my favorite place too," he admitted with a salacious grin.

"Fuckkkkkkk," I moaned while bucking against his palm.

Truth Greene's smile would do me in every time. It didn't matter how much control I thought I had. That was my kryptonite. That was my Achilles's heel.

I pushed his hand away when my sensitivity overwhelmed me, and Truth didn't hesitate to bring his sticky fingers to his mouth.

"Fuck, I forgot how good you taste, darling," he groaned while sucking his digits clean. "I think I miss it more than you do."

Relief flooded me like a river while I caught my breath. Finally, we were on the same page. That was all I needed to hear, and I pulled my panties all the way off to welcome Truth home. Only I couldn't because he held me back when I tried to reach for him.

"I miss it, but I'm still not fucking you, Alise," he said firmly while shutting my legs. "Now take your hot ass home. I got paperwork to finish before we leave tomorrow."

I was finally sober, and my mind was made up. I was running away. Everyone said it was a bad idea, but it couldn't be a worse one than marrying a man who wouldn't touch me. What was the worst that could happen? Sure, I knew he'd find me again, but at least I could get a tolerance break before I went back to being taunted 24/7.

So I packed my car with the essentials: A few clothes, some food, some of the good weed that Boogie grew. Then I headed for the border. Atlanta would be my closest and best bet. It was populated enough for me to shake his crazy ass for a few days.

It was a solid plan and I was about half way to seeing it through, but my car started tripping as soon as I passed Oxford.

"What the hell?" I scoffed. "I know I'm up to date with my maintenance."

My plan included everything from playlists, to gift ideas for important dates, and mileage reminders, so I knew it wasn't an issue with my maintenance. But for some reason my car was jerking and stalling. It had stopped completely by the time I reached Abernathy. I had to fight to get to the safety of I-20's shoulder. I spent an hour trying to get it back started but it wouldn't budge. That left me with two options. Either I could call AAA and risk Truth finding out about my escape attempt, or I could call my sister who was six months pregnant and hear another I told you so.

"I told you that shit wasn't going to work out," she sighed. "Where are you?"

"About ten miles outside of Georgia on 20 east," I grumbled.

"God damnit, Alise!" she fussed. "I'm too fat for this shit. Hold on. Let me call Boogie, and I'll call you back."

I cracked open a soda and a pack of chicken salad snackers during my wait. It was hot as hell and the hour I spent in the sun had left me depleted. Luckily Boogie called me before I could get half way through my lunch.

"So your car stopped?" he asked.

"Yep. On 20 east."

"You told Andrea you were about ten miles outside of Georgia?"

"That is correct."

"Ok cool. Well, I have good news and bad news."

"Bad news first," I sighed.

"Alright, bad news: I can't come get you and neither can Andrea. You tried to run."

"That's fair," I sighed while kicking at a rock. "What's the good news?"

"Good news is that your husband is on the way. He should be pulling up right about now."

I looked down the road, and lo and behold, Boogie was right. Truth was riding in the 4Runner with his windows down, blasting SchoolBoy Q.

"Evening, Miss," he teased with a laugh. "You need a ride back to Birmingham?"

"What did you do to my car?"

"Oh, this old thing?" he asked while slapping his palm against the hood. "You mind telling me where we're at?"

"We're in Abernathy, ten miles outside of Georgia."

"Exactly!" he exclaimed. "You were ten miles from the nearest border. Which triggered your engine kill switch."

"BIT–" I started before calming myself down.

I took a deep, belly-ballooning breath. I was beyond pissed off, but I didn't want to get in the habit of public meltdowns and calling my husband a bitch. Even if he rode my nerves like one.

"Truth, why is there a kill switch in my engine?"

"To keep you from leaving the state, duh. I'm not stupid, Alise. I know you take the saying, *"My way or the highway,"* literally. Now come on, get in the car. We got shit to do tomorrow."

For the first time in my life, I felt true defeat. I couldn't talk, finesse, or wiggle my way out of this. Truth was one step ahead of me at all times. I was outdone. Truly outdone.

"Can we at least go get Marbella's?" I asked as I climbed in the passenger seat.

"Sure, I can do a burger," he shrugged.

Truth

I felt bad.

I mean, I felt bad two days ago in my office when I saw the disappointment in Alise's eyes after telling her no, but at least my Lexapro was kicking in then. Now the feeling was overwhelming because I had officially worn down my wife. Her fight was gone.

Did I mean for this to happen?

No, no I did not.

I just wanted to keep us both safe. Sex with Alise clouded my judgment and I couldn't afford to be off my shit right now. It was a critical time for multiple happenings. I was campaigning for a senate seat, Alise was preparing for Jackson Marks, and family responsibilities were shifting as Andrea got closer to her due date. Plus my feelings were still hurt and rightfully so. Because Alise tried to leave again as soon as shit between us got too tough.

"Where are we going today?" Alise sighed while typing out an email.

Symphony was on an honor's trip and she had sent Alise a virtual postcard. While Alise liked to pretend that she was allergic to emotions, that girl was indisputable proof that she wasn't. She nearly sobbed when she saw the picture of Symphony trying pumpkin leaf salad.

"Decatur and Florence," I replied before pecking her temple. "Thank you again for being such a good sport about this."

"Of course," she said with an annoyingly placating grin. "I'll get ready in a second."

I hated when Alise tried to manage me and I would fight her on it if we had more time. Unfortunately, we didn't. Simon would be knocking on the door in ten minutes to discuss the day's itinerary, and while he and Alise remained cordial during the tour, I did my best to limit their interactions. Alise didn't like him because she could smell dishonesty on folks. Simon was the best in the business but the skeletons in his closet were numerous and possibly even infinite. Then it didn't help that his wife tagged along because she suspected him of cheating.

But to be fair, he absolutely was.

"Dress or pants suit?" Alise asked.

"Dress!" I called back. "It's warm outside."

"Yellow or purple?"

"Yellow," I mumbled while biting my fist.

Purple was my favorite color and Alise was my favorite person. She also happened to be the owner of my favorite ass. Sunny yellows made her look ethereal, but seeing her in purple devastated me. I always knew I couldn't withhold sex from her forever because dancing with her at my birthday party really tested the limits of my abstinence, but we needed to have a good, honest talk before I gave up the goods. Purple wasn't facilitating honest talks.

"Ok, what do you think?" she said while doing a little spin.

The dress passed all my cut concerns because it fanned well past her knees and you couldn't see a lick of her cleavage, but we were interrupted by urgent knocking before I could give the rest of my opinion.

"Truth! Or Alise!" Simon shouted. "Open up, this is an emergency."

Simon tumbled over the threshold in a sweaty, anxious heap as soon as I pulled the door open.

"What happened?" Alise asked immediately.

"Oh, Mrs. Greene. Don't you look like a little ray of sunshine?" Simon smiled before his expression dropped. "Go change, they're already calling you a child bride."

"What the fuck are you talking about?" I growled.

The magazine was thrust into my hands instantly. Bham Now had a joint article released with The Investigator, detailing everything about me and Alise's courtship and subsequent marriage. Everything from our first dance at Trixxie's, to our private date at Marbella's, and even our failed cabin weekend. The article claimed that I began grooming Alise as soon as she became legal even though I didn't bother to look at her until she was 21.

It was disturbing to say the least.

"Truth," Simon started. "We need to get ahead of this. We need to come out with a statement, a backstory, all of our ducks need to be in a row-"

My fists began to curl around the paper as Simon continued to rattle off action items. It shook between my hands for a split second before I ripped it in half with the clipboard it was resting on. I couldn't believe that someone took the time to stalk us. I felt like I had failed Alise, because now her business was put up for community review.

"Simon, shut up!" she hissed while pulling me back. "Give him a fucking minute. He's obviously not here."

Alise was right, I wasn't present, and I was grateful that she took control of the situation.

However after a few minutes of organizing my thoughts, I knew I didn't want this to be the norm.

"This was fun, but I'm going to withdraw my candidacy," I said while patting my knees.

"Absolutely not," Alise protested with a headshake.

"Finally, something we agree on," Simon scoffed. "Truth, you can't just withdraw."

"Actually, I can!" I exclaimed while rising to stand. "My love life is being dragged through the gossip rags, and that's enough for me. It doesn't matter if it's reliable reporting. Shit like this leaves a mark, and it can affect Alise's college admission."

"Tru, honey," Alise sighed. "None of this is real, and getting in the senate is your dream. You have communities depending on your success. Besides, if Jackson Marks reneges over something as tepid as a Bham Now article, that means they were never the school for me."

"You're starting to grow on me, jail bait," Simon laughed.

I was about to check him for that shit, but I ended up not having to. The smile that crept onto Alise's face gradually shifted from calm to manic, and then she silenced him with a simple sentence.

"I value your personhood a little less every time you open your mouth," she chuckled.

He swallowed his upcoming reply.

"Ok, all of this sounds fine and dandy," I sighed before picking up the ripped article. "But what do we do about this?"

"Their source is a mole," Alise announced after reading through the article on her phone. "There are too many details for it be anything else. How else would the cabin trip be in here?"

"I don't have anyone on my team that stupid."

"You never know," Alise hummed while subtly eyeing Simon.

Suddenly I remembered that the Letz's were divorcing, and that the reason listed was adultery. It was such a simple observation. A snap judgment in a sea of ongoing mess, but regardless of how quick Alise came to that conclusion, she was still correct.

"Simon, can you give us a minute?" I asked. "I want to try and retrace our last few months."

"Of course," Simon said immediately. "I'll be in the lobby doing the same thing if you need me."

"Thanks," I nodded.

He shut the door behind himself and while I had sixteen questions ready to go as soon as he was in the hall, Alise held up a single finger with the silent command to wait. Two minutes later, Simon knocked again.

"Sorry, I forgot my pen," he explained. "And I wanted to remind you both that we still have to get going by nine."

"Noted," Alise grinned. "We'll be down in a second."

"Ok, good," he replied awkwardly.

I waited this time, and once Alise was sure that we were alone, she started automatically.

"He knows who it is."

"You think it's him?"

"No, I'm not saying that," she corrected. "He has too much to lose if you go down for this. But when I mentioned a mole, his leg started shaking. So I think he knows who it is. Is there anyone on the team that he's particularly close with?"

"I don't know. Simon fucks most of the women he meets. He could be more than friendly with quite a few people."

"Ew, that's unfortunate."

"It is," I agreed. "Because we don't have time to interview every potential offender."

"We were never going to do that anyway," Alise chuckled. "What we need is a trap. These gossip rags pay good money for the right information. So we just need to give the mole a grub to hunt. So what would you like our first public fight to be about?"

"This is some real Scooby Doo shit," I mumbled. "I don't know. Can we fight about you popping up at my office?"

"Better idea, let's fight about your refusal to fuck me," she shrugged.

"Now, Alise," I warned. "Don't start. You know why I won't fuck you."

"And you know why I left," she countered with grit in her voice.

She brought her arms around her body like a shield to soothe the pain of a memory I couldn't quite pinpoint, and while I knew my wife had the potential to be manipulative, this didn't seem to be one of those instances.

"I really don't," I said softly while pulling her closer. "I wish you'd tell me."

She surrendered into my embrace briefly before the ten minute warning alarm went off, but once our peaceful bubble was broken, she packed all that vulnerability right back up.

"We can talk about this some other time," she mumbled while walking back into the bedroom. "Let's get this tour figured out first."

I didn't think I was important enough to accumulate a press cloud, but apparently I was. A thicket of reporters stood in the hotel parking lot waiting for us to exit, and the sheer amount of camera flashes and noise they were generating made Alise grind her teeth.

"It's going to be fine," I whispered. "Just walk in front of me and I got you. Don't stop for any reason, ok?"

"Ok," she said with a shaky exhale. "I think I'm ready."

"Ok," I confirmed. "On the count of three. One, two, th-"

"There they are!" a rogue journalist screeched. "Justice Greene, would you mind telling us how and when you met your wife?"

"Sources say you used your relationship with her family to influence her. Is that true?"

"Did you get married to prevent her from testifying against you in court?"

"Would you like to comment on the theory that this is a sham marriage brought on to boost your approval ratings?"

It had long been my belief that journalistic integrity was in the toilet, but this was on a whole other level. They were relentless and the questions were beyond disrespectful. However I didn't give a damn as long as no one touched my wife.

"Alise Greene! Is it true that your husband asked you to defer your enrollment to the prestigious Jackson Marks?" someone asked.

That made Alise stop in her tracks.

"Sweet pea, no!" I chided. "Stick to the plan."

I tried to scoot her along, but her tough little ass wasn't having it. She stood tall and made me do the same by digging her nails in my back. Just like she did the very first time we touched.

"My husband has never once asked me to dim my personality or my goals to fit his agenda," she said firmly. "Our age difference is a bit unfortunate because it leads to unsavory conversations like this, but Justice Truth Greene has never once tried to manipulate me due to my age. We are just a regular couple. The only hardships brought on by our age difference are entertainment preferences."

The crowd seemed to back down just a bit, but when I made the mistake of leaning down to kiss her forehead, they were right back to it.

"Mrs. Greene!" numerous reporters shouted.

It took us ten minutes to get on the bus, and I was so irritated that I was shaking. Alise plopped down in the seat next to me looking just as frazzled, with her hair everywhere, her clothes jostled, and her mascara smeared. Today was already off to a rough start and we hadn't even set our trap.

"What did we learn today, sweet pea?" I asked calmly with my eyes still closed.

"Don't talk to the reporters. Ever," she sighed.

"Glad we had this talk, darling."

The rest of the tour stops went well despite the morning ambush we had to endure. The Black and Hispanic communities we were visiting welcomed us with open arms, especially when Alise flexed her linguistic abilities. By the end of the day, we were surprisingly full from plates of gifted food and drinks, tired, and ready for bed. Unfortunately we still had one last thing to do before we could relax.

"You are so damn hard-headed!" I yelled.

That wasn't a lie. Alise was hard-headed but to have to pretend that it bothered me was crazy.

"And you're controlling!" she shouted. "I couldn't even wear my purple dress because you were worried about appearances."

"Hey now," I mumbled between us. "Don't do me like that."

"Truth baby, focus. This is a fake fight. I know you like the purple dress."

"Right, my bad. Please continue."

"Another thing!" she hissed, playing up her dramatics. "I was defending you! What did you want me to do? Let them call you a pedophile?"

"If it meant avoiding that shit show, then yes!" I shouted back.

We wouldn't know how well Alise's plan worked until the morning, but based on the watching crowd of staff and the passing glances, I was confident we'd catch our fish.

By the end of the night, I needed a hot shower and an Xanax. My mind knew it was fake, but my body couldn't tell the difference. Especially because some of those emotions were real. I was still mad at Alise even though my anger had dampened dramatically since March, and my heart still lurched with the fear that she'd leave again every time she raised her voice. It wasn't fair to her because I knew it was my BPD showing up and out, but that almost made it worse. She wanted to validate how I was feeling because she understood the root cause, and I wanted to fight about it so we could finally figure out what happened and move past it.

It was a hellish cycle.

Luckily we were taking a little break from that reality, and as we laid in the bed of Florence's highest rated 3.5 star hotel with the A/C blowing, I was able to find a little peace.

"Do you think that was a good enough fight?" I asked.

"I think so," she yawned while snuggling in closer.

"Good, because I don't want to do it again."

"I know," she said softly. "I'm sorry for encouraging your anxiety."

"No, it's not your fault, sweet pea. This is a stressful time for everyone."

"Except for the mole," she added.

"Right, except for the mole."

Alise reclaimed her rightful place in the center of my chest and then the blanket was thrown over my exposed shoulders. The lip oil was on and sleep was beginning to claim me. I didn't want it to though, I needed more time with her like this.

"Close your eyes, Tru," Alise cooed knowingly. "We got a hole to close in the morning."

"Wa, I can't believe this shit!" Simon exclaimed. "I'm about to hire security because it almost seems like they're following us."

"It does, doesn't it?" Alise sighed calmly. "I just wish I could pinpoint a particular person."

Now that I knew for certain that he had something to do with the seemingly miraculous leaks, his voice was starting to irritate me to no end.

"You and me both," Simon huffed. "We need to start interviewing support staff to get to the bottom of this."

"That could take ages though," Alise said with a demure head tilt before bringing her teacup to her mouth. "The tour is happening now."

"Tour or not, I'm getting to the bottom of this barrel," he announced with a certain amount of fervor. "Sit tight for a second. I'm about to go shake some shit up."

He left out the door with a loud bang that made Alise jump in her seat, but she recovered gracefully and righted herself before her tea could spill.

"What say you, sweet pea?"

"I know who done it," she grinned brightly. "Just give me a second to finish my earl grey."

"Can I get you some fruit to go, darling?"

"Ooh, strawberries please."

Two cups of fruit, a fire-ass caramel dream cappuccino, and ten minutes later, we were down on the second floor of our lovely inn, waiting for Simon to come to the door. Conversations were hushed and reigned in soon after we knocked, and I could tell they were intense by the sheen of sweat on Simon's forehead.

"Hey y'all, what's gong on?" he said calmly. "You need me for anything?"

"Mind if we come in?" Alise said with that sugar sweet voice of hers. "We have a theory we want to tell you about."

She had inherited plenty of dangerous things from her parents, but that voice was the most critical of them all. Mama Joy was a Southern enchantress and so were her daughters.

"Yeah, of course!" Simon exclaimed with a big wave. "Come on in."

He shut the door behind us firmly and then introduced us to his wife. Well, he introduced Alise. I met Shirley plenty of times before but she worked to avoid Alise for some reason.

"It's nice to meet you Miss Shirley," Alise said warmly. "I'm so glad you could join us this time around."

"Oh me too!" Shirley smiled. "Me and Simon have more time to go on adventures now that I'm retired. It's been wonderful."

"I'm sure," Alise nodded while slowly looking around their suite. "Especially since you get to see all the news before it hits the blogs."

Shirley's smile slowly faded into a muddled, confuddled lour.

"I'm not sure I follow? You mean that God-awful gossip?"

"Yep, that's exactly what I mean," Alise smiled before reaching into a dresser drawer. "Why else would you have all these pictures?"

She threw the folder on the floor and hundreds of pictures of me and Alise over a year's span scattered across the carpet. Among the most mention able were the tabloid headers and some very intimate shots from my office when Alise brought me lunch.

The angles on those had me rethinking my sex ban.

"I can explain," Shirley said, raising her hands into the air. "Simon, he-"

As soon as she said that, Simon tried to run.

I realized then and there that the way my family regarded marriage was a special case, because I'd never leave my wife for dead. It disgusted me more than his cheating. Which is why I launched a nightstand at his ass before he could make it down the hall. It smacked him square in the back before crashing against the wall, and he fell forward into the splintered wood with a spectacular full-body plop.

"Not so fast, hoe," I barked, dragging him back by his ankles. "You said you wanted to get to the bottom of this so let's do that."

Shirley was waiting on us with tears streaming down her face when we returned. She was still worried about her husband even though he abandoned her.

Unfortunately, I could relate.

"So I'm going to make an educated guess about what happened, but you can feel free to jump in at any time," Alise started. "Anyway, my theory is that Simon knew that you were seeing someone, but because you were dishonest about it and he is incapable of minding his business, he came up with the plan to hire a PI to figure out who I was. The only problem is that most PI's are already on Burry payroll, and none of them were stupid enough to double dip. That's where Shirley came in. See she and Simon also have an age gap, although it's much smaller in comparison to ours and much more volatile since their relationship started when she was only 16. Unlike Moi, Shirley didn't have a good foundation and she didn't know any better, so she let Simon lead her through whatever. Mistresses, scandals, abandoned dreams. You name it, this nigga has probably done it. She wanted to be a PI, but that wasn't a respectable job for the wife of a prosecuting attorney, so like with everything in life, Shirley settled. She became a regular ole reporter for The Daily Tribune, but the PI skills were still there. She probably feared she'd die without using them until Simon came up with this little number. But I guess eventually she got bold and started turning us over to the rags instead of keeping it between them. That's the only thing I can't figure out a why for."

"You're going to be an excellent attorney, sweet pea," I smiled.

"Thank you, Tru," she chuckled before pecking my cheek.

"So what was it?" Alise asked while removing a blade from the lining of her bust. "Why'd you decide to do too much?"

"Please don't kill my wife," Simon whined from his position under my wingtips. "She doesn't deserve to die because of this."

"Hush," Alise tutted with a light wave. "Shirley, do you want to keep letting this man talk for you? Or do you wanna use your big girl voice?"

Shirley seemed like this was the hill she was willing to die on until I pulled my gun out of my ankle holster and aimed at her pitiful husband. I shot one silenced round into his right hand. Then she started talking fast.

"I did it because of Aster," Shirley admitted. "The only reason Simon wanted this campaign to go well was because he's still lusting after your mama. I was tired of hearing about how proud Aster was, and how grateful she was to Simon for making it happen. The praise was nauseating, but the extra spending money didn't hurt either."

"Wow," Alise scoffed. "That's fucking pathetic. You too old to be this damn foolish and jealous. I don't even think cutting you would be worth it. You already let this nigga cut you down for thirty years."

"Pack this shit up," I sighed in agreement. "Simon, you're fired. And depending on what's in those pictures, you might even be dead. Excellent work, sweet pea."

Ride Or

We finished out the rest of the community tour after modifying Simon's original plans. It went off without a hitch. Truth was well loved and he talked a good game because he could back it up. His years in service as a circuit judge lent a great deal of support to his campaign initiatives. Initiatives like ending the school to prison pipeline that had Alabama in a chokehold, and ensuring safer work environments with better pay. He had been crowned the sweetheart of the South and I couldn't be prouder of my husband.

I just wished he would fuck me.

I started my Freshman semester at Jackson Marks in a month. I wouldn't be far from home since the campus was just outside of Atlanta, but I knew I wouldn't be able to focus if we didn't figure us out before then.

"Alise!" Truth chided as I pulled the shower door open. "What are you doing, woman? I'm in here!"

"Yeah, I can see that," I whispered while once again palming his pec. "I can see all of that."

The sight of Truth naked and wet was just as satisfying as it was a year ago. I hoped the novelty of seeing him like this never wore off. Especially the thrill I got when I ran my fingertips over his scars and soft skin.

"Alise," he groaned while tipping my chin forward. "What are you doing?"

He asked me that like I was the one pulling him into a kiss. Like I was the one stealing air out of his lungs. Like I was pressing myself against him. For once I wasn't the initiator, even though I was guilty of egging him on.

"Truth," I moaned softly. "Can we take this to bed?"

I lazily traced the edges of his lips while I waited for a response. If Truth had taught me anything, he had taught me patience. So I took joy in moments like this. Moments where anticipation clung to me as I watched the water create sacred pathways down the length of his body.

"Alise, I-" he started while leaning in for another kiss.

One that never came.

"I can't fucking do this," he groaned. "Get out and put some clothes on. We're taking a drive."

Somehow my patience lasted the entire five and a half hour drive back to the cabin. I didn't know where we were headed at first, but it came rushing back once we passed all the pretty waterfalls. They were just as majestic as they were seven months earlier, and the beauty of the summer florals only added to them.

"Why are we out here, Mister Greene?" I sighed.

"I told you we were taking a drive."

"To where?"

"To the cabin," he sighed. "The place where this whole mess began."

"Truth, no!" I protested. "We can't just pop up there with no reservation! Money aside, we're both too dark to risk that trespassing charge."

"Girl, hush," he chided. "The cabin is ours. I bought it for you as a Christmas gift. You would know that if you stuck around."

"What did you say?" I gasped while staring him down. "Did you just say that you bought me a fucking treehouse?"

"Don't act so shocked," he scoffed. "We both know love makes people do crazy things."

We spent the rest of the hour ride in silence, and I was honestly grateful because I needed all my strength to face what was to come. The cabin was still beautiful, even more so in the summer time with fronds of cosmos and sunny dahlias surrounding the support posts. They were so beautiful that they distracted me from the reality of the situation, but all that anxiety came rushing back as soon as I touched the front door. I stood frozen in the entryway. The memory was now painfully clear.

"I'm right behind you, sweet pea," Truth cooed. "It's alright."

He scooched me inside with a firm hand placed in the small of my back, and then the door was shut behind us.

"You look uneasy," he whispered.

"That's because I am," I admitted.

"Ok, what about this place do you not like?" he sighed. "Is it the decorations, the location, is it me?"

I remained quiet and began retracing my steps from seven months ago. My hands dragged across a drinking glass and I recalled the exact moment I noticed Truth got my favorite plum wine. Then I walked back through the living room towards the bedroom, but I froze again when my fingers touched the door. His admission was still fresh in my mind.

"So *what, this is just another conquest for you?*"

"*Yes.*"

"I want to go home!" I sobbed. "Take me back home."

My sobbing continued long after Truth pulled me into his arms. He was comforting, but my current reality warred with painful memories of the past. Nothing had ever cut me so deep.

"Alise, tell me why you left," Truth commanded while guiding me to the couch. "I want to know exactly what happened. Down to how your feet felt on the floor."

"It wasn't my socks," I cried as I plopped down. "I heard what you said."

"What did I say?"

I regretted leaving so soon the first time, because I was wholly unprepared for how comfortable this couch was. I zoned out while tracing the embroidered velvet roses covering the arms.

"Alise, focus!" Truth snapped. "The couch ain't going nowhere. Now what did you hear?"

My tears started again when I looked at him. None of this was helping, not even being given a ring and his last name.

"I heard what you said to Simon about me being a conquest. I heard you say you were just getting me out of your system."

His eyebrows scrunched together tightly while he waited for me to continue with my explanation, as if he was still missing something.

"That's it!?" he shrieked. "That's why you left?"

"What the fuck do you mean, that's it? Do you think I'm made of steel, nigga? Of course that's why I left! I'm not a fucking side dish!"

"Oh My God, Alise! I LIED! I LIE ALL THE TIME! IT'S A SPORT FOR ME AT THIS POINT! You think you're the only one who prefers a private life? You're not! I've always felt weird about Simon, I wasn't going to tell him the truth about you. He would've tried to convince you to marry me the next week and fake a pregnancy for increased approval ratings!"

"How was I supposed to know that?" I hollered back.

"You fucking ask!" he hissed. "You ask, and we talk about it, maybe you throw something at me, and we move on! You don't just up and leave because of a phone call!"

"I didn't want to give you the chance to embarrass me! It was bad enough that I had fallen in love with you! What was I supposed to do? Wait and see if you were playing me?"

"Love is always a risk, Alise," Truth sighed. "You weren't the only one nervous to see how this would play out. I bought you a cabin to profess my love for you, and that was a big fat risk and a failure, because you left!"

"Well, I'm sorry!" I screamed. "I was scared, Truth!"

"So was I!" he yelled. "I'm sorry too."

TV shows rarely acknowledge how exhausting fighting is, and because emotional outbursts are against my religion, it was unexpected. I stood in the center of the living room catching my breath for a few seconds while Truth did the same.

"So now what?" I asked after a sip of water.

He picked up his phone and began furiously typing. I didn't know who he could be talking to because his expression was still irritable, but Boogie had already handled Simon. Whatever he was doing must've been serious though because when I tapped his arm to repeat my question, he held up his hand to stop me.

"Ok, the groceries will be here by seven and I let Mariah know I won't be coming in until Wednesday. Now take off your clothes."

"Excuse me?" I scoffed.

"Oh, did you need me to say it another way? Fine, how's this? Get naked, sweet pea. All I want to see for the next 72 hours is waistbeads and nail polish."

"What happened to us not hunching?"

"Yeah, that's dead. I was upset because you left, but we talked about it, we apologized, and now we have three days to remedy the last seven months. So do you want to keep chatting, or do you want me to eat your pussy from the back?"

Now that was the question of a lifetime. Luckily I had enough sense to answer with some tact.

"Can you help me take off my bra?" I gulped.

"Absolutely."

Truth meant what he said about remedying lost time, because my nipples were sucked into his mouth as soon as they were freed. He bent down to one knee, never once losing contact with me, then pulled me forward to straddle his lap. I was burning up by the time we made it into the bedroom, and while he had kept his promise about the soft bed, the only thing I cared about sitting my ass on was his face. He didn't seem to mind that preference much because he was sucking on my clit like a Jolly Rancher.

"God Damnit! Why are you so fucking good at this? " I whined, until I realized what I had asked. "Wait, don't answer that. Just keep eating, friend. Just keep swimming."

He laughed at my Finding Nemo reference and the sound of his amusement coupled with the curl of his smile pushed me right over the edge. My hips bucked to chase my orgasm, and while it was a glorious nut, I was embarrassed that it was achieved without a lick of rhythm. It was record time for the salacious tongue of Truth Greene.

"Oh no," I whimpered. "I'm too sensitive."

"Yeah that happens after seven months," Truth chuckled. "Not that I'm complaining."

"Hush," I chided while adjusting our positions. "Arrogance is unbecoming."

"Says the hypocrite," he hissed as I mounted him. "Shit, that's still a big stretch."

My back was flush with Truth's chest which gave me all the leverage I could ever need to fuck him deep and slow, and he was happy to help maintain my chosen pace.

"Just like that, sweet pea," he whimpered. "Fuck me just like that."

Heaven's chorus rang loudly in my ears as his hips rose to meet mine and the urge to brace myself for the peak grew strong. I didn't want to cum again so soon but I realized I didn't have much of a choice. My stamina was gone, and edging wasn't an option. Truth delivered wave after wave of consistent, heady pleasure, pump after delicious pump.

"I love you," I cried while flicking his nipples. "I love you so so much and I have for a while now."

"I love you more, darling," he grinned, showing off all those sharp white teeth. "I've loved you since our very first kiss."

"I'm sorry for leaving."

My apology came out wobbly and strained due to the overwhelming influence of our shared pleasure, but I meant it all the same.

"It's ok," he cooed against the shell of my ear. "I'm sorry for stealing you."

"You're not," I panted as our speed increased.

"You're right, I'm not," he admitted huskily. "Especially not right now. Jesus fucking Christ, Alise Greene. What are you doing to me?"

I was riding him like a merry-go-round horse, and I asked myself the same question as I ignored all the signs warning me to stop or slow down before Truth really put this birth control to the test. But in my perseverance, I found both the answer to his question and a gloriously loud joint release. Once the twitching stopped and our bodies cooled, I felt well enough to give him the cliffnote summary.

"I'm welcoming you home," I smiled.

Epilogue– Two Years Later

A LISE

"That's right, baby. Come to your mama!" I cheered.

I watched with swelling pride as my tiny wobbly kitten jumped from the corner of my desk into my lap.

"Yay! You did it!" I exclaimed, cherishing the soft mewl I got in return.

Cleo was an abandoned runt that I found on Jackson Mark's campus last spring. The black and gray cotton ball was barely hiding amongst some hedges but luckily I found her before the hawks did. I had nursed her back to health after weeks of bottle feeding and couch cuddling, and now she was leaping off of desks. Tears were trickling down my cheeks. I still wasn't ready for human children, but raising Cleo often felt just as fulfilling.

"What's going on in here?" Truth queried while peeking around the door frame. "Is your fleabag scratching up the furniture again?"

He liked to pretend that Cleo was his biggest opp, but I never paid him any mind. She had real diamonds on her collar and I didn't pay for that shit.

"Did you need something?" I laughed. "Or are you just acting ornery so I'll give you some attention too?"

"Actually, I came to deliver a package," he tutted. "But I can go if you don't want it."

He held up the glittery pink box with one hand, beckoning me forward with an almost hypnotic circle.

"Gimme!" I exclaimed while snatching it from him.

There was only one thing that came in a box like that, and it was-

"Oh, shit you got some new fairy wings? Want me to go grab my loin-clothe?" Truth asked while rubbing his hands together.

Despite our initial trials and tribulations, our marriage had grown into quite the healthy partnership. We had shitty TV marathons, took morning walks together, conspired against my sister and her crazy-ass husband, and yes, had a healthy sex life. Sometimes it was a little too healthy though, because there were nights were I had to rush and submit my assignments with whipped cream still coiffed on my nipples. Still, I hadn't turned anything in late yet.

"Aye Birdman, this ain't that kind of party," I chided as he began to loosen his jogging pants. "I'm just trying them on. Besides, we have to leave for Boogie and Dre's vowel renewal in ten minutes if we want to make it on time."

"All I really need is five," he countered while throwing his hands in the air.

"Fat chance, future Senator Greene. Go put a shirt on."

Truth didn't win his first election run. Unfortunately our Bham Now scandal was a bit too much for a lot of the more conservative constituents, but that was alright. It gave him time to work on rebuilding his image, and it gave me time to focus on getting through my first two years of law school. Plus he would've lost his mind if he had to leave for DC during that winter when I caught the flu. So everything had worked out the way it needed to.

That included Boogie and Dre. My beautiful niece, Imelda Joy, had two doting parents who were undeniably in love. Plus if my suspicions were right, she'd have a sibling join her sometime in the near future. Uncle Nick was always asking if I knew something about that, but I was still great at keeping secrets. Increasingly honest husband or not, I didn't see that ever changing. Mystery kept life fresh. Which is exactly why I always answered Mama's favorite question in a different way.

"I love my grandbaby and I'm grateful, but Alise, when are you and Truth going to have a baby? Joy needs a friend like you and Mae."

The honest answer was four to six years, however I gave her a leisurely. "Some time soon."

Luckily it satisfied her and she walked off to pester Dexter, who was seemingly enraptured with Liberty. Maybe I'd look into that later.

"You know Nick is gonna be elated to hear you say that," Truth teased while pulling me close.

The familiar scent of cotton, bergamot, and rosemary comforted me as I sought to drown out the celebratory noise around us. Folks were yapping, smacking, singing, scooting, and hooting but I didn't care one bit. Because it was one of those few but increasingly frequent times where I didn't have to fake a smile.

"Ah because we're supposedly strengthening the merger?" I asked in response to his question.

"Mhm," Truth laughed while kissing my temple. "I got a merger of my own for yo ass too. A nice, strong, hard merger."

I felt it press against my back and I was overjoyed that Truth was once again living up to his name.

"Fine, but don't get mad at me when you have to deal with the consequences," I grinned.

"Unlike somebody I know how to follow the rules," he whispered while tapping my ass. "Remember that time you thought it'd be cute to run off to France and try on ugly rings for a day?"

"Oh, please," I scoffed as we swayed to the music. "You got your lick back for that. Terrence still has 4 years left on his bid. I wonder why his appeal hearings keep getting denied even with good behavior?"

"Beats me," he shrugged lazily. "Now let's go find out if the garden shed is empty. We still got some remediation to do."

"Yes sir, Senator Greene," I smiled as we walked through the gardens. "Let's see how strong this brand of eyelash glue is."

The end

Thank you!

Hey y'all! Last year I released Burry The Hatchette and you all showed me so much love that I ended up in the top ten for mafia romance. I was so happy that I cried, and while it would be cool to have that happen again, I'm grateful regardless. The support has been overwhelming and it's kept me going on the days I'm too tired to talk. So whether this is your first time reading a book by me or your tenth, thank you. I can't wait to see you at the end of the next one.

About the author

Aria is a die-hard romantic and her life goal is to always be drying her eyes from something sickly sweet. She has been dreaming up stories since she was seven years old, with the first one being a Toy Story fanfic. She focuses primarily on writing disability inclusionary and body-positive contemporary romance, because everyone deserves to get lost in love. Her dream is to one day write magical stories that center Black Folks full-time, but for now, she labors in fraud as a working stay-at-home mom. You can find her looking for epic eats, reading, writing, or enjoying time with her family in her free time. She's currently living out her own happily ever after in Saint Louis, Missouri with her middle-school-sweetheart turned-husband, and their adorably chaotic son.

Like what you read? Let's connect!

https://dazedreamers.com

https://www.instagram.com/ariadazewrites

https://www.tiktok.com/discover/aria-daze?is_

Also by Aria Daze

Glory

"I WANTED EVERYTHING ALL the time. Boys, girls, fae, theys, and thems. I wanted to eat braised short ribs and redskin mashed potatoes while sipping an elaborate drink that contained no alcohol. I wanted to be enshrined in a candle too pretty to burn and memorialized in affectionate poetry detailing my midnight skin. I wanted to hold Cash and be held by Frankie. I wanted them both. Both."

Gloria Esther King is living up to what it means to be a preacher's daughter: Wild, sneaky, and promiscuous. She had no plans to give up the single life, but the twenty-seven-year-old re-evalutaes her life choices, finding herself stuck between heaven and hell after a routine night out goes wrong.

One For The Team

Despite what her recent ex-boyfriend thinks, Chrissy Hawkins has options.

As the beloved mascot for the Minnesota Hares, she's surrounded by beautiful men every week. But none more so than Blessing Harrel. The high-energy hockey center has had his eye on her since she joined the team even though she remained needlessly loyal to her so-called boyfriend. However, he isn't the only one pursuing Chrissy, and it's an unfair fight where Emery Greene and Thaxton Paul are concerned. All three of them are shooting their shot both on and off the ice. So what will happen when neither of them can take a back seat on their feelings for Chrissy? Will she choose? Or will she take one for the team?

Burry The Hatchette

"Andrea Hatchette, a woman after my own soulless void of a heart. Will you do me the honor of being my wife?"

Lots of women dream of moments like this. A calm evening. A party on the lake surrounded by her family and friends. A handsome, rich, educated man asking for their hand in marriage in the middle of a fancy-ass yacht with a big-ass ring. Except for Andrea. Marrying her lifelong enemy, Nathaniel Burry, is her worst nightmare. Still, she knows she has no other choice if she doesn't want to be disowned and thrown from the company she helped build. She supposes there could be worse fates than marrying a billionaire. Right?

Meanwhile, Nat has a plan. Being forced to take a wife isn't the picture of peace he had five years previous, but he's willing to make the best of it with Andrea. After all, even villains deserve happy endings. Can these two find middle ground and make it work, or will they drown in a storm of their own creation?

www.ingramcontent.com/pod-product-compliance
Lightning Source LLC
Chambersburg PA
CBHW050341030726
47503CB00008B/2565